Lake Moon

For Mrs. French, and Bill —

My old friends

Lake Moon

With very best wishes —

J. M. Williams   *Johnny*

John M. Williams

October 26, 2003

—

Mercer University Press

MMII

ISBN 0-86554-802-1
MUP/H606

© 2002 Mercer University Press
6316 Peake Road
Macon, Georgia 31210-3960
All rights reserved

First Edition.

∞The paper used in this publication meets the minimum
requirements of American National Standard for Information
Sciences—Permanence of Paper for Printed Library Materials,
ANSI Z39.48-1992.

Library of Congress Cataloging-in-Publication Data

Williams, John M., 1952-
  Lake Moon / by John M. Williams.—1st ed.
    p. cm.
  ISBN 0-86554-802-1 (hardcover : alk. paper)
  1. Southern States—Fiction. 2. Guitarists—Fiction.
3. Musicians—Fiction. 4. Singers—Fiction. 5.
Death—Fiction. 6. Grief—Fiction. I. Title.

  PS3623.I558 L35 2002

                                          2002008539

For Erin, Martin, and Ellie

The Man from Out of Town

August 1983.

A Greyhound, twenty-four hours from Houston on the last leg
of a continental trip, wound through the maze of downtown,
seeking home.

Hotlanta. Summer in the city.

At the station a man alighted and collided with a wall of
heat. He passed through a blast of diesel exhaust and instinctively held his breath. Two minutes into town, he felt the clam-
my sweat under his shirt already. He was tall, slender. Somewhere deep below words lurked one thought: *I can't do this.*

His name was Doug Earley and no one recognized him.

As he emerged onto the sidewalk he understood at once
that everything had simply continued without him. He gazed up

and down the busy street, undulating in midday heat. *I can't do this.*

What you talking about? You got to do this.

But in those few seconds the fragile scaffold of his plans, born far away and nursed over hours and hours of tired America rolling by the window, collapsed.

Or rather, rearranged. The Johnsons. Alma. He couldn't face them yet. Maybe not at all.

He needed to hear the record first. He looked around, wondered where he could find a telephone book.

The third try—a newsstand. Without knowing exactly what he was looking for, he searched through the worn yellow pages of the section until "Excalibur Light and Sound" caught his attention. Then his eye, running down the list, froze at "Lake Trash Records." He looked back up the page. The number was the same.

He didn't need to write anything. Up in Chamblee. He returned the book to the clerk. After just those few minutes in the air conditioning, his glasses fogged as he stepped back outside and icy pearls of sweat rolled down his spine. Lashed by the scorpion remorse, he started away.

———

The sound of a Dobro twanging through a decaying spring afternoon from a shadowy porch, talking, saying something slow, beyond remedy, distrustful of words. Around the cabin the woods are newly green; over it, the sky pale blue. Out front the lake broadens from a funnel-shaped, flotsam-choked lagoon towards a wide bay. The smell of a septic tank infiltrates the air.

Overhead, too regular to be heard, comes the high rushing whisper of jets; closer, and similarly, the lap of water. As the shadows lengthen over the inlet, the peace is broken by a sudden splash, a flash of silver, then the return of the unquiet quiet. A momentary lapse in the Dobro's prowling tale, the turn of a head, too slow—then the intimate gesture so practiced it seems to have

2

worn a groove in the air: the arm moving the tumbler from table to mouth, and back.

The Dobro resumes.

———

Amazing how the music came back. As though it belonged, like a spirit, not only to its time but to its place. Eleven years of not hearing it at all, and now here it came flooding back in a rich surge like something rising from the ground, the streets, the houses—the place itself. Like a fragrance trailing all its secrets—casting into doubt those eleven years—his current dubious self trumped by the older one left behind.

The music was trying to explain something—and just that urgent, talking quality of it, like somebody *telling* you something, brought Glenroy back. All those static years reduced to one or two abstractions in his memory—now rushing back into life—everywhere—he *was* this place. Glenroy.

Doug pushed the emotion back as he got off the bus and began walking. So familiar all of it—the road, the houses, the Korean signs, the passing cars as though he had stepped through a hole in time and it was the same people on the same errands in the same hurry.

The location gave him some trouble. The numbers simply skipped it; he made a second pass and they skipped it again. He stepped into a convenience store and the half-bored, half-suspicious Indian clerk nodded toward next door. Down the drive, set back from the street.

Ah. A shaded, nondescript brick house, set oddly perpendicular to the road—the sort, and so situated, that one could look at and not see, as he had. No sign, no address number. Just a couple of cars parked in the back. Doug crossed the mossy yard to the front stoop and there at last saw a small brass plate: *Excalibur.*

He hated telephones and it did not seem at all absurd to him that he might have come up here for nothing. No doorbell—so he rapped lightly, waited, then tried the door: it opened with a loud crack.

He found himself in an ice-cold room serving as a lobby and presenting him with so many things at once he stopped his breath, like someone addressed simultaneously by a roomful of people. Crowded walls. A desk to one side, cluttered but unmanned—two or three lipstick-smeared cups. The sensation, as with any studio, of music from within, felt not heard—like the awareness of someone in the dark.

Funny, but Grube held no particular emotion for him one way or the other. In his mind he had now and then rehearsed an encounter with him, but he had never really talked with him then and had no idea what he would say now.

A young woman appeared and looked at him. His wet shirt clung icily to him.

"Is the owner here?"

"There's two."

"Is either one here?"

"One is. He's doing a mix."

"Just tell him there's somebody to see him when he gets a chance."

She nodded, and disappeared.

The closing door left him alone with the teeming and intriguing walls.

They were covered, every inch, in promos, posters, plaques, memorabilia—new and old. He approached the near wall and began to study it piecemeal, keenly. Young groups: faces arrogant with ambition, a reminder of the never-satiated nature of this business, eternally digesting novelty and youth. And the names: Scary Thought, Acid Crack, The Nice Bazookas, Goose Dooky, Bored Shitless, The Love Nuggets, PU, The Lumps, The Drains, Do-Do Monkey—there was no bottom to the well, no bottom at all. They just kept coming.

He rounded the corner, moving back in time: The Cranks, Slap Happy, The Pluggs, Oblibia, The Drips, Free Meal McGill, the duo Slim and None. And then he began to recognize faces. He studied them and a thousand myriad details, enthralled. It was a private experience; there was no one to tell: I knew him, I remember.

Must be the right place anyway. He crossed the room to the opposite wall, and then suddenly: Lonnie. 8x10 head shot, about 1968, the time of his hit. The emotion came with swift and sudden power. Doug fought his burning eyes, prayed that Grube would not find him like this. He took off his glasses and wiped his eyes against his shoulders, one, then the other. Almost too much. Lonnie. A trivia question now, yet something more than what other people were. Bigger. Had been. Gone now. Smiling like a million dollars from nowhere. It took a moment for the charisma of the photograph to fade and for the others, around it, to appear. Doug found himself looking at his own skinny, diffident self, with the guys—then an older shot, with Artie. God, Artie. What the women call a sweet man. How they had jammed together, just the two of them, for hours. Soaking up all his tricks. Let go—like jumping off a cliff, let it take you.

Doug swallowed, looked away. He wiped his eyes again and tried to collect himself. This was overwhelming; he hadn't expected it, hadn't prepared for it. How was all of this not engulfed and obliterated?

His focus had drifted but now returned, and his gaze was locked directly on it.

It occupied its niche in the patchwork wall simply—yet harboring something so extraordinary it seemed odd to be a piece of anything. It was one of the other black and white shots the woman had taken that day at the lake, at the end of the session. The photograph itself he might have been seeing for the first time, but he retained an oddly clear memory of the day: a rain-cooled late afternoon in May, the drive down there sullen. Then a half hour in the dying light. And there they stood—Glenroy, Dartt, himself—two white, one black—no smiles, no idea whom they were looking at.

Along the bottom in ink now fading someone had written: The Trybald Trio, 1972.

As his trance waned, his gaze moved to others of the Trio, all rather late, one in performance, and he realized there hadn't been many photographs, especially from the early days. But he didn't dwell on the thought because his eye had alighted on another image now: a promo from the same time, a little later: "Streetcar." A busy photograph, too many people—too many pawns crowded around King Dartt. And then just below it—the hand behind this was accurate—the king again, but bearded, in a hat, solo. D. D. Knight? For God's sake. Doug stared, trying to determine what was so different, and then realized it was Dartt's expression: the look of one trying to please.

Doug retreated to the center of the room, wanting to stop, close his eyes, try to absorb all this, but it was too late. His eye had caught sight of something else, not just there but on *display* there, in a glass-covered case above the main door lintel—something he recognized immediately: a shell-pink Fender Strat, its neck cracked, a gash across its heart, strings awry. Somebody had simply picked it up, that was all.

He stepped toward it, drawn to a photograph on the wall below it: a young man, head back, laughing, reddish-blond hair falling about his neck, darker swaths along his cheeks and shading the soft curve of his chin and throat: Glenroy. Doug stood there, looking. He had never seen that picture but he had seen *that. Good Lord, had he been* that *young?*

A voice from behind: "God *damn.*"

Doug turned quickly; the man had materialized without a sound. Ponytail now, different glasses, heavier—but the same nose. Boyd Ange.

"God almighty damn."

He approached, enfolded Doug, pulled away looking at him in amazement.

"I'm not seeing what I'm seeing. God *damn*—" almost tears "—to walk out here and find you standing here, man. God *damn*." He embraced him again. "Why didn't you tell her who you *were*?"

Dumbfounded, Doug could only shake his head.

"I'd have come right out."

Doug, at a loss, smiled. "How you been doing?"

"Man, I've been doing great—the question is, how the hell have *you* been doing?"

He shrugged.

"Where the hell have you *been*, anyway?"

"L. A."

"Playing?"

He nodded.

"What?"

A shrug. "Jazz, fusion stuff."

"Listen, I was really sorry to hear about your mother."

"Thanks."

"I figured you might be around, but I didn't want to, you know…"

"This your place, man?"

"Half mine."

Doug nodded. "I guess I know the other half."

Boyd's expression turned quizzical. "Mm, I doubt it. I don't think you'd know Buddy."

"Buddy?"

"My partner."

"Oh." Doug gave a little laugh. "Man, I thought…I don't know."

"What?"

"*Him.*"

"Him?" He studied Doug for clues. "You don't mean Grube?"

Doug shrugged.

Boyd laughed. "Aw man—where you been? Shit, that little fucker's been gone for ten years. You'll never see him in Atlanta again, I promise you that."

Doug stared at him, then gave a little laugh himself.

Boyd held his hands before him, like bookends, trying to encompass the situation. "Look, just tell me now: what are you doing? Are you here? You going back? I mean, what's happening? How the hell did you find me anyway?"

"I just looked in the phone book, man."

Boyd reflected, then laughed. "Lake Trash."

Doug nodded.

"Man, you should have known he wouldn't have used that."

"I didn't really think about it."

"So what's the deal?"

"Well…I'm not sure."

"That's good enough for me."

Doug looked at him uncertainly.

"Man, there's so much—there's so *much* I want to talk to you about." He studied Doug, as though for the first time. "You look good, man, you look good."

"Thanks."

"You know you're what they call a cult figure."

Doug gave a puzzled frown.

"And I've become a collector." He waved his arm around. "You been looking at my little gallery?"

"Yeah."

"What do you think?"

"Blows me away, man."

"Did you see *that*?" Boyd cut his eyes upward to the guitar.

"Yeah."

"That's something, isn't it?"

"Yeah. That's something."

"Man, I've got some ideas. Want to come down and look at the studio?"

———

The house just kept going down—steps, a room, more steps. The descent ended at the control booth of the cave-like and equipment-crowded studio, with a view, over the sound board, of the main playing room. They seemed to have the place to themselves.

Boyd sat down in his rolling chair. "You're not in a hurry."

Doug shook his head equivocally.

"Sit down." He was rolling himself around the little space. "Listen to this."

Doug sat in a big stuffed chair, its wide armrests stacked with music magazines and catalogs and sundry clutter. From a cabinet against the back wall Boyd took out a DAT tape, snapped it into a unit on a stack to the side, turned to Doug with a smile, fingers on the volume control, waiting. A deep electronic hiss came into the room.

"...severe thunderstorm warnings, cancer, snakes in the water, mad dogs, rusty knives, the wrong pills—some of the things you don't have to worry about when you're dead..."

A poor recording, the voice bizarre. Then some weird guitar chords, and the voice singing over and over, "Everybody's dead, everybody's dead..."

Boyd was grinning at Doug. "Bet you don't know who that is."

"You're right."

"I'll give you a hint: he's extremely drunk."

"No shit."

"I'll give you another hint: he had two sons. Acknowledged anyway." Doug lowered his eyebrows quizzically and shook his head. "Okay, I'm going to show you something only the privileged few get to see," Boyd said, and rolled back to the cabinet. He took a mass of keys from his belt, unlocked a strong box, took something out, and rolled it over to Doug.

"...everybody's dead—you and you and you and you, and you too, Fred..."

9

Boyd handed Doug a yellowed box of old six-inch Scotch reel-to-reel tape. Doug turned it over. In pale blue ink someone had rather carefully lettered a list: "Everybody's Dead," "Sameold Sameold," "Bad in the Way," "If It Does, It Does," "Too Many Cooks," "Shitfaced on the Porch."

"There's only one of these," said Boyd, and presented Doug a snapshot. Black and white, 1960 printed on the crinkly margin: a handsome man with hair combed back, unbuttoned cotton print shirt, caught at an odd moment.

"This is one of the last pictures of him. Maybe the last."

Doug studied it, shook his head.

"Sonny Trimble."

Doug looked up. "You talking about Glenroy's daddy?"

"And Louis's."

"Oh yeah. Louis. You know something, man? I think I've even heard this stuff before."

"You may have. Glenroy had it—before him, Louis. Thank God Glenroy was whatever he was enough to leave everything in Trybald. I got it from Eunice."

"Eunice?"

"His mother."

"You went to see her?"

"Oh, I've been to see her many times. I'm a regular visitor."

"She's still there?"

"Still there. First shift. Going strong—don't ask me how."

"Hm."

"She's given me most of what I have. She trusts me—plus, I could tell she didn't really want it around."

"She by herself?"

"No, she's remarried. I think he's some kind of home-grown preacher. This is the second time, actually."

Doug grew reflective, and Boyd rolled over and stopped the tape.

"Where's he buried?" Doug asked.

"Sonny?"

10

"No, Glenroy."

"Well, they're all there together—in Trybald. People...go there. Leave things on his grave."

Doug looked at him in quiet amazement.

"You know—I tried to find you when he died. I tried hard."

Doug made an odd face. "I heard some guy talking about it in a club one night. I asked him and he told me. Out there, nobody's ever heard of him or the Trio. Hardly anybody."

"Maybe that'll change."

Doug was looking ahead.

"Anyway, I'm sorry you had to hear it like that. I wish I could have found you."

He let out his breath in a sigh. "Wouldn't have mattered." He paused. "You know, I never really heard the whole story."

"How he died, you mean?"

Doug nodded.

"Well," said Boyd, "the thing is, nobody's ever really going to know—exactly. My opinion? It was the wiring, like they said. It was old—all that heart pine—what else could it be?"

"I remember there was a fireplace."

"Man, it was August."

Doug gave a little grunt, stared ahead.

"Anyway, it started in the kitchen, they're pretty sure about that." He paused. "Smoke inhalation all the way. He was probably asleep. Passed out, more like it. At least I hope so. Anyway, it's not like he was, you know..."

Doug grimaced. "Burned all the way down."

"Oh yeah."

"He was living there?"

"Yeah, he was living there. I used to go down there a good bit. He'd get pretty wasted by late afternoon and it could get fairly weird—he sort of stopped bathing—but we'd talk."

Doug gave an odd laugh. "Was he playing any?"

"Yeah, he was playing a lot, actually."

11

"Who with?"

"Well, a lot by himself—I took him a Dobro and he got sort of interested in that—but with various people—down at the Renfroe brothers' place."

"Who?"

Boyd smiled. "Oh, quite a crew, let me tell you. Professional alcoholics and potheads, and surveyors on the side. Plus, they grew the best weed in Georgia—nobody knew where—probably still do. Just these three brothers from Gosom living down on the lake: Danny, Rook, and Stubb. Nice guys actually—just not exactly *with* us. Each one had his own cabin around a little cove called Hatchett Creek. I haven't been there in a long time, but I bet you they're still there and haven't changed a bit. Rook was the oldest—for some reason dogs always barked at him—he was married; Stubb was the middle one, and Danny was the youngest. Danny—he would sit in a chair all day holding a cup of beer, sort of smiling, and everybody would just go around him. The cabin in the middle was Rook's and that's where everything happened. It had a big terrace out front, a barbeque pit, and an old refrigerator they kept a keg in—had a big tap on the front with duct tape all around it. There was all kind of crap all over the place—washing machines and God knows what all—an old truck with the hood open and a tree growing up through the motor, a van on blocks with a really bad redneck-psychedelic paint job—that kind of thing. They had a ratty old houseboat on oil drums they'd go out on all night fishing and raiding trot lines. It was a constant party—starting about Wednesday. They'd fry fish and barbeque, and there'd be people all over the place, mostly from Gosom. You could swim out front—there was an old dock, sort of rickety-looking, and you could count on about half of them ending up naked. The band would set up on the terrace—it was all pick-up, but occasionally some fairly decent people would show up. They'd come get him in a boat and he'd ride over sitting in the middle like Cleopatra in her barge."

Doug laughed. "Sounds like his kind of place."

"Oh, he loved it. And let me tell you, he was *God*. And he was still getting better too. He'd get blown away and if he could get a pretty good band cooking behind him he'd just stand there and play this stuff like you've never heard in your life. Just amazing. I tried to record it a couple of times, but it didn't really work. You were just either there or you weren't."

"What kind of stuff was he playing?"

"Everything. Blues. Rock'n'roll. A lot of it just stuff he made up—you know, just like he used to. He'd just come up with something out of the blue and off he'd go. Chances are you'd never hear it again."

"Was he trying to get a band together?"

Boyd shook his head. "Nah. He wouldn't do it. Of course everybody was trying to push him into it, but he wouldn't do it. They were just—*good* anyway. I think the whole *band* thing, finding the right people and all that—he didn't even want to think about it."

"Sounds like he was doing all right."

"Yeah—he was, basically. Had two women taking care of him—they would take turns. The Renfroe boys kept him in reefer and I kept him in vodka. I'd give him fifty bucks here and there. He'd go up to Allred's and buy baloney or whatever. There and the Renfroes were the only places he ever went. Except for Eunice—every now and then he'd fire up Big Blue and go in to Trybald to see her. How, I don't know, by the grace of God I guess, it kept running. You know, it's still there."

"What?"

"The Valiant."

"Where? You mean…"

"Yeah, down there—just sitting right where it was, one side of it charred black. Nobody's touched it, nobody's been out there, they just left it."

Doug looked puzzled.

"Isn't that funny? It bothered me at first, and then I thought—well, maybe it was meant to be left alone. I've been trying to buy the place but they won't sell it."

"They?"

"Jernigan Mills. They own that whole side of the lake."

"I thought…"

"What—Grube?" Boyd laughed. "Shit. That's what he wanted you to think. But he just leased it. I found that out when it ran out."

"You paid it?"

"It was me or nobody."

"Glenroy didn't know."

"He considered himself getting even with Grube." He smiled. "If I *could* buy it, I'd just put up a gate and leave it, just like that."

"Mm." Doug was reflecting again. "Must have been—how long?"

"Labor Day—a little after—to August. Almost a year. That winter, I got him in the studio."

Doug looked up.

"I want to play it for you—we just took a few of his best ideas and worked them up. All instrumental. He could write—one day the world's going to recognize that."

"Mm."

"You won't believe *him*—but the band—what band? They weren't even…you know, it's always money. It never pays to be cheap—I've learned that. I see now exactly what I should have done. I should have borrowed three times as much money and bought the best musicians I could get." He shook his head. "How was I supposed to know?"

"It might not have worked with those guys."

"I'll never know. I basically did it all wrong. Fucking Grube. I should never have gotten mixed up with him. It took me a year to get untangled from all that shit. It really goes back to that Streetcar deal."

"Yeah, I saw Dartt's picture out there."

14

Boyd laughed. "Yeah, good God."

"He went solo?"

Boyd snorted. "About two gigs and three tons of bullshit."

"What kind of deal you talking about?"

"Him and Grube, man."

"They had a deal?"

"Hell yeah, they had a deal. And I've never really decided how I feel about it. Because it goes two ways."

"What you mean?"

"I mean, on one hand you look back and you think, that's what killed the Trio. But on the other hand, you remember Grube just let me have *Lake Moon*. The whole thing. The concept, everything. And Dartt played his ass off. Of course, after you and Glenroy left, we spent about two weeks, all day every day, mixing out his songs—and he's still punching shit in the whole time—and I'm saying, yeah, they're great—and I never got a cent out of it, by the way, but I didn't care. I would have *paid* to make that record. And then Grube—whatever else you say about him—he *knew*. And by the time Dartt found out what we *did* with those songs, it didn't matter. Because by then we were already into the Streetcar thing. Which I never got paid for either, incidentally."

"Streetcar made a record?"

Boyd gave a little laugh. "It never happened." He sighed. "It was December before we went in—I remember because we had to listen to Dartt all that time. So finally Grube, owing pretty much everybody by then, got it set up and they went in, and *Jesus*. All the songs were Dartt's and I mean every single thing had to be perfect. Every note. And the guitar player sucked, and the drummer sucked, and we'd just keep doing it over and over. Even when something was plenty good enough, he'd hear some minuscule little thing he didn't like and we'd do it again, and it'd be worse. I remember two weeks went by and we had absolutely nothing. Grube was shitting in his pants. After he disappeared we kept going, and it took about three or four days to realize he'd hauled ass. That's when we found out he hadn't put up a penny. I mean, the entire thing was bullshit. And then all these people started appearing from everywhere looking for him."

"Did Glenroy know about any of this?"

Boyd shook his head. "We never talked about it. He never asked."

Doug considered this.

"Man, it was *bad.* I knew Dartt would do something but I wasn't smart enough to figure out what. You know what he did? He took all the Streetcar stuff—probably been jerking off to it for ten years—which, who cares, right? But we were still in Tomorrow and I had everything in there. Everything. Just lying around. Unbelievably stupid. He didn't take it all, thank God. Mainly just his stuff from Lake Moon, which is all he wanted, but all the outtakes too. All of them."

Doug's brow furrowed.

"Not that there were all that many. God came to earth for that session."

"I remember some of his songs…"

"Except for those."

"You kept everything?"

"Hell yeah, I kept it. Man, there's nothing I don't keep. Anyway, that's where the bootlegs came from. I think he was also trying to trash the record."

"Bootlegs?"

"Man, where you been? There's all kinds of bootlegs out there. There's a whole underground thing." He laughed.

Doug looked puzzled.

"But of course it had the exact opposite effect. Which really pissed him off—but now he sort of tries to cash in on it too."

"You still see him?"

"Nah, not too much anymore."

"Is he playing?"

Boyd shrugged. "I'm not really sure. But I did go see him a few times. He got a job with some kind of delivery company and he'd been working his way up the ladder. He really changed. Mainly the way he looked. Cut his hair. Bald on top."

"Bald?"

"Yeah. And glasses. You'd look right at him and wouldn't know him. I was just trying to get the tapes back. Mainly one from way back—back before you even knew you were a band. Down at the cabin."

"A tape?"

"You know, microphone hanging from the ceiling kind of thing. But it's the very first stuff the Trio did. And I had it. Naturally I hadn't made a copy. I offered him five hundred bucks."

"For real?"

"Which was a mistake, because all that did was let him know how valuable it was to me."

"You ain't never gone see that shit, man."

"I know. I also wanted to find Moon Tuna—she had some photographs of the Trio—real early stuff. But he either really didn't know or wouldn't tell me where she was."

Doug just shook his head.

"Well, anyway, let me show you a couple more things." He rolled back to the cabinet and returned with another box of reel-to-reel tape.

Doug took it, looked it over. Again, on the back was listed a number of songs: "Jeez Louise," "Grapefruit," "Squatty Body," "Amy, Smile," "Mother Roach," "On Hard," "Bad Gas," "Take Forever One Time," "Say Hello to Bob (I Believe You Two Have Met)." He smiled.

"This is the only one of Louis's tapes left. At least that anybody's ever going to find. You know, he made a list—he had over a hundred songs."

"Damn."

"He was only twenty. I've also got a tape Debacle made—about 1966. It's fascinating—you can hear Glenroy trying to do all this stuff he can't quite do yet. Absolutely no fear—he just keeps going no matter what. And Louis could really sing."

"We used to listen to some of that."

"Then there's an Epitome tape from late '69. They're light years better."

"Man, it's incredible you got all this."

Boyd laughed. "I spent a week going through their closet in Trybald. You wouldn't believe some of the stuff I found."

"Probably not."

"Of course, I've got all the Trio stuff: the Auditorium, a live performance from '71—before I had any idea what I was doing—all the stuff from the "Jeez Louise" session, including a couple of jams that I think capture the band—the live band—better than anything, even if it was in the studio. I've even got a copy of The Decisions' studio demo."

"Shit," Doug laughed.

"What I want to do is take the best of it and make a commemorative package—a double album with a booklet."

Doug gave a puzzled frown.

"I think it'd be really successful."

"Hm."

"Don't you think so?"

"I don't know, man."

"Of course, it'd be nice if we could reissue *Lake Moon*—we missed the tenth anniversary, but whatever."

Doug didn't reply.

"But that's obviously not going to happen. At least now. I'd be amazed if Grube still had the rights, but I haven't been able to find out who does. It's been out of print so long. And hey, I want to do an interview with you."

"An interview?"

"For the booklet. You were there for the whole thing. And you're the only person who really knew Glenroy."

"I didn't know him."

"Come on."

"Not really. The cat to interview is that dude, Jimmie..."

"Jimmie Myles. Oh yeah, we've had quite a few talks through the years."

"Well, he can tell you a lot. I can't really tell you anything."

"That's not true."

"Just listen to the music—that's all."

"Oh I do. Believe me, I do." He was smiling at him. "Man, I can't believe you're sitting there. So—what's it been like out there?"

"I've played a lot of music—a lot of different people."

"Done any recording?"

"Some."

"You're not playing with anybody now?"

"Well, yes and no."

"Yes and no." He gave a short laugh. "Are you going back or not?"

"I really don't know."

"Well, look—it's just something for you to think about, okay? But I could get you together with a lot of good musicians. People who know about you. Who'd give their nuts to play with you. And it's just an idea, okay? But what I want to do is take Glenroy's stuff off that last session and put a new band under it."

The frown was back.

"We'll put you right to work." He laughed.

Doug shifted in his chair.

"Think about it?"

"Yeah, okay."

"You know—it was *you*. I mean, with Glenroy."

Doug sighed. "I can't help him now."

"That's what I'm saying. Maybe you can."

Doug shook his head sadly. The room fell quiet.

Beyond the control window the small studio, with its chrome stands and sundry equipment, a piano, a B-3, cords coiling over the wooden floor, foam walls, sat still and mute, like a picture.

"You've got a nice set-up, man."

"A lot of work's gone into it." He laughed. "I mean, it's mostly wannabees and bad gospel groups, I don't know. But I love it."

Doug nodded. Silence reigned for a moment, except for the pervasive hum of the room that seemed to become suddenly audible.

"You know anything about Alma?"

"She's around."

"I was wondering how she was doing."

"Good, I think. I see her sometimes."

Doug glanced at him.

"Place where I have my insurance. She works there."

"She married?"

"Was. She has a daughter—probably about seven or eight. The guy was a bastard. He's gone. Been gone."

"Where's she staying?"

"Perry Homes."

Doug slowly shook his head. "I was just wondering how she was doing."

"Hey—how are you getting around?"

Doug shrugged. "Bus."

"Look. I've got a car. I know you've got some places you need to go. Let me take you."

"Naw, man, I..."

"Come on—you've been gone eleven years; you can't refuse me that."

Doug looked up, seemed about to say something.

"I'll take you by there. I can find it."

At last he barely nodded, and something in his pained expression relaxed. "I had one other place..."

"I'll take you."

"And—there was one thing."

Boyd lifted his eyebrows. "Name it."

"The record."

"The record?"

"Yeah, I'd like to see it." Pause. "And hear it. If you've got it."

"If I've *got* it?" Boyd smiled. "How long's it been?"

"I've never heard it."

Boyd's expression was incredulous.

"Just in the studio—the playbacks."

"Do you even have it?"

Doug shook his head.

———

A few moments later, sitting alone in a small room, he held it and saw immediately the whole idea, that it made sense, belonged precisely in the flow of things—though it didn't feel like him, but someone else, someone whose story he had heard of, not lived. As he gazed at the strange figures against the lake, both seeing for the first time and remembering, together, he found no emotion tasteful, but only looked with innocent expectation across the room as a deep electronic hiss and some faint pops came into the air like wind blowing open a door.

Lake Moon
The Trybald Trio
Marathon Records. Recorded May 1972, Tomorrow Studio, Atlanta, Georgia. Produced by Rob Grube. Engineered and mixed by Boyd Ange.

Side One	Side Two
1. Jeez Louise (L. Trimble/R.Grube)	1. Lake Trash (A. L. Preast)
2. Moolah (D. Dartt/G. Trimble/ D. Earley)	2. Do Like Me (L. Trimble)
3. Grapefruit (L. Trimble)	3. Rainy (G. Trimble)
4. Mother Roach (L. Trimble)	

———

"This is good right here," said Doug, and Boyd pulled over against the curb. They were just off Edgewood Avenue, under a Kool billboard with sanitized Negro models. Doug nodded to Boyd. "I appreciate it, man."

"I'll be happy to help you look for it."

"Thanks, man, I think I'll just walk."

"You want to say five o'clock?"

Doug nodded. "Sounds about right."

"If you're not here, I'll wait."

Doug smiled and started off down the sidewalk. The neighborhood, a little world of self-contained life, hadn't changed much. It seemed, if anything, louder; even on this weekday mid-afternoon many of the yards blared with music. Children played. Young men washed their cars. A few old folks haunted the porches. The streets had a sameness, and he merely walked, turning or not turning by instinct, hardly thinking at all, but following some inner map. He walked and no one really took much notice of him at all.

Which was unexpectedly reassuring. You belong where no one notices you.

A little strip of shops came up, among them a café. Cool Inside, it promised, ice melting over the letters. He stopped, peered in, found himself looking at a woman looking back at him. He stepped inside.

It *was* cool. And the woman, in white, her hair in a net, holding an empty silver pan, was smiling.

"You too late, honey. It's after three o'clock."

The place was vacant and the serving line only empty holes.

But the woman seemed about to laugh. He smiled back, looked around the room feeling transported back twenty-five years.

"You ain't got any ice tea?"

"Honey, I got enough ice tea you take a bath in it."

"Where the tub at?"

She laughed.

He lingered about twenty minutes, at a front booth, watching the world outside like an old play. The woman, and her coworkers, had a good look at him then left him alone.

When he stepped outside he felt for a second he had walked into some sort of exhaust vent, or the wake of a bus, then realized it was the day itself. He remembered: you never get used to it.

Walking again—a block, then another—then more feeling than hearing the sound he cocked his head, like one catching a scent. The almost-sound, a snare drum, came from somewhere indefinite, from some other street, or was maybe just a lost part of the day itself. He stopped, surprised by memory.

Mr. Guthrie. 1965. A gifted man, gnawed by something within himself, but fair. His listening, exacting features in the closed little room became those of the taskmaster Haskell Harr, known only by his schoolmasterly picture on the tattered book. The piece was "The Glenwood Boy" and Mr. Guthrie sat listening attentively to a rendition of it unlike any he'd ever heard—snapping smartly, with dynamic nuance and finesse. When it was over, he shook his head with a little smile, having written nothing on his pad, and exhaled a long sigh.

Walking again; the sound faded and disappeared—he turned a corner and knew immediately: this is it.

An old street, shaded under a canopy of oaks, the sidewalk cracked and root-buckled. The houses on one side were lower than on the other, and he noticed that the street followed the base of a little ridge, his side the high side. His mind replayed his old stored image.

Which, of course, turned out to be less than accurate. The house did not loom but simply sat there, elevated, its yellow paint weathered, and though it extended farther back than one might have supposed, it was smaller than he remembered. He stopped at the foot of the concrete block steps rearing up the barren slope to the porch. The yard was all dirt, scarred, gullied, roots exposed like writhing snakes, not a blade of grass. A water oak grew in the space between the sidewalk and street, its fallen acorns sculpted into drifts against the fractured sidewalk, cracking underfoot.

Tired potted flowers formed an orderly row along the porch railing like convalescents taking the air; behind them sat two or three disused chairs. The answer to his knock was slow in coming, but at last he heard someone pecking at the locks and chains behind the door, which cracked open. A light brown face appeared there, with reading glasses and a halo of white hair—a woman he had met once. Her expression metamorphosed from suspicion, to curiosity, to wonder, to fragile recognition, in one unfolding moment.

"*Doug?*"

"Yes ma'am, Miz Johnson—it's me."

A moment of astonishment, one beholding the other.

Then she recollected herself. "Well, my heavens, come on in where it's cool." She opened the door fully and he pulled back the wobbly screen door and stepped inside.

The room smelled oppressively familiar, and "cool" was generous—it was the murky half-cool of a shaded house. A pervasive hum suggested that somewhere in the back things were better. Religious pictures and effects dominated the knickknacks scattered over the sterile room. He took it all in quickly, had no desire to look closely, as somewhere within him a clock had begun a countdown: just so many minutes, and no more, could he stand this.

"I just happened to come up here, or I wouldn't even have heard you."

Doug smiled weakly, nodded his head.

"Are you—back in Atlanta?"

"I'm not sure, Miz Johnson. I'm just trying to take care of some things."

"Did you just get here?"

"Yes'm—just a couple of hours ago."

"You been out in California all this time?"

"Yes ma'am, I have."

24

She stared, then bestirred herself. "Can I get you something to drink?"

He nodded.

"Well, just sit down—I'll be right back."

The sound of muffled television surged and diminished with the opening and closing of the door. While she was gone Doug perched angularly on the forward edge of a hard chair. As the door re-opened and the television noise repeated, Doug stood up. Behind Mrs. Johnson, this time, appeared a man. He carried his bulk resentfully, his hair like his wife's gone white. Dressed in baggy shorts, tee shirt, and slippers he gave the impression of someone who had, indignantly, just bolted upright from something.

He stopped, and only stared as Mrs. Johnson handed Doug his lemonade. Doug gave her a little smile of thanks, then held the glass in his spidery fingers as Mrs. Johnson looked solicitously from him to her scowling husband.

"How you doing, Mr. Johnson?"

He nodded curtly. "Getting by. How about yourself?

Doug shrugged. "I guess I'm still around."

"Why don't we sit down," pleaded Mrs. Johnson, and they did, in a triangle, Doug perched again.

Silence.

"Look like it want to be as hot as it can the day you come back," Mrs. Johnson offered. Doug nodded. "I hope we can get a shower—it's been so hot and dry."

"Yes ma'am, that would be nice."

"Well, I'm just gone come right out and say what's on my mind, if that's all right," said Mr. Johnson.

"Please—that's why I'm here."

"That's why you're here? I got to say, that's just what I was wondering, and I'll tell you one thing, I didn't never expect to see you sitting there."

"Well Henry, he's…"

"Just let me say what I got to say to the man." A sharp look at his wife, then slowly back to Doug. "The way I was raised, it's a son's place to take care of his mother."

Doug nodded.

"And a son that don't even come to his mama's funeral..."

"Henry, he's just..."

"I done told you to let me talk." Back to Doug. "What kind of a son is that?"

"A bad one. A real bad one." This abjectly—then looking up with a plea: "But I didn't know. I really didn't know. I didn't hear about it in time. I've moved a lot. When I found out I left the next day. I just walked out on everything..."

"You good at that, ain't you?"

"Henry..."

"Well?"

"No," said Doug. "He's right. But I didn't hear about it till it was too late. I've been on a bus for four days."

The older man breathed heavily, his hands squeezing the knobs of his chair arms, and didn't say anything else.

"It was a very nice funeral," inserted Mrs. Johnson.

Tears glistened in Doug's eyes. "I always thought I would see her again. You got to know that. I know I can't ever pay you back—but you got to know I loved her, in my own way, and I've got to live with myself." He shook his head. "I won't ever see her again."

"Won't nobody," said Mr. Johnson.

"Miss Vonceil knew how you felt," Mrs. Johnson said, her own eyes wet. "She talked about you all the time. Wasn't hardly nobody in the world but her Doug to her."

Doug leaned aside and took a wad of folded money from his trouser pocket. He held it up briefly, the outer bill even at a glance having the rare look and air of a high denomination note—then set it on the coffee table.

"I'm sure it's not enough, but it's all I can do right now. There'll be more coming."

"Child, you don't have to do that. We took up a collection at the church, and she's buried out at Morningstar…"

"Ain't nobody refuse it," cut in Mr. Johnson. "Ain't none of what we talking about free."

"But Henry, can't you see he's…"

"I just don't want to hear it. They's all kinds of sacrifices been made, all the way around. We give that money, and anymore else you put with it, back to the church and they be *glad* to get it. We ain't talking about rich people here—not nowhere near it."

"Thank you. That's all I can say. Thank you."

"We appreciate everything you sent," said Mrs. Johnson.

Doug shook his head. "It was nothing."

A silence fell then. It seemed strange that after eleven years it could all be said in so few words.

"She was a kind soul," Mrs. Johnson said, "full of love—wasn't one bone in her body mean or spiteful to anybody. She didn't have no easy life, and her last years was hard—but she was a good soul."

Doug nodded, then at last took a drink of the lemonade; the ice at the top had melted and it was watery. He reflected. "Morningstar—where is that?"

"It's out from East Point—it's a little cemetery there at the church. You know my own mama was raised right out there."

"No ma'am—I didn't know that."

"It's not big—her grave is off on the left edge by a big chinaberry tree. You can find it."

Doug nodded. A brief silence. "I was wondering…Monroe Goode—did you know him?"

"Who?" growled Mr. Johnson.

"Monroe Goode. Just—somebody I used to know. I believe he might have visited here once or twice."

"Never heard of him."

"I think I know who you mean." Then to her husband: "You remember, Henry. He was that *man* that called on Miss Vonceil a few times. He would come around to the back door."

"That thing? Good God, what you want with him?"

"I was just wondering if he had been around lately."

"Oh no," said Mrs. Johnson. "It's been *several* years."

"Shii-" hissed Mr. Johnson, hands still on the chair arms, turning his head away.

Doug set down his glass, rose, wiping his hands on his pants. The Johnsons rose as well, Mr. Johnson slowly. He was sweating, conflicted between not having said a tenth of what was impacted within him and his need to get back to the air conditioning.

"California—it ain't like Georgia atall, is it?" said Mrs. Johnson.

"No'm—it's not. It's different. But, I don't know, you get down to it, it's about the same."

Mrs. Johnson seemed amazed. They were at the door—not quite goodbye.

Doug hesitated. "I wanted to ask you about somebody else." He stopped, they looked at him. "Alma Lowe."

"Never heard of her," said Mr. Johnson.

"Henry—" Mrs. Johnson softly to the rescue again. "You know Alma." Her husband looked at her, frowning and puzzled. She looked at him, then back to Doug. "She's been good to visit."

Doug nodded. He seemed about to say, ask something—but didn't.

Then, goodbye—he made it to the porch, the door closed, it was over.

———

He stood there, gazing from that height over the shady, tree-lined street. *She's been good to visit.* He felt alone—but free. He looked in one direction, then the other, then descended the steps and started away, hearing again or imagining the solitary snare pattering at the edge of the heavy afternoon.

Free—but alone.

Alone.

1965. At fifteen, an introverted and beanpole kid in glasses, Doug stood by himself at the edge of a milling schoolyard. The sea of white students behaved as though he were non-existent, their eyes moving over him like an irregularity in the air. Only seven or eight other students of his color attended the school, none of whom he really knew. Like anyone treated non-existent he felt non-existent, and so he started as four white students crossed the semi-circular drive and approached him over the lawn.

He knew them. They were the other drummers in the band, their leader a lanky blond kid, with talent, named Stan Chambers. They had neither accepted nor rejected Doug but only reached a silent and uncomfortable truce.

Stan looked embarrassed.

"I guess you're first chair."

Doug barely nodded, standing in tense, expectant silence.

"I'm not saying you don't deserve it."

"I just played it the best I could, that's all."

"I guess we all did. I was a little off—I wasn't really concentrating. I had a lot on my mind. But anyway, I don't know, maybe you are the best."

"You can challenge."

"Yeah, I know."

The boys shifted around uncomfortably.

"We can't play 'Dixie' anymore."

Doug stared at him.

"My father says that's not right."

Doug shrugged. "It's just a song. To me."

"Well, we can't play it."

Doug was at a loss.

"My father says challenging you was not the way to handle it."

Doug didn't reply, watching him carefully.

"I guess maybe we ought to fight."

"What?"

"That's what he says anyway."

"Fight? You mean—fight?"

"I guess so."

"Why don't you just challenge?"

Stan reflected but could only say, "That's what my father said."

Doug waited uneasily.

"After practice I guess we can go down to the woods behind the practice field."

Doug shook his head, perplexed.

"Okay?" Stan's eyes met Doug's in a fleeting, daring flash.

Then the boys were gone.

———

Absurd.

Stan stood a few steps beyond his friends in a clearing in the woods below the schoolyard, facing Doug who stood alone.

Doug looked at him. No one said anything; everyone was uncomfortable. Stan took a step. The invisible force impelling him was palpable, and nothing new.

"Okay. I guess it's time to do it."

But he didn't do it—they only waited. Birds made noise in the trees. A small plane droned overhead.

"You say it's your father wants us to fight. What do you want?"

"We might as well just do it!"

"I can't see any reason for it."

"What good is it doing standing here talking about it?"

But they only stood there.

At last, Doug shook his head. "Man, this is crazy."

"Okay, that's enough talking!" Stan took a step, shoved Doug on the chest.

Doug's upper body swayed backward, but he held his spot. Some feeling came into his voice. "This is crazy!"

"Let me take your glasses," one of the boys offered, coming towards him.

"I ain't take' my glasses off—I can't see! There ain't any reason to do this."

"Come on!" Stan called, advancing again. "Come on!" He threw his weight into Doug's midsection, trying to take him down.

They grappled awkwardly, then pulled away from each other and held up their fists.

"You started this!" Doug cried. "I didn't do anything to you! It's just crazy!"

Stan took a swing; Doug dodged, grabbed his arm, and held it until they were wrestling once more. A little pinch, a twist, a kick: they were both getting mad now. Suddenly they were on the ground, limbs flailing and kicking, then on their feet again, smeared with dirt, circling each other. Fists lashed out, but few connected, and soon they were entwined again, groping furiously for advantage.

Finally they separated once more and this time Stan landed a grazing blow on Doug's jaw, which Doug, hurt and stunned, his glasses askew, abruptly returned with a roundabout to the side of the head that sent Stan reeling backwards.

"Fighting dirty, huh?" Stan cried in pain. And he charged, his head low, into Doug's stomach, but Doug negated the force of the charge by bending his body and giving way, taking hold of his adversary's waist from above. They wrestled, then extricated themselves and stood facing each other yet again, breathing heavily now, their clothes dirty and torn, leaves and twigs and dirt in their hair. The gallery, as it had all along, watched in taut silence. Doug barely had time to adjust his glasses, and then Stan charged again.

But more or less the same thing happened. Finally, after about twenty minutes, there was nowhere for it to go. Weary, feeling the futility of it, they faced each other again.

"Hey come on, that's enough," one of the watchers finally said.

And that was all they needed. Neither of them really hurt, nothing changed, the artificial heat in the little clearing dissipated into awkward embarrassment. Doug watched the four boys walk away, then headed home.

———

He had planned to slip in the back, but as he came down the sidewalk he saw his aunt and Vonceil on the front porch and, too late, realized they had seen him.

"Lord, child," exclaimed Aunt Regina. "What happened to you?"

"Nothing."

"My foot, nothing. You been in a fight?"

"It wasn't nothing."

"You ain't hurt, are you?"

Doug shook his head contemptuously.

Miss Vonceil, worrying a handkerchief in her hands, rocked slightly, smiling.

"Was it a white boy?" asked Aunt Regina.

Doug barely nodded.

Regina sighed heavily. "Lord, Lord, Lord."

"It ain't like that."

"What happened?"

"He started it."

"I'd a guessed that. Was it a big boy?"

"No'm."

"Was it just one?"

Doug nodded.

"Them pants torn?"

"A little."

Regina sighed again, shook her head, and looked down the street.

Doug started up the steps and Miss Vonceil, whose eyes had never left him, asked proudly, "What did you learn in school today, Doug?"

"Nothing," Doug returned curtly, crossing the porch, "I didn't already know." The screen door banged to behind him.

The house smelled of food. At the kitchen sink he washed his hands, splashed his face, drank a glass of water—then went to the room he shared with his cousins. Andrew, the elder, was off somewhere, but Kenny was lying on his bed with a transistor radio and an earplug. As Doug entered, Kenny removed the earplug and sat up eagerly. The radio played on, distant and static.

"You been in a fight?"

Doug hesitated, eyes narrowed. "Yeah."

"Did you lick him?"

"You mean them?"

"Aw, come on."

"Naw, it was only one. Big football player. Had to bust him."

"Naw, unh unh."

"I ain't lying to you."

"Tell me what it was really."

Doug sighed. "What it was really? Nothing. Just a bunch of crazy nothing made me tear up my good pants."

The walls of the room teemed with pictures clipped from newspapers, magazines, catalogs. Around Doug's bed, and Kenny's, a few photos of famous drummers and other musicians formed a collage with fabulous, glossy catalog pages of drum sets, like Joe Morello showing off Ludwigs. In a corner, squeezed into the small room with fanatical economy, sprawled something closer to the real thing, though nothing one might see in a catalog. The only legitimate pieces were the bass drum, hi-hat, and snare, three fatigued specimens he had saved enough money to buy from a friend of a friend; all else was the product of ingenuity, fancy, and junkyard luck: tubs for tom-toms, the top of an old bird cage or a bicycle basket with some of the wires clipped for sizzle, or hanging hubcaps filled with pennies, for cymbals—even one real cymbal but with a triangular slice of it missing that he had found one afternoon discarded behind a music store—all of these propped or suspended in position by concoctions of wire and tape and rod.

"Did you lick him?" Kenny asked again.

"Nobody licked nobody."

"What was you fighting about?"

"Account of he made me."

"How come?"

"Because I'm better than he is."

"Play something for me. Just one time."

"Can't do it."

"Come on—please."

"Naw, man, I got to get changed and cleaned up—ain't got time for none of that."

"Come on, just one time. Please."

"Boy, I done told you, I'm busy."

Kenny was grinning, bouncing on his knees. "Please, please, please."

"You better stop all that, or I ain't playing nothing."

Kenny stopped. "Just go round the world one time—two times!—that's all you got to do. Then I be quiet."

"Boy, you ain't nothing but a pest—some kind of mosquito flying around me."

Doug wormed in behind his set, sat down on his sawed-off kitchen stool, and took up a pair of mangled sticks, one held together with tape. He kicked the bass drum a couple of times, eyeing the suspect pedal with its wad of masking tape. Kenny was watching alertly.

He started slowly, borrowing some random riff floating by, gradually working it into a more complicated and hypnotic rhythm—then keeping it alive with his left foot made his way all around his set bringing forth a wondrous staccato and simmering eruption of sounds, then back to the unabandoned rhythm, his hands and feet working like some bizarre machine—then a final trip around the world, a flourish, the end. He stood up.

Kenny fell back on his bed, kicking his feet and laughing with delight.———

Walking again, listening.

Snare drum—tight, remembered rudiments rising like a succession of geometric shapes into the air—rising and floating away—impelled by a fleeting and whimsical energy, sounding muffled from the cold afternoon outside, mingling with the odor of the septic tank, rising like the chimney smoke.

Then gaining momentum, luring the feet, the toms, finally the erratic lightning flash of cymbals, becoming a locomotive bearing down a mountain presenting only two options: jump on or get out of the way. The house rocks and shakes.

The big room inside, cool around the far edges, lies open and littered with the remains of food, beer cans, bottles, overflowing ashtrays, roaches left everywhere—amps, mike stands, cords, a mike hanging from the ceiling on a coat hanger, leading to a battle-weary Teac reel-to-reel, two girls vague on the couch: a young man with Samson-like black hair excitedly shoulders a black Fender bass, and the power instantly doubles. They ride it, talk and answer, chop it down, build it back—play with it.

Laughter.

Then the other, blowing out a stream of blue smoke, takes his guitar and begins to tell a new story, though the same—and in a moment the innate and pregnant rhythm has exuded itself into music, naturally, and the bass player is singing about a monkey on his back, cleverly, and it is a song, then like a fish jumping it is gone forever.

Laughter.

———

The afternoon, slouching toward suppertime, had lost some of its infernal edge, but still hung humidly over the earth. Off to the southwest the bruised sky sent a promising rustle through the tops of the trees, as the woman stood in the dank kitchen thinking, without much heart, of food. Her daughter worked in a large notebook, wielding a big red pencil. On the table the peanut butter sat open, speared with a knife, beside a box of graham crackers. The girl had a smear of peanut butter on her glasses.

"Look at you—I don't know why you so sloppy."

Soup, on the back burner from habit—let it take its time. Sitting at the table she drank iced tea, leaving her hand around the cold glass, watching the girl. Eventually a hissing sound came from the stove and she rose to turn it down. She took a box of Saltines from the cabinet, cocked her head, then sat down again at the table, waiting.

"Gayle, honey, go see who that is at the door."

Gayle looked up at her mother in surprise.

She gave her an encouraging nod.

The girl laid down her pencil, went to the hallway, paused looking over her shoulder, then disappeared.

The woman stared at the still-life on the table, listening. These weeks had left an expectant rawness along her nerves. She waited what seemed a long time, and when the girl reappeared she stood there in the hallway looking at her mother.

"Was it somebody?"

The girl slowly nodded.

Rising, the woman hesitated, then went to turn off the stove. She passed through the hallway, where the floor sagged around the furnace grid, to the threshold of the front room. She stopped there, in the murky air hardly moved by the window fan rustling the curtains. He stood as little past the front threshold as one can stand and be in the house. Her first thought was: he hasn't changed. Different glasses, but he still looked young, still slender, even in his face, still tall, graceful. She wondered how she appeared to him—feeling herself completely changed, heavier, older. Gayle stole like a shadow to her side.

"Alma."

Her face went through a war of emotions, and it took all the strength she had, and some borrowed from Gayle, to make indignation the final one. She lifted her chin, breathing deeply.

"I see you ain't dead."

He shook his head. Then for an instant he almost panicked—another suffocating room, decorated with religion and resign. He swallowed.

"How you doing?"

"I'm living my life."

"You look real good, Alma."

She shrugged. "You here because of Vonceil?"

He gave an ambiguous nod.

"You late."

"I know." He flinched from her gaze. "I didn't hear in time."

A dozen chastisements passed through her mind, a dozen explanations through his, but neither spoke.

At last she took a few steps into the room, Gayle shadowing her, and sat down. Gayle attached herself to the side of her chair. Some moment had passed.

"Might as well sit down."

Doug took a seat on the green sofa he remembered, leaning neither forward nor back. His eyes made one quick sweep around the room, paused at a framed snapshot on the bookshelf. Beside it sat a little bag tied at the top with a piece of yellow yarn. Alma and Gayle watched him. He glanced across their gaze, shifted slightly wiping his sweaty palms on his pants.

"Gayle, this Mr. Earley. Somebody I knew before you were born."

Knowing perfectly well who he was, she stared at him.

"Why don't you go see if DeLois home." Gayle was slow in responding. Alma turned to her. "Go on now. You can finish your homework later."

Slowly, looking over her shoulder, the girl retreated down the dim hallway.

"You got a pretty girl."

Alma nodded.

"What's her name?"

"Tawana Gayle. Call her Gayle."

Doug sent a searching glance to her, looked away.

"What about you—you got a family?"

He shook his head, began to ask something, but had a mouthful of silence.

37

"Her father is gone and won't be back. There's a man I see sometimes."

He nodded.

"You been in California?" A nod. "All this time?" Another nod. "You got a job?"

"I've been playing in bands, Alma." He gave a little laugh. "What else have I ever done?"

"I couldn't say what all you done since I ain't seen your face in eleven years."

He absorbed her scorn. "How about you?"

"How about me what?"

"How have you...been doing?"

"All you got to do is look around to see how I been doing."

He responded with a tight-lipped expression.

"I've got by. They ain't came and took nothing."

"You haven't changed."

"I guess some things don't show."

"Alma, look..." She had her queenly look again, head high, nostrils angry, waiting. "I came here..." His voice faltered.

"Why *did* you come here?"

He couldn't think of a way to answer. "You've got a right to hate me—I know that."

"Hate? You come back here after eleven years talking about hate?"

"I'm just saying how it is."

"You don't know how nothing is. How you know what I feel?"

He raised his arms, let them fall.

She was crying, wiping her cheeks with her fingers.

"Alma..."

"Alma what? You eleven years too late!"

He let out a breath, wiped his palms, leaned back into the couch, let her cry.

Words struggled mutely within him. "Sometimes—the world feels like a bottle we're in—and the sky just some cotton stuck in the top."

"What we—the aspirin?"

"Naw, we the bugs somebody caught."

"What they gone do with us?"

"They don't tell you that."

Alma sniffed loudly. "Maybe you a bug—I ain't."

"It's just the way I feel sometimes."

"Is that what you came back to tell me—that you feel like a bug?"

"No, Alma, it's just talking. It's just words—it doesn't mean anything."

"Like the way you ain't called, you ain't took the trouble to write, to let me know where you was, if you was alive or dead?"

"Alma..."

"I've had stray dogs come through my yard I treated better than that!"

"I can't *explain* it."

A soft rumble of thunder rolled across the sky.

A moment passed. "You like something to drink?"

"Yeah—if you got something." He pulled himself forward.

"Just stay where you at—I'll get it."

She brought him some tea, and her own glass, and sat down again.

"You in a band now?"

"Well," Doug sighed. "Yeah."

"What that suppose to mean?"

He shrugged. "Maybe I'm not sure where it's going."

She observed him. A moment slipped by. "Why not?"

He sighed, considering his response. "Everybody's real good. It's good music." He paused. "Kind of music you hear it, you say that's good and that's it. It's a lot of work learning it."

"I thought you enjoyed that."

39

"I do. I don't mean it like that. It—occupies your mind. It's..." He shook his head. "I don't know." Pause. "Seems like lately it just left me."

"What?"

"Whatever it is. It's not the music. It's *me*."

"You what?"

"Just sitting there bored."

She studied him. "Everybody get bored sometimes."

"I don't mean that. I'm talking about being sick of something. Like I'm just watching myself."

Alma looked puzzled.

"I don't know how to explain it."

"I'm sure it will pass."

"Probably will."

A moment of silence. "How long you staying?"

He grimaced. "I don't know."

Alma observed him, waited.

"You remember Boyd? The guy that..."

"I remember Boyd."

"I went to see him—matter of fact, he brought me over here."

She listened.

"He said something about some studio work." He made a face. "Old stuff. It's...Glenroy is who it is."

"Glenroy?"

He exhaled. "Yeah. I thought all that was dead and gone a long time ago."

"What you mean, Glenroy?"

"Some studio stuff he did—put down a new rhythm track."

She seemed amazed.

"The way he holds on to all that..." Doug shook his head. "Like going through somebody's drawers, seeing what you find." She watched him. "I listened to the record. It was better than I remembered. But it's something that ain't coming back

again. None of it is. There won't never be another one like
him."

"Even if that's true, you still got the rest of your life to
live."

He smiled wanly.

"Maybe *you* have to be the one."

He looked at her—for an instant their eyes touched—he
blinked, looked away.

"You going to see your mother's grave?"

He nodded.

"You know how to find it?"

"I went by the Johnsons…"

She looked at him. Thunder rumbled, closer.

A car pulled up at the curb.

"Where you staying?"

"I'll figure something out."

"You had anything to eat?"

He shook his head.

She stood up, leaned to see out the door.

"He gone take you out to Morningstar?"

He turned, looked out the window. "Yeah," he said and got
to his feet.

They stood there.

"I can fix you something. For when you get back. If you
want it."

"Alma—you're too good for this earth."

"Don't say that. Don't say that to me."

He lowered his eyes.

"You hungry for anything in particular?"

Footsteps, then Boyd appeared at the door.

"Everything."

———

*"Vonceil Earley—1920–1983—She Hath Done What She
Could."*

Abrupt spits of lightning slashed the black sky, and they took shelter inside the back door of the austere, unlocked church. The rain fell furiously for a while, soaking the little cemetery.

When it let up, the air was cooler and time had slowed. Their conversation resumed: the picture of Glenroy, the idea, on the porch, sipping the afternoon, having a toke, tracing phantom melodies, sinking by degrees, in the groove he had worn in the procession of days, toward the dark.

Or was it like that?

"He was a lot smarter than people knew," said Boyd.

"He was smart."

"He would say the strangest things sometimes. Like people were watching him from the woods."

"Maybe they were."

"And the wind was the voice of the dead."

"Might be."

"But he could see himself. He knew. I think Sonny was a talented man—he just didn't have any luck and he didn't leave any. It was Eunice he depended on—and he *was* like her in a lot of ways. But it was fire and ice with him—nothing in between. And I know he felt very alone."

"Lot of that going around."

"He would say it's all luck—a lot of things happening at the right time—and you only had a minute. And it never came back."

Thunder rumbled, past them now.

"Of course he was drunk."

"Of course he was right."

———

Mr. Guthrie, frowning at the podium, State Contest, April, 1968, Sightreading. Not a happy man. The rehearsed pieces had not gone as well as they should—not just errors, but the wrong errors. He still felt embarrassed. Was he slipping? He thought of his great bands of the fifties and early sixties—tight, disciplined units—where were they now? Time to retire? No—concentrate on the piece...

Surprise! 5/4.

What kind of... Clearly, his winning streak was too long—the sonofabitches were out to get him. The band watched him—a lid dancing on a hissing pot—paralyzed. His five minutes were gone; now he had three to explain it. He pointed out the unusual time signature, was not allowed to tap or hum it, so chopped it with his baton, growing redder by the second, looking around at the fishlike faces. Then the key, the basic conception, the transitions, the solos—his time was up. Any questions? Too many to ask. The judges nodded; he scowled at them and raised his arms. He counted off, and with a sound from the clarinet section like a duck undergoing a surprise proctology exam, they were off.

But where? The attempt was pregnant with chaos, which gathered beneath the fragile would-be structure Mr. Guthrie attempted to hack out of the air. The worst players dropped out first, like weak runners, and cowered in the skeletal shadows of their music stands, looking at the music of their struggling betters, as though that would help, until there were only the six or seven best players left attempting to carry it off, then three, then two, then one.

The sound of one snare drum filled the room, the eyes of the player flicking from the conductor's hands to his music like a lizard's. His frozen colleagues watched him in shamed amazement—or, from the front, dared a glance over their shoulders. It seemed, for a moment, the director would let him take it to the end, the crisp rolls and tight little figures, but in reality it was only enough for it to feel like some sort of justifying statement—then he waved it dead, and viciously attacked a sudden itch on his arm.

For a lingering moment, the room echoed with the sound.

———

Fire. A low, sprawling building in full flame, painting the night sky red, drawing a throng of onlookers. The fulfillment of the building's life, its rare and long-awaited bloom.

The sign above the canopied entranceway begins to blister and melt; a section breaks off and falls, like a spoken word, flaming to the pavement.

THON!

———

A back porch, drowning in twilight—a guitar, an arm rising and falling with a cup, and two eyes peering into the sweet oblivion of dusk. A voice singing—clear words gradually disintegrating into nonsense. The muffled cries of children playing down by the creek, stealing the last breath of daylight.

Somewhere, something is dripping.

———

And a living portrait:

Green shoots spearing the charred stobs, sawbriar snaking up the chimney, waist-high grass swaying easily in the yard and against the blistered side of the mired hulk facing a billion years to remember its ten seconds of being a car, a careless rustle in the trees all around. Water smacking along the pier pilings, and against the bleached-out, half-sunk basketball, bobbing Clorox jugs, bottles, cans, shards of Styrofoam, and driftwood of the snaky slough. Jets high above, spring birds nearby, the wind whispering: sounds that circumscribe and nurture a heart of fallen silence.

The Trimbles of Trybald

Jimmie Myles

The old days? I close my eyes—Glenroy and Louis, that's who I see.

We lived a block apart—a world—though we didn't know it then. There's a line, and sometimes you can't say exactly where it is, but it's Milltown on the other side, and they were on that side. Of course, at the time we were just buddies. I never thought about it. That came later.

I remember when they built the lake; we thought that was pretty hot shit. My old man would take me down to where they were building the dam and say, all that will be under water one day, which was pretty hard to believe, but damned if it didn't come true, and now we have Atlanta's scenic sewage in our very own backyard. And I still don't know who the hell Walter M. Moon is. Or was.

When we were kids our neighborhood wasn't really all that far from the outskirts of town. Once you crossed the tracks it was mostly woods—of course, it's all subdivisions now. The old story. Thank God for memory because that's where most of everything worth a shit is.

I always liked Eunice. You know she started working at the mill when she was fourteen. She was this weird combination of religious and wacky, and she was real funny and she didn't treat you like a kid. She seemed more like somebody you knew than somebody you knew's mother. I used to think Glenroy and Louis were so lucky—they had this cool mother and they could do whatever they wanted. They never ate meals. There was just food around and when somebody wanted something they just got it and walked around eating it. If you spent the night over there you'd get to stay up as late as you wanted, and everybody would just sleep wherever they ended up. I always thought that was amazing—not sleeping in the same place every time. Their house was full of conch-shell lamps and artists' renditions of heaven, and, I don't know, spray-painted cattails and shit, and had a very distinctive smell. It always felt sort of dark, like a cave. Eunice played piano for the church—that little church at the end of Calhoun Street. Probably still does. They had a piano at home and she would play for us sometimes and sing gospel songs—she had this twangy voice, and sometimes if Sonny was around he would sing harmony with her—they should have been Earl and Pearl or something—but what I mainly remember was how she could play the piss out of that piano. Just tear it to pieces. She taught Louis, and he got pretty good, but of course Glenroy never touched it. And it was funny how piano was okay—but later on when Louis wanted to get an organ for the band she put her foot down. No sir. Sacrilegious.

I saw her about a year ago—she still looks like she did when we were kids—funny-looking. It's like she has two bodies: a fat woman's body from the waist down and a skinny woman's body from the waist up. I guess when she looks in the mirror she just sees the lower half because the whole time we were growing up she talked about losing weight. I used to think, what she needs to do is figure out how to rearrange it, and I'd imagine a giant pair of hands grabbing her by the ankles and squeezing her upward and then tying it off like a balloon.

She always wore these sort of calypso pants and had some kind of mill tool in a little scabbard on her belt. She used to talk all the time about First Shift—like that was about the most prestigious thing you could imagine. She finally made it and you could tell she was proud of it; she would drop little references to it and got a more complicated-looking tool. I still have no clue what she or anybody else does in there—but whatever it is, I bet she's gotten pretty good at it.

Now Sonny was a whole different story. He seems like a dream to me now. Actually, he seemed like a dream then too. He wasn't around very much—of course he never worked, never did anything at all—but when he was there he was a gas. Crazy, funny. The proverbial sweet drunk. He had the same sort of lunatic personality as Eunice, except with him it wasn't a streak, it was the whole deal. I guess that's what attracted them to each other. Because you wouldn't have really thought they were each other's type. I've always assumed it was just a base for him—not that he didn't love his boys—but his deal was on the side, you know? I mean, I knew even then—everybody knew—that he was no-count. When he was home, mostly he would just sit on the porch, but he had a group of drinking buddies and would go off with them for days. I remember, before the lake, there was an infamous joint down on the river called Thad's they'd go to, and he could disappear, seriously, for a couple of weeks. Eunice basically ignored him. He had a huge box full of records—old 78s and 45s—which he played a lot when he was home; and sometimes he would sing for us. He played guitar and harp, as he called it, and he made up songs with ridiculous words. There was one about a gorilla in a Cadillac—I don't remember exactly—I just remember laughing my ass off on their back porch, leaning against an old foot-pedal sewing machine.

Glenroy was always the leader, but Louis was the one who could get away with anything. They just had different personalities. Louis built models; Glenroy torched them with lighter fluid. When we played, it was always Glenroy's game—these day-long things like army or pirates or spies or Flash Gordon—but usually it was The Girls: Amazon-types who were always kidnapping and torturing somebody. Totally Glenroy, that shit. Don't ask me where he came up with it. Anyway, whatever the deal was at the time, he would get so into it he wouldn't break character all day, even when we went home for lunch. "Hand me the chips, Joe." Whenever we got to whatever the mission was that day—a pirate ship or alien planet or The Girls' hideout—which was always the same cluster of trees standing out in the middle of a pasture like an island—in fact, we called it The Island—way on the other side of Burton's Pasture, we'd have to split up. He loved to split up. "Let me get there first and you come in from the sides." If he didn't get there first he got mad. He always carried one of those little sticks with a knob on it in his belt, and the penalty for any breach of his rules was a thump on the head, which he never got away with inflicting because who was going to stand there and let him do it?

When he was older he got in fights a lot and was usually in some kind of trouble—real trouble, not the charming kind Louis got into. Everybody loved Louis; he was just the lovable type—real funny, with this weird sick sense of humor. Seems like he had tonsillitis all the time, but as far as I know he never had his tonsils out—they probably couldn't afford it. And he had asthma and always carried one of those little inhaler things with him. When I think of him, for some reason I see him then—that blond-headed kid with those blue eyes. So different from Glenroy's—brown, about the color of bourbon held up to the light. The whole time we were growing up Louis said he wanted to be a pharmacist, but you could tell way back that

Glenroy would never make it out of high school. You could just tell.

It was seventh grade—Louis was a year younger—that we started to grow apart. My old man had never approved of them and started leaning on me to stay away from them, which really pissed me off, but it wasn't that—it was more of a natural process. Glenroy was already veering into a world I didn't know anything about, and basically was scared of—and here I was trying to play football and be this horseshit jock guy—and of course Louis never did any of that. And it's true—you couldn't help but be aware of it: they were mill people. You just reached a point where you understood what that meant—where you *felt* it—like not being able to take a bath with your sister anymore. All these milestones, growing up—you're in such a hurry—it's sad.

But it's great at the *time*. I'll never forget Brenda Buell, in the woods behind her house. I felt ten feet tall, but I've never been so scared in my life: I was terrified of her father—a linebacker turned contractor with a den full of his college football pictures. Then it was Debbie Neese and then Carla Watts—it turns out getting pussy is a full-time job, and it really was a couple of years I didn't see them much at all—in the hall, maybe, just in passing.

Then the damn Beatles came out.

All of a sudden everybody was forming combos. Boots, wigs, everything. I knew immediately I had to get in on that. It was a lot easier way to get girls than football, where you had to run laps. There was never any doubt I'd play drums—I thought it was the coolest thing in the world. I had a pretty crappy set I badgered my parents into buying me for my fifteenth birthday. The first group I was in was called The Crestliners, a name we got out of a *Field and Stream* at Lawrence Green's house. We had our first session in his basement, which we thought went extremely well, even if we did spend more time talking about our hair and trying to think up a name than we did playing. The *Field and Stream* was a

49

bolt of inspiration. The whole thing lasted about a month. We played one party and then Lawrence had to quit because he wasn't doing his homework. That killed it because he had the only amp.

Amps are hard to come by at that age. The next group I was in, everybody had to borrow equipment from older siblings, which is a kind of generosity that dries up fast, we learned. We managed to play about two twist parties, and then at the height of our coolness that fell apart too.

You can usually tell when something is destined to be—at least you can looking back—and that's how it was when Louis came by to see me. It was, like, a week after that band broke up. It was really a surprise at first. I had hardly talked to him for two years. But he knew all about what I was doing and he was real interested in it. What made the biggest impression on *me* was his hair. I don't know how he did it, but somehow while nobody was looking he had managed to grow it out longer than anybody else's in Trybald. And got away with it.

We set up in their living room. Eunice was the only mother I guess in the world who actually encouraged her kids playing in bands and she gave us the run of the house. Sonny had been dead two or three years by then.

Well, it was obvious in about thirty seconds that this was a different ballgame. A little thing called talent—which Louis had a lot of; that was the first time I realized it. Of course he'd always played piano, but he'd learned guitar, too, from Sonny, and he was a million times better than anybody else I'd ever heard. It turned out he'd been teaching Glenroy too, who'd been playing about a year when we first started. Of course he was sloppy, but *fast*—and he could figure things out in no time, which drummers always appreciate. They each had a Silvertone and one little amp they'd gotten for Christmas. God knows how long Eunice had worked to buy them. There was a little power struggle at first—they both wanted to play guitar, and I can honestly say it's one of the few arguments I ever heard them have. Of course Louis I guess you could say lost and started playing piano, which we miked into the PA, which gave us a really great sound. There was a guy named Nix Vaughn who played bass. We had a lot of fun that first day and became friends all over again. We christened ourselves The Vandals.

We started playing gigs. Right off the bat we were the best band in Trybald, which I realize is not saying much, but there were actually quite a few bands around. Besides the piano, which we actually loaded up and took to our first few gigs, we had several things that made us distinctive. One, we actually knew the songs—because slave-driving Glenroy made us practice all the time. We also played what people wanted to hear, but Glenroy was always looking for good B-side stuff that nobody else did—and some of those became our best songs. Those and Louis's—because he was already writing tunes by then, and this was back when almost nobody did original stuff—not and lived to tell about it anyway. But everybody always loved Louis's songs—and some were real favorites like "Grapefruit" and "Jeez Louise," which I believe is the first song he ever wrote. Finally, over Eunice's objections, Louis got a Farfisa, and you could tell it was us a mile away. Also, Louis was by far the best singer anywhere around and the girls dug him.

I couldn't name the exact minute Glenroy got better, but it was almost like that, it seemed like it happened so fast. I guess it didn't—but all of a sudden it was like all of those things he'd been trying to do but couldn't pull off, he *could* do, and he was a million times better than any other guitar player around, and playing these unheard-of solos. Of course he worked on it all the time; that's all he ever did. Always listening to Chet Atkins and The Ventures and anything with guitars in it. And he thought about nothing but the band, ever. He was always trying to improve the sound and think up ways to add to the show. He was a big believer in that. Got to give 'em a show. We went through all kinds of outfits—surfer shirts, dickies, ascots—which he'd seen in a magazine somewhere— you name it. We started doing a more or less regular gig on

Friday nights at the Youth Center, which would be packed—it's not exactly like there was a whole lot else to do in Trybald—and we'd get maybe five dollars each, something like that—which actually seemed like a lot back then, for something you would have done for nothing in a heartbeat. Probably even paid to do.

Something Glenroy thought up that became a sort of trademark was our entrance. We'd get everything set up, then leave and wait for the place to fill up. An announcer would get on the PA and say something like, "Ladies and gentlemen, we have just received word that the band has arrived—they're on their way and should be here very soon. We appreciate your patience"—and then do it several more times until they were chanting our name. We would bust in and run to the stage and go right into, usually, "I Want Candy." They loved it. We always did "Wipeout" too—my moment of glory. Louis would go "Br-r-r-r-r-r-r, wipeout!" and I'd play like three seconds of the solo, the girls would scream, and I'd stop. We'd do that off and on all through the night. Make 'em wait. Usually we wouldn't actually play it until our last song—just in case anybody had any crazy ideas about leaving. For three minutes I was God. I lived for that. We tried all kinds of other things too—colored lights and even dry ice once which turned out to be more trouble than it was worth.

One thing we did a lot of was go hear other bands. We knew what everybody in Trybald was doing, so on weekends if we weren't playing we'd go to Atlanta. Of course it's always enjoyable to hear a band that's worse than you, but it was the good ones Glenroy was interested in. He'd sit for hours watching a good guitar player and always wait around after the last set and talk to the guy, who would almost always show him what he wanted to know. Then he'd spend days in his room working on it—whatever lick or technique it was. And if he was having trouble he'd keep going back again and again until he had it. And then he'd sort of gloat about it.

He had the drive, so he was the leader—not that there was
ever any doubt. Louis sort of sank back and they both just kept
getting better. I held my own, and I got better too—you can't
help it when you play all the time and have somebody like
Glenroy pushing you. But it was serious work—basically more
than I was willing to do. Glenroy wanted to practice all the
time, I mean *all* the time. My old man hated the whole thing,
which is probably the main reason I stayed with it. The real
problem as far as the band was concerned was Nix. I mean, I
was more or less in over my head—I admit that—but he was
really in over his from the beginning. He was kind of fat and
sweated a lot and always had this desperate expression on his
face when we played. We had a ton of music to learn, and it was
getting harder, and Glenroy had these exact ideas about what he
wanted everybody to do, and Nix couldn't cut it. He would
stink at practice and write everything down and swear he was
going to learn it by next time, but of course he wouldn't. So
we'd have to stop and work on the same shit over and over, and
it was about to drive Glenroy crazy. Everybody crazy. I mean,
the bass player—you know what I'm saying? He liked being in
the band, and he would try to pull me into a confidential little
confederacy of two, but it didn't work. I just felt sorry for
him, and he was really getting on my nerves. He made it
boring, which you can't forgive—and there was just something
about this fat, sweating, desperate guy that didn't fit. Probably
that he was fat, sweating, and desperate.

Glenroy had been hanging out with Gosom people for a
good while, and some of them were musicians who started
coming by our practices or showing up at our gigs. They were
the first people from Gosom I'd ever really gotten to know.
Like everybody from Trybald I had basically believed the
myth—that they were a lower life form and never did anything
but have chain fights in parking lots—but of course it wasn't
true. They were just your basic hell-raising good-time low-life
sort of people, and I liked the scandal of hanging out with them
at least as much as hanging out with them. One of them—

Wayne Lane—was a good bass player, and there was another
guy, Jimmy Hendricks, who played rhythm guitar. The
inevitable happened. I've seen this so many times—Glenroy
just had them over without telling Nix. The music was great—
but of course you're thinking the whole time, how are we going
to tell him? You're wondering if you can do it by mail somehow. So of course he drives down the street and hears us and
comes to the door in tears. Big scene. But basically Glenroy
just told him, and that was the end of that.

But, bam, we had gone up about ten notches. We had a lot
bigger sound and both of the new guys could sing, so we started
working out all these background vocals. We changed our name
to Moonshine and started playing a lot more, quite a bit in
Gosom, and things got really hairy at home. My old man just
couldn't handle the Gosom part of it, especially the skanks who
were always hanging around, and of course we were drinking a
lot. But I wasn't ready to quit yet. At some point we changed
our name to Debacle—Louis's word, of course. He was writing
more and more good tunes, and Glenroy was already pretty
much a local legend.

In mine and Glenroy's senior year—1967—the senior class
voted for us to play the spring prom. It was a pretty big deal
because it was a kind of official acceptance—plus it was an
opportunity for Glenroy to rub their faces in it. So we said we
would, and then immediately the whole thing was vetoed by
Slug Spears. He was the assistant principal—Slug was our
affectionate little name for him. He was a fat, bald, gross,
stupid, lazy, mean, scab-head, nose-picking, ass-crack-scratch-
ing son of a bitch—but other than that, he was a fine person. A
retired Army something, who had picked the bullying of
adolescents as a second career. He loved to rope things off and
line people up in files. He and Glenroy were bitter enemies. He
had kicked Glenroy out of school dozens of times. Eunice
despised the man even more than we did, and every time he
kicked Glenroy out she would go down to the school and cuss
him out in front of everybody. He was so afraid of her he got

where he would run and hide when he saw her coming. So when she went down to demand to know why we couldn't play the prom, they had to look for him for about twenty minutes. He was up in the vocational-ed shop, so she marched up there and they had this huge scene by the table saw. He didn't have the balls to say it was because he hated our guts, so he said it was our hair, and our name was unacceptable. Glenroy was there and called him a fat turd and told him to go to hell. Slug expelled him on the spot, like an umpire throwing somebody out of a game. After things cooled off, Eunice went back down there and got a deal out of him. Glenroy was supposed to cut his hair, and do a whole list of things like pick up trash on the school grounds on Saturdays, and go to summer school. Needless to say, Glenroy never graduated, and we didn't play the prom.

Eunice was very upset about that. She was fanatical about her boys finishing school and not working in the mill—or ending up like their father. Glenroy and Eunice were always very close, and he tried to assure her—which of course he really believed—that it didn't matter because he was going to be in a famous band. But it shook her up. But what really blew her away was when he moved out. Good God, she took that hard. They both bawled about it, but he still left that spring and moved out to the place where Wayne and Jimmy were already living—an old sort of halfway rundown plantation house with a pecan orchard, out County Road 41, which back in the old days was a busy market road running between the river and the railroad but by then was just a lonely back country road skirting the east edge of the lake, which at that time was still fairly new. It was the home base of a pretty strange guy named Al Hamby, and everybody called it The Mansion.

I never understood the arrangement exactly—never worried about it—I guess Al was renting it from somebody, I don't know. I never asked. It was a little seedy—but it was a beautiful, real secluded place, set back from the road and hard to see in the summertime through the pecan trees, with a dirt drive that wound through them like a tunnel. I haven't been out

55

there in years—some lawyer probably bought it and fixed it up with little porcelain bathroom fixtures and stained glass alcoves or some shit—or maybe it just fell in. The pasture sloped down to the lake—no dock, just a few boats pulled up on the bank and a sandy sort of beach where people went swimming. I have no idea how many people were actually living there; they came and went, and bikers passed through all the time.

Al was probably in his thirties, which seemed grandfatherly then—and was a biker himself. He always had about ten bikes, or pieces of bikes, around, and worked on them constantly. Harleys, a Ducati, a Norton, and especially an old Indian that was his baby, and looked brand new. He hardly ever rode it. I never knew where he was from, but it wasn't from around here. We got along fine—he was actually a nice guy, quiet, soft-spoken—but I never knew him all that well. He was sort of a small guy, bald on top with a frizzy ponytail—tattoos, an earring, the works. He was into Zen or Tao or whatever it was and had actually been to India, or said he had, and spoke in proverbs. The bikers brought in a little bit of everything illicit, which was my first exposure to it, and I knew some of them were growing reefer in the woods. Al himself didn't smoke or drink, but he did eat mushrooms, and occasionally you'd see him in the pecan orchard in lotus position with his disciples around him. Which is what they were. He had that sort of personality. We basically just used the place as our headquarters for the band. We kept everything set up in one of the downstairs rooms and we spent a lot of time out there for a couple of years or so. I graduated from high school and started really growing my hair out. The situation at home kept getting worse, but I didn't care. I had a job that summer working on a chicken farm, which along with our gigs kept a little money in my pocket.

The locals were Gosomites, and some of them attached themselves to the band. They started helping with the equipment and following us around, which was nice but became a pain in the ass because they always expected to get in free everywhere we played and were constantly getting into fights. No shortage of Gosom girls around either. I remember a couple of them—real tight—named Sandy and Tina. You never saw one without the other. They would start out about mid-morning with a quart of something apiece—they were into Dr. Bombay gin—and finish it off that afternoon. Sandy was sweet, real smart, but she turned sinister when she got drunk, and her lip curled into a sneer, which was the only way you could tell she *was* drunk until she passed out, which she always did. Tina was different—a big, rawboned girl who was mean sober and in league with the devil drunk. She would pick out the guy she wanted that day, like a spider—but there was one guy who was sort of her main squeeze—a big, red-headed guy. At some point she had gotten pregnant and had the baby—a little girl who was always dirty and crawling around on the floor playing with a hash pipe or something. The boyfriend, who may or may not have been the father, ended up disappearing—who could blame him? More than once I saw them get into a fight, and I mean they fought with their fists, slugging each other in the face. I admit it: she scared the hell out of me. Then something happened—I never knew what—but she and Sandy apparently had this big argument, and we never saw Sandy again. Tina stayed around but seemed to sink into a depression. Nobody messed with her.

Glenroy fooled around with the Gosom girls, but I didn't do too much of that myself. I was still dating several girls in Trybald—one I guess more than others, named Frances Thorne. I think it's fair to say she was more keen on our little romance than I was, but she was the eager to please type and had some notable assets, and she helped with the home situation because her family was respectable and my old man knew her old man—they were in the Rotary Club, and all that. Louis, who was also spending a lot of time at The Mansion, was by then bound with invisible wires to a girl named Amy Hughes. She was beautiful—the introverted, sleepy type—and I admit I always had the hots for her, but she and Louis were like a single organism. She was fanatically jealous. Her twin brother had been killed in a car wreck in the tenth grade, which had given her a sort of tragic clout.

I quit the chicken farm and went through a series of jobs. Glenroy and the other guys painted houses sometimes—just long enough to get some money. Glenroy spent all of his on equipment. He had several guitars and was constantly trading them. Eventually he ended up with the Fender he always played.

When you play with somebody all the time you don't really notice their playing unless you stop and consciously listen. I used to do that sometimes with Glenroy, and I would think about the early days, and it would blow me away how good he'd gotten. As a band—what's the expression?—we had reached a plateau. Except for him. I was still more or less enjoying it, but I did get real tired of it sometimes. We played fairly regularly out at a place called Journey's End, on a little peninsula back closer to Trybald. It had originally been a VFW or something, then it had been vacant for a while, then the owner—a disreputable specimen of local trash named Thad Stroop—had decided to develop it into a hangout. Thad was a nasty guy, probably about sixty back then—always dirty, scraggle-whiskered, bleary-eyed, and dog drunk. He had a far-flung reputation as a no-count debaucher of youth, which he reveled in. He loved being the kids' depraved old buddy, and was kind of free with his hands around the girls—but he usually got away with it because Journey's End was the cool place to be, and there was a sort of decadent prestige in knowing him. Plus, he could get a little crazy. More than once I've seen him get pissed off and go to his trailer and then come weaving out with a shotgun. I think it cost two dollars to get in. They served barbeque and beer inside, which he couldn't legally sell to three-fourths of his clientele, but everybody knew he paid off the police and they left him alone. I don't know if he made any money out of the place, but he didn't need it. His family owned hundreds of acres all around the lake—in fact, a lot of their land had *become* the lake—and all that was left was him and a brother somewhere. They'd sell off pieces now and then for subdivisions. Never worked a day in his life. He lived by himself in a trailer behind the club and according to legend had big sacks of money stashed away inside. We played at Journey's End almost every weekend for two years at least, and unless it was a bad night, we'd get a hundred bucks—twenty or twenty-five apiece.

I say "we"—but actually the personnel shifted several times during the Mansion days. Glenroy and Louis and I stayed together, but the others came and went. We had about five different bass players, and sometimes we had a fifth member and sometimes not. Personally, except we each got less, I liked having a good rhythm guitar because that's when you cook. We changed our name a lot too—which was Louis's department: after Debacle we were Wall-to-Wall, then Undecided, then Epitome. The next spring—1968—Louis graduated and started staying out at The Mansion most of the time. The psychedelic era had found its way into Georgia: the hair got longer, rednecks discovered dope, the parents freaked out. God knows what they imagined went on out there. Probably in their wildest ravings they had it about right. Mine entered into a conspiracy with Fran, who was supposed to rescue me, so needless to say, that relationship went nowhere.

I guess it all could have gone on indefinitely—but nothing does. At some point—this would have been 1969, fall—a guy drifted into the picture and attached himself to Al. He was a big huge guy with long stringy black hair and a beard—not really the lumberjack type but a sort of psychotic rhinoceros. He wore big biker boots and blue jeans they must have made out of tent material, and carried a huge wallet in his back pocket chained to his belt. He had a vicious gleam in his eye, which was dangerous because he was the sort of person who had no idea what to think about anything on his own. God knows how he found Al—like a luna moth, I guess—but he made himself into his personal bodyguard. His mother must have named him something, but everybody called him Igor.

He was the kind of guy it was tense being around because he thought everybody was making fun of him, which they were, which he actually liked because he loved to throw his weight around. But it was a drag because it was constantly this crazy, Charles Manson-looking guy going, "What do you mean by that?" Whatever—we just minded our own business and stayed away from him. About all you could do was wish he would go away. Then there was this other guy who came and went at The Mansion named Prairie Dog. He would pass through and stay a while, then disappear, and about the time you forgot about him you'd look up one day and he'd be back. He was one of those people who spend their entire waking lives stoned and seem to have no purpose in the universe but wandering around, smoking dope, and copulating. Ideal life, pretty much. His woman at The Mansion was a vaguely Latin girl named Tawana and they always hooked up when he came through. She was all over him. The problem was, Igor had been hitting on her, but— surprise—she wouldn't have anything to do with him. So to crazy and stupid, add frustrated.

So we should have seen it coming. They'd already had a few little spats and you're thinking how could anybody have anything against this guy? It's always a woman. It happened very fast. It was one afternoon—Al was gone somewhere and we were practicing. All of a sudden we heard things crashing around in the back room and we ran back there and Igor and Prairie Dog were rolling around on the floor trying to strangle each other. It was a horrible mismatch—Prairie Dog was a little guy. We finally got them broken up, and then before anybody knew what was happening, a knife flashed out of nowhere and Prairie Dog was groaning on the floor. Igor was standing there looking about half crazy and half terrified. We took Prairie Dog to the Emergency Room in Trybald, and after a couple of hours the doctor came out and said he had a fifty-fifty chance. It scared the hell out of me. Thank God, eventually he pulled through, and after he was fully recovered he disappeared for good—Tawana too—and that was the last we ever heard of them. Of course, meanwhile, Igor had hauled ass. The cops came to the hospital and asked us a lot of questions. When we got back out to The Mansion there were sheriff's cars everywhere and they were going all through the house. They'd been looking for an excuse for two years; about twice a week a patrol car would come around the driveway real slow. Al didn't let anybody keep their stash in the house—a rule not always followed—but luckily all they found was some paraphernalia. They arrested everybody, but we all ended up getting off, except for Al who had to go to court and got a suspended sentence and had to pay a fine, which we all chipped in on. Meanwhile, they caught Igor about a week later somewhere in South Carolina, and we all testified against him and I think he ended up going to jail. I always figured he'd come back for revenge after he got out, but we never saw him again.

Well, that was it—it was never the same after that. My old man, who had bailed me out, went berserk, but I had already moved into a little house in Trybald and stayed away from him as much as possible. We started seeing the cops a lot more at The Mansion—the word "paranoid" was in its heyday— though there weren't nearly as many people around anymore. It just wasn't the same. And the band was in a bad rut—doing the same shit, playing the same songs—kind of like a bad marriage. Glenroy had gotten so restless it was almost like work just to be around him. God, he could be unbearable. Wasting time, getting nowhere, everything half-ass. The other guys, except for Louis who was always with Amy making little tapes of his songs, were like me: lazy, stoned most of the time, never bringing anything new into the band. It seems like we argued all the time, and when I look back I remember a lot of really boring days where we basically did nothing at all.

Then there was Fran, who was really heavy on this marriage thing. I started avoiding her and she started catching me. It was something I needed to deal with, but didn't. Then, winter was coming, and I found myself thinking about how cold The Mansion got. I was afraid of getting drafted and my old man was trying to get me to go to college and get a deferment. I don't know—something about college, I just couldn't get into it, but I was almost twenty-one and I had been out of high school for over two years, which more or less felt like one long blurry afternoon. Glenroy worried about getting drafted too, but Louis never had to because of his asthma. All they wanted to do was keep playing music. I was pretty miserable. Except for playing I didn't have much to do with Glenroy and I couldn't get near Louis because of Amy. She could hardly stand for anybody to even talk to him. It was like we were just going to keep on playing at Journey's End for the same stoned drunk people for the rest of our lives.

I remember—it was late March. 1970. There had been the usual early taste of spring, a string of warm days and all the fruit trees blooming. Then the bottom fell out. It rained for three days and there were floods everywhere. The lake rose—then a front blew through and it cleared up and turned cold and windy. I remember the lake looked like chocolate milk and was all the way up in the banks and full of logs and crap. Maybe it was the sun being out. I don't know. But the thing is—it was so uncharacteristic of him. He had his impulsive side, but he didn't even like water or boats or any of that. He couldn't swim. If you made a list of things he might do, it would be dead last. Maybe it was Amy's idea, but it wasn't like her either. Just some kind of bizarre, off-the-wall wild hair is all I can figure. Anyway, that's pretty much what we all con- cluded—we never knew for sure. It was that little sailboat that belonged to somebody and had been pulled up on the bank all winter. It was just too windy. Too choppy. Too cold.

That day will always stand out in my mind. I remember a freight train was going by when I got there, the paramedics were already there, and some sheriff's cars. I can see Amy—it's the last time I ever saw her—wrapped in a blanket, looking at nothing, not crying, just trembling. She had stayed with the boat and somebody had picked her up. And Glenroy was off to one side, by himself, looking up from time to time with a strange expectant expression on his face. But he knew. And so did I. I could tell the second I drove up. Even if it did take two days to find him. It made absolutely no sense at all.

Louis had just turned twenty.

Monroe

The calendar insisted it was October but New Orleans didn't buy it. The young man wearing the tee-shirt and shorts he had slept in sat at his one tall window, where a sheet gathered back and tied let in the sounds of the day: cars and the periodic groan of a bus from the avenue, slamming doors, thunderous children on the stairs, muffled televisions, and, as though no wall were there, a radio from the next room. The tired surrounding buildings and little jagged puzzle pieces of sky comprised the view. A breeze, like a weak breath, nudged the makeshift curtain.

Behind him a battered saucepan on a hot plate began to hiss. Then, from the couch came a rustle and a groan. Doug glanced, then turned back to the window, absently watching the glimpses of life pass across the slice of street. Against the far wall, by a mattress on the floor, spread the orderly clutter of his dismantled drums: conventional and eccentric.

———

His drums. In June, the VW bug, all hatches yawning on Regina's tiny lawn, had refused to accommodate all that plus the suitcase and hang-up bag. The boys had tried every combination and then, defeated, stood aside studying the impasse. From the porch Vonceil sat kneading her hands, watching the proceedings with an expression of vague pain.

"You're going to have to put something on top," said Stan.

"Yeah, I'm thinking about if it rains," Doug replied.

They studied it.

"You know, we could try taking the heads off the bass drum."

Doug looked at him, then at the drums, calculating. "Let's try it."

It turned out to be the key. A half hour later they had all the equipment in the car, some accessories and the hang-up bag in the hood, and the suitcase wrapped in a scuzzy shower curtain tied to the top.

"Now all you need is some pans to hang on the side," said one of the boys.

Doug smiled, then went to the porch.

"I'll stay in touch," he promised, and felt her slip something into his hand as he leaned down to embrace her: a kerchief bound with yarn, bulky with coins.

"You won't be gone long?"

He sighed and said, "I'll come back," but he could hardly stand to look at her—the anxious expression so helpless with love.

As he pulled out of the yard he had one last glimpse of her—her arm raised wanly to say goodbye—and of the boys standing there at the start of a different road than his own, and whom he had the prescience to know he would never see again, gave them a beep and lurched away down the street.

At the corner they watched his one working brake light feebly come and go, like a firefly, as he slowed, turned, and disappeared, leaving a wake that lingered a while, then dissolved into the afternoon.

——

Would it ever be cool again? The past four months seemed one long nightmare of futility and sweat. Another groan sounded from the couch and the person sleeping there rolled over. Doug looked over his shoulder.

He couldn't exactly account for how the man had attached himself to him—in the little club where Doug sometimes sat in. But he had. All night long he had been drinking something from a jar whose unidentifiable pungent smell lingered even now. By the time Doug had got him to the couch he was raving, waving his arms, but had soon surrendered to oblivion—though an oblivion pierced, all through the night, with cries and babble.

Another moan, a pained lament against consciousness, escaped his guest, and Doug looked again. The man opened his eyes and lay staring for several motionless minutes at the ceiling—until finally his eyes began to dart about. At last, with a sudden bolt as though someone had thrown a switch, he jerked upright and looked around the unfamiliar room in panic. When he saw Doug he stared at him with wide, crazy eyes.

"That thing after me all night," he announced at last.

Doug looked at him with a little frown of uncertainty. "What thing?"

"Damn *turtle*," he answered—like, what the hell do you think?

"Turtle?"

"A big un too. Just coming along. Coming along. Ain't no way to get away from it. Everywhere I go—here he come."

The man swallowed and rubbed his hands over his face. His hair and scruffy whiskers framed his yellow-red eyes with gray.

"Nobody but a fool kill a turtle," he said.

Doug studied him. "Did you?"

"Way back long time ago. Ain't nothing bring worse luck."

"Why's that?"

"Shit. That thing come back get you, boy."

"So why'd you do it?"

"Hell, I don't know. Wasn't nothing but a nap-head, didn't even know why my pecker got hard."

"On purpose?"

"With a brick—I reckon that's on purpose. That thing been after me ever since."

"And brought you bad luck?"

"What you *talking* about. Boy, you don't know what bad luck is."

"I think you might have been talking about some of it last night."

"What I say?"

"Don't ask me."

The man snorted. "That's because I be talking in tongues, boy. Spirit talk. My soul be off in another rim."

"I believe that."

He rubbed his face again, then regarded Doug quizzically. "I just need you to answer me one thing," he said.

"What's that?"

"Who you is?"

Doug laughed. "You mean you don't remember?"

"Tell me and I'll see."

"I was playing at Come-Back's last night. When it closed, they said you didn't have anywhere to stay."

"Did?"

"Mm hmm."

"I don't 'call your name."

"Doug."

"My name Monroe. Monroe B. Goode—even when I don't be."

"Yeah, I remember."

"I done told you?"

"Yeah. Last night. Several times."

"Hell, I ain't studying last night."

"What was that you were drinking?"

"I ain't exactly sure—something go in lamps."

"Kerosene?"

"*Hell* no, wasn't no kerosene," Monroe replied indignantly. "Something else, I done forgot what it call. All I know, it sho eat you up."

"You ought not to drink things like that. The real thing's bad enough."

"Only real thing I know what's in my hand. Ain't like I go in the big store and just try to make up my mind."

The water had at last begun to boil and Doug got up to make coffee.

"You hungry?"

Monroe sniffed. "I might could eat a bite—I won't lie."

Doug dished up some beans and back-door biscuits and brought the plate to Monroe with a spoon. "I'll get you some coffee in a minute."

Monroe studied the plate momentarily with a scowl. "You ain't got any vi-ennas."

"Sorry."

"I ain't complain." He started eating.

Doug fixed the coffee, and a plate for himself, and sat down again. They ate for a few minutes.

"That's what you do—play them drums?" asked Monroe.

"Try to."

"I used to play 'em."

"You did?"

"I play ever instrument."

"Maybe you ought to be in a band."

"Shit, band. I ain't play with none of these young fools around here."

"I'm not getting too far with it myself," Doug said. "Must have killed a turtle some time."

"Might did. Or somebody got you conjured."

"Maybe they do."

"Less you just born under a bad sign."

"I wouldn't know."

"Most likely somebody got a little trick laid on you. Ain't no problem—I take it right off."

Doug laughed.

Monroe eyed him sharply. "What you laughing about?"

"I ain't laughing."

"You think I can't take a trick off?"

"Well—how?"

Monroe continued looking sternly at him a moment. "Well—it depend." He paused. "It ain't exactly free."

"You saying it costs money?"

"You ever heard of anything don't?"

"How much?"

"That depend on how good you want it took off."

"Talking about *good.*"

"Well..." Monroe reflected. "I say twenty dollar." He looked down at his plate, ate a bite. "If somebody *had* twenty dollar." He ate another bite.

"I ain't got twenty cents."

Monroe shook his head. "Then you better watch your step."

"I try to."

They ate for a while in silence.

"You looked under your bed good?" Monroe asked.

"What?"

"Talking about somebody got the hand on you, I'm just axing you looked under your bed."

"For what?"

"Could be a lot of things. Conjure ball. Hot powder. Something somebody put the touch on."

"No—I haven't." He gestured over his shoulder toward the mattress. "Anyway, *that's* my bed."

Monroe frowned, looked around. "How 'bout this here?"

"The couch?"

"You looked under *it*?"

"No."

Monroe sopped his last piece of biscuit through the bean juice, set down his plate, and stood wiping his hands on his pants. "Come grab this other end."

"Look—that stuff..."

"You better do like I said—if you got any sense atall."

Sighing, Doug put his plate aside and came over to the couch. They worked it away from the wall, revealing a ton of dust and trash. Monroe pushed through it with his foot and turned up a broken comb.

"Looka *here*."

"What?"

Monroe blinked several times studying it. Frowning, he bent down and waved his hand slowly over it. "It don't feel hot. Might be just a comb."

Doug laughed.

Monroe gave him an evil glance, then looked back. "'Cept it's sho funny the way it's broke."

Doug leaned over to grab it.

"Don't touch that thing! You crazy?"

"It's just a comb."

"You gone think just a comb when your eyeballs come out your nose."

Doug straightened up, while Monroe gauged the room with an expression turned serious. "I believe I *do* feel something in this room somewhere," he said. "I didn't pick it up till just this minute."

"You want to help me push this couch back?"

"Just leave it where it's at right now—I got to concentrate right this minute."

Slowly then, he began to step across the room, holding his hands parallel to the floor, proceeding cautiously, cocking his head every few steps.

"They's a hand in here sho nuff. Who you know out to get you?"

"Nobody."

"Nobody you *know* about," Monroe said, and angled toward the corner of the room that served as the kitchen. "It's coming from over in here." He stopped, facing the little table that held the hot plate, coffee makings, a few cans, and some utensils in a shoe box. "All this yours?"

"Most of it."

"Which ain't?"

"One of those pans was here. I didn't steal it, somebody just left it."

"What about what's in this here box?"

"It's mine—what there is."

"This knife yours?"

"What knife?"

"This long nasty-looking thing."

Doug came up and looked over his shoulder. "Okay, yeah—I think that was here too."

Monroe laughed. "Ain't no reason to look no more."

"What you talking about?"

"You don't know nothing, do you?"

"I know you crazy."

"You gone think crazy when that thing come walking across the room."

Doug rolled his head with a little laugh.

"You better listen what I say. And I hope you was telling a lie when you said you ain't had but twenty cents."

"Wasn't no lie."

"Then you better be looking for some mo'."

"What you mean?"

Monroe let out his breath patiently. "You mean to tell me you ain't never heard of nobody conjuring a knife?"

"Never *believed* it."

"Boy, I could tell you some stories make your short hairs stand up and squeak."

"Like what?"

"Like my uncle, lived over in Gretna, got to carrying on with a woman married to a man stayed gone all day working. Till he found out and went to a root doctor and told him my uncle name and where he stayed and the day he was born, and he laid a trick on a butcher knife and slipped it into his house. My uncle didn't know nothing about it, till one day he opened a draw where his underbritches was at, and there it was talking to him just as plain as I'm talking to you, saying, *"Pick me up, pick me up,"* and as soon as he did it wasn't his hand no mo', that thing was coming after him."

Monroe illustrated.

"So what happened?"

"He got lucky. It wasn't a strong enough hex—just kind of glazed him on the side. Drawed some blood, but didn't hurt him bad. But he knew he had to find somebody turn that mess around fast—didn't matter how much it cost."

"Why didn't he just throw the knife out?"

Monroe laughed. "Boy, you *don't* know nothing. First place, ain't but a fool carry it around. He wouldn't a made it out the do'. Second place, nobody don't just throw away a conjure knife. That thing be back in the house before you get turned around good, and this time *mad*. You got to do it right."

"How much did he pay?"

Monroe searched his memory. "Fifty dollar."

"*Fifty dollars?*"

"Might a been forty. It was 'long in there somewhere."

"You ask me, the man got the forty dollars the only one with any sense."

Monroe shook his head sadly. "Boy, you so ignorant I don't even know where to start."

"I just don't believe this stuff."

"That's where you fucking up, right there."

"Aw, come on."

"All right—that's fine. You don't believe it, go ahead on. I go somewhere they appreciate a old man. I ain't *got* to stay around here, listen to some young fool don't know his dick from a pine cone." Monroe gazed contemptuously at Doug, then returned to the adrift couch, took up his empty plate in both hands and licked it. He burped. "I need me some chicken and rice."

Doug sighed, returned to his chair. "What is it you're talking about doing, anyway?"

"Ne-mine—you don't need nobody help—go ahead on."

"Just tell me."

"That's all right—when they find you I'll go by the police and say yes sir, that's him, that's the one."

"All right—just tell me."

Monroe looked at him. "Boy, don't you know they ain't nowhere in this world the evil can't get—not one inch nowhere in this world? And evil don't walk up and ring the do'-bell—evil slip up from behind."

"You need money—is that it?"

"We ain't talking 'bout *me*, we talking 'bout *you* need that mojo took off."

"I just need some good luck—I need a break."

"That's what I'm talking about."

Doug sighed. "How much?"

"I done told you, twenty dollar."

"I done told *you*, I ain't got twenty dollars."

"You ain't got to pay me right this minute."

"Good, because I ain't got it and I ain't got no way to get it, and if I did, I already owe the landlord a hundred and fifty."

"I do it for ten."

"You ain't listening."

"Yeah, I'm listening. I ain't going nowhere. I done seen I'm gone have to stay around here a while."

"Stay around here? I ain't got room."

"Ain't nothing wrong with this couch. Got to wait on the new moon anyway."

"When is that?"

"I got to study on it."

"Aw, man…"

"Turn your luck *all* the way around." Monroe suddenly stopped, held up his hands. "Listen!"

"What?"

"That's my *man*."

"Who?"

"Singing that song."

And only then did the pervasive radio enter Doug's hearing: a bittersweet ballad part of the air that summer.

"Oh yeah?"

"My *man*. Got him started in his first band."

"What you talking about?"

"Talking 'bout I got him started in his first band."

"You know him?"

"Got him started in his first band, mus' would 'bout had to. Hell, I knowed him when he wasn't nothing but a little shithead dancing on the street corner for nickels and dimes. Got him started in his first band."

"He's from New Orleans?"

"That's what I'm telling you."

"Who is he?"

"Name Lonnie Ray. Wasn't for me, he'd still be jukin' on the corner."

"Come on."

"I ain't lie to you. I know the man. I take you to hear him."

"When?"

"Anytime he's around—'cept not right this minute." Monroe reclined on the ill-positioned couch, tugged the rumpled sheet over him. "I just need to lie here a minute. Don't make no noise and stay away from that box."

"If it's so evil, seems like we ought to see about it now."

"Naw, it a wait. Me just being here enough. Now hush and let me see what kind of 'vice the spirits give."

In half a minute he was snoring.

Doug got up and walked over to the kitchen area, reached into the box, and picked up the knife. He held it only a couple of seconds, then quickly put it back and didn't go near it again.

———

Don L.'s slouched just off the northeast edge of the Quarter, and for a Wednesday night had a good crowd—some tourists, but mostly locals. No cover charge, but a two-drink minimum. Doug ordered a coke, then looking around realized with relief that Monroe had disappeared. Empty chairs offered themselves, but randomly among the patrons, so he stood against the back wall, eyes drawn to the band.

They sounded good. And he realized with amazement that the singer did indeed sound like the song on the radio—an easy, distinctive voice. Was it possible?

But it wasn't so much him as the band itself that held Doug's attention. Four ingredients: a perfect dish. A good blues guitarist, who seemed to know every lick of all time, a funky bass player, and a first-rate drummer. The singer played guitar too. They were comfortable, tight, and seemed to be having great fun—especially the drummer.

The longer Doug listened, the more awed at their polish and poise he became. Eventually he took a seat at a newly vacant table, then as the room thinned worked his way gradually forward until he was sitting near the front. He got away with his one coke all night, spoke to no one, and no one spoke to him. From time to time he caught sight of Monroe working the tables, occasionally doing a little shuffle, drawing laughter—but he would look away. The music was too good, and the thought *I want to do this, exactly this* too pervasive for words.

Early in their last set they played their hit, "This Time Tomorrow." The singer's story of lost love and the lonely wasteland of life—simple, wistful, heartfelt—touched some haven of memory and longing within Doug. After that, he was in the man's power. Around midnight they finished and only then in the dissolving spell did Doug look up and realize how the crowd had thinned. The sensation, not matching his feeling of a rapt audience around and behind him, startled him. Only a few couples intent on each other, and a few odd drunks, remained. Monroe had melted into the night. Some lights came on; the room looked shabby and dirty, and Doug felt conspicuous.

Then the singer did an unexpected thing: he took off his guitar and wiping his face with a towel came directly towards Doug and sat down. "Anybody that sit out here listening like that need me to buy him a drink."

Doug was overwhelmed. The man had extraordinary presence and he regarded Doug with a smile.

"I...don't drink."

"Don't drink?"

Doug shook his head.

"What's that?"

Doug looked down. "Was a coke."

The man grinned. "Don't meet too many that way. Me, I can't say that. Didn't they make you?"

"Nobody said anything."

"It's because you sitting there looking so serious."

A woman from the bar set down a tall icy glass and a short glass before the man and looked at Doug.

"How about just bring him a big ol' co-cola, honey."

She nodded and left.

He killed the shot. "You a spy or you just like us?"

"I just like you."

"Man, we ought to take you around with us."

"That'd be fine with me," Doug said. "I been hearing your song."

"Yeah, we slipping. Number thirty-two this week." He grinned. "There go the man wrote it right there." He gestured toward the guitar player at the bar, then held out his hand. "Lonnie Ray White."

"Doug Earley."

"Doug Earley—staying late." He laughed. "You here by yourself?"

"Well," Doug said, looking about, "I came with somebody…"

"Uh oh."

"No—not anything like that."

"You live here or you visiting?"

"Call myself living here."

"What do you play?"

Doug looked at him curiously.

He grinned. "I know you play something—I can tell by looking at you."

"Well—drums."

The man nodded. "You look like a drummer. You any good?"

"I think so."

"You just think so?"

"Yeah—I'm pretty good."

"You got a band?"

Doug shook his head.

"You playing?"

"A little pick-up, that's about all."

"Where at?"

"There's a place called Come-Back's. They let people sit in."

Lonnie laughed.

"You know it?"

"Good God, there ain't a single one I don't know."

"You played there?"

"Everybody's played there."

"Another place called The Blowout."

Lonnie nodded. "Where you from?"

"All over. We moved to Atlanta when I was thirteen."

Lonnie smiled. "When was that—about a year ago?"

"I'm nineteen."

He laughed. "Nineteen. Man, you got all kind of time." He finished his drink and offered his hand again. "Hope everything go good for you."

"Thanks."

"Come back, hear us again sometime."

"I will."

"Well, let me go see about my money."

He rose, then paused not quite full height as a commotion erupted at the door.

"I was done *here!*"

"We're *closed!*"

"Oh my God," said Lonnie.

"I was done here! Let me in or I call the po-lice!"

Laughter.

"It's all right, Leon!" Lonnie called out. "I'll get him a drink."

Monroe made an indignant entrance and swam toward the bar.

"You know him?" Doug asked.

"I got to tell you the truth or you gone let me lie?"

Doug shook his head with an odd laugh. "He said he knew you—I didn't believe him."

Lonnie looked with amused curiosity at Doug. "Don't tell me *you* mixed up with him."

"Well..."

"Oh my God."

"I'm not sure what to do about it."

"Head the other way."

"I don't think he has anywhere else to go."

Lonnie laughed. "Shit. Don't let him fool you. He's got more places than an alley cat. He'll be panhandling at mine and your funeral both."

Monroe, holding a battered paper cup, wavered toward them through the tables.

"What the hell you doing bothering this boy?" Lonnie demanded.

"Bothering, hell."

"Corrupting him, leading him astray."

"Shit—I help that boy more than you know."

"Aw, what he need with some old chewed-up ain't-never-hit-a-lick-at-a-snake piece of garbage-eating trash like you?"

"Trash, my butt."

"Hell yeah, trash. Between you and a plug nickel, I be *goddamn* if I wouldn't take a plug nickel every time and come out way ahead."

"Watch out!"

"You so sorry the wind don't even waste its time blowing you down. You so dirty they got to hose down where you even *thought* about going."

"You don't know your ass from a cantaloupe." He turned to Doug. "I *told* you I knowed him."

"What you talking about, old man? I ain't never saw you before in my life."

"Shit."

"Sober."

Laughter.

"Go ahead on—laugh at a old man. You stand before God one day."

"We *all* stand there, old man. Some ahead of others. What *you* gone tell him?"

"I tell him they's some he made poor, and some he made mean—and they down here all mixed up together."

"Tell him they's some that's both."

"Them that's poor *got* to be mean. Them that ain't, just mean because they like it."

"How you call somebody mean just bought you a drink?"

"'Bout half water."

"Now the man *complaining*," Lonnie appealed incredulously to Doug.

"I ain't complain, I ain't call nobody mean. All I did, walk in the door." He sat down, took a long draught from his cup, and emitted a grunt of satisfaction.

Lonnie mimicked the sound.

"Act like he don't know me," Monroe grumbled. "*Shit.* Got him in his first band—ain't never seen the first dime from it neither."

"You believe that?" Lonnie asked Doug.

Doug shrugged.

"First time I met Ray was with him—about a hundred years ago—he been talking about how he got me started ever since." Lonnie laughed. "Man live in a *fantasy* world."

"Ray?"

Lonnie gestured over his shoulder. "The guitar player," he said. "Speaking of him, we about to go over to my place—you want to come with us?"

Doug stared at him, surprised. "For real?"

"Yeah for real," said Lonnie. "Less you got something else better to do."

Doug shook his head. "No, I ain't got nothing to do."

"Come on then. It's early, Earley. We have us a little pick-me-up."

"That's right," said Monroe.

"Except you ain't a drinking man, but that's all right. And you—" to Monroe, "if you was just a little bit sorrier you'd have it made. The devil'd send you back."

"Look out!"

"Think you can walk?"

"Boy, I be walking when they pushing you around."

Lonnie laughed and went to the bar to square up.

———

Ray, it turned out, had plans, but they were joined at the door by the drummer, whom Lonnie introduced as Artie. Awed, Doug could hardly take his eyes from him—a stocky, permanently grinning man.

Lonnie drove them in a green Chrysler Imperial to his apartment. They climbed the stairs in almost pitch dark, and Lonnie fumbled with the key and let them in.

They crossed through the dark living room to the kitchen where a dim light burned. Lonnie produced a bottle of whiskey and some coffee mugs as the others sat down around the kitchen table.

"You sure you won't have a little nip?" Lonnie asked Doug.

Doug shook his head.

"I will," said Monroe.

"I guess Artie and me have to drink by ourselves."

"*I* have some," said Monroe.

"But if that's the way it's got to be, then that's the way it's got to be."

"Right here—*I* take some."

"Oh—you want some too?" Lonnie took the bottle and poured a few drops into his cup.

Weaving, Monroe frowned. "That ain't nothing but fumes."

Lonnie poured a little more, then teased him a couple more times before filling his cup almost full.

"That better, old man?"

Monroe grunted and drank three-quarters of the cup in one long swallow. He finished with a deeper grunt and set the mug down.

"Some sho nuff whiskey," he rasped, wiped his mouth, and slipped into silence.

Meanwhile, from a cabinet below the sink Lonnie brought out a hand mirror and set in on the table. He took a seat beside Artie.

"Me and Artie gone do some of this—you want some?"

Lonnie somehow had it in his hands, which Doug was seeing for the first time: white powder in a little piece of tied-up cellophane and a razor blade. He stared in fascination, felt a tightening in his groin, and shook his head.

"I didn't think so," Lonnie said with a grin. "That's all right. Ain't nobody making you. It's just something make you feel better."

He watched Artie prepare two lines, as Lonnie took out a twenty dollar bill and rolled it tightly up. Monroe, staring straight ahead, had gone catatonic.

Doug observed the process attentively, and when they were done Lonnie carefully retied the cellophane and replaced the paraphernalia below the sink. He and Artie sipped their whiskey, smiling.

"When you gone let us come hear you play?" Lonnie asked with a sniff.

"Man, y'all don't come—I'd be nervous."

"Nervous? You got to get over that. You talking about doing this and getting paid for it, right?"

"Yeah—I hope so."

"All right then. Ain't no room for nervous. Shit, me and Artie know everybody ever *thought* about playing music in this town. Might could help you out—you never know."

"How long you been playing, man?" asked Artie.

"Since I was a kid."

"Hell, you *still* a kid." He grinned. "Lonnie says you from Atlanta."

Doug nodded.

"You just come down here by yourself?"

Doug nodded again.

"Man's got some nuts," Artie said with a grin to Lonnie. "How come you pick New Orleans?"

"Hell, the man want to play music—where else you pick?"

"My mother's from here. We lived here a couple of years when I was growing up."

"The man coming back home," said Lonnie.

"Whereabouts?" asked Artie.

"I was real young—I don't remember."

"Well, you let me know some time when you're playing."

Doug shrugged. "I guess I'm down at Come-Back's about every night. Most nights I play some."

"I be sneaking in one of these nights."

"Here, I got something I'm gone give you," said Lonnie. He went into the living room and came back with a 45 in a plain brown sleeve. "For your very own—you tell them you knew me, even came to my house."

Lonnie Ray White: "This Time Tomorrow"—R. Hoover. On the flip side: "Lake Trash"—A. Preast.

Doug looked up admiringly at Lonnie.

"Ain't no telling what he say when they start asking him what was he like," said Artie.

"He a say—man, he was something else. So good-looking everybody around him have to wear shades. Kind of man women just be *throwing* pussy at him. And sing? The man send shivers down your spine."

Artie laughed.

"What's this B-side?" asked Doug.

"It's an old blues my uncle wrote. We played it tonight."

"Your uncle?"

"Augustus Preast. Everybody called him 'Coral Snake'—cause he dressed real colorful and had a *bite*." Lonnie laughed. "And what you want to do, before you play *that* (pointing to the record) is hear *him* sing it."

"Does he live here?"

Lonnie laughed. "Naw, man—he's been dead thirty years. I'm talking about the record."

"Where can I get it?"

"You can't." Lonnie stood up. "If anybody besides me got one, I don't know about it. I'll see if I can't find it."

"Aw man," said Artie, "you'll wake up Thelma."

"Won't be the first time. She a go back to sleep."

"Man, we don't need that."

"Why you so scared of Thelma? Shit man, what she gone do?"

Artie shook his head.

It took him a few minutes, out in the living room, searching through an overflowing box on the floor beside the record player. "Come on in here!" he called.

It was an old 78 in a heavy cardboard sleeve; he took it out and blew on it. "This record was made in 1936—in an orange warehouse somewhere around Orlando, Florida. Had to stop while the train went by. Called it 'Lake Trash Blues.'"

Doug and Artie came into the living room, leaving Monroe, comatose, at the kitchen table, hands still around his mug.

"Don't play it too loud now," said Artie.

Lonnie grinned and set the needle on the spinning disk. Crackling static and loud pops filled the room.

"Man, turn that *down*," Artie said.

But Lonnie just kept grinning.

Doug didn't remember Lonnie singing the song, but it wasn't at all as the band had played it—it *couldn't* have been: eerie, haunted, the bottleneck slide guitar sinister, like a shard of glass on the spine, the voice quavering and possessed.

Lake trash on the river, river riding high
Lake trash on the river, river riding high
Woman come down to the river
River burn like fire.

"Found him in a canal—never found out what killed him—or who—just another dead nigger back then. Wasn't but twenty-two years old. Only cut ten sides, and I got 'em all but a couple—"The Sweet Thing That Kills Me," "Sally Takes Her Time"—we did those tonight too. College man come by here one time, tried to give me a hundred dollars for 'em—I just laughed at him."

"Got her claws in his liver!"

They all turned toward the kitchen.

"Got his soul!"

That woman lake trash, boy you leave her 'lone
Lake trash in the morning, lake trash all day long

Mess around with that lake trash
Eat the meat right off your bones.

"Her hand curling round the house, wind blowing the trees! She hungry, she crying in the wind—got her claws in his liver!"

"Shut up, fool!" hissed Artie. Lonnie laughed—Doug stared.

"Fire under the porch, coming up through the floor! That house ain't empty! Winter coming on—ain't no leaves, the trees all snakes!"

Lake trash talking to me, empty holes where her eyes
Lake trash talking to me, lake washed out her eyes
Dog howling where her teeth is
She done told your mama lies.

"Pickled his face! Smiling out of a pickle jar!"

The bedroom door blew open and slammed against the wall. A strapping woman in a white nightdress and crazy hair was standing there like an avenging angel.

"Get that drunk fool out of here! Get *all* you drunk fools out of here! Get out this house!"

"Aw, baby…"

"Get out! Somebody got to get up in four hours and work twelve—you sitting around drinking? Get out of here!"

"She calling me! She calling my name! She coming after my liver!"

"I get your liver, you damn drunk fool!" she cried, taking a few steps into the line of sight of the kitchen, meeting the wide-eyed, horrorstricken gaze of Monroe at the table. She turned to Lonnie. "I told you don't *never* bring that crazy drunk thing back in this house!"

"Get this thing off me! She coming!" He was waving his arms.

"You better *all* get out of here—you hear me?" She spun, stalked back across the room, slammed the door—she was gone, leaving the electrified air.

"She just got to missing me," said Lonnie.

85

"Yeah, she gone miss you so bad one day she gone be gone," said Artie.

"Shi-i-t."

"Here she come! Got his face in a pickle jar!"

"Shut your damn mouth!" cried Artie.

Someone was thumping on the floor above, and muffled shouts were coming from several directions.

Be a piece of lake trash, lake trash when I die
Be a piece of lake trash, lake trash when I die
Floating down the river
Come by your house by and by.

Doug went into the kitchen, held out his arm. "Come on, I'm gone take you home"—then thought to himself, *home?*

"She calling for my soul!"

"Ain't nobody calling you. Let's go."

Monroe got to his feet, his eyes crazed with panic, but let himself be led.

Lonnie stood up too. "I'll run you home. Ought to just leave him in the park."

————

It peeved him that he hadn't become aware of them sooner—he would have put everything into it.

Artie's face was all grin. "Man—I'm gone have to *quit*."

"I didn't know you were out there."

"That's because we didn't want you to," said Lonnie.

"Man," said Artie, looking at Doug's kit. "You got some funky-looking shit there."

"It's just junk, most of it."

"Don't sound like any junk I ever heard. They let you keep it set up in here?"

"Some of the time."

"What you do, you bring it over to my place sometime. We'll sit down together. Just you and me."

"What you trying to do?" asked Lonnie, "Run everybody out of the building?"

Artie slowly nodded. "I ain't got about five or six tricks I want to show him. That's all. After that, you ain't be able to stop him—not as quick as he is and feet like that. The man know how to tell a *story*." Artie grinned at him.

Doug smiled back, warmth spreading up through his body and burning his face.

——

About a week later.

Lonnie: "We've got a young friend out there tonight who's asked to sit in on a couple of numbers." Artie, grinning as always, was already getting up, holding out his sticks. "Doug Earley! Doug?—" peering into the audience—"where you at?"

A total shock. Doug froze. The fear locked him up like ice—but after the initial second of panic, when his eyes made a quick and furtive reconnaissance of the path to the door, he understood. There was no way out. It was more than a challenge or a dare; it was some kind of rite.

He met Artie at the edge of the low stage and took the sticks. A little applause in the room—but he didn't hear that—he saw only the welcoming faces of the band, and thought, *if I can just hold my own.*

"I don't know your stuff," he protested to Lonnie.

"Aw man, we're just going to do a little jam. Ain't nothing to it."

He didn't even have time to settle in good before Lonnie started counting it off—whatever it was. Doug jumped irresistibly in—and they were a band.

It came quickly—hardly a minute into the song, with no warning or preparation or thought—like possession: somebody else playing inside him, taking over.

He had never played with anybody like this, never felt this before—it was the first time. Where he was, who he was, dissolved as they made their way deeper into the song and it overtook him utterly. At the end, when the others dropped out, he could see in his mind the complete picture of what he needed to say from the first instant the world fell away around him.

When another fifteen seconds would have been too long, he sensed it acutely, nodded, and they came back in around him to take it home.

Their laughing faces, like a portrait, he would remember forever—and the joy, as the audience screamed and whistled.

"Man, I better find this boy a band *quick*," said Artie, "or *I* be looking for a job."

———

March, 1970. Mardi Gras had come and gone, and a cool, humid spell settled over New Orleans. Doug, in his fourth band, had a Sunday afternoon garden gig in the District—some tournament—and the casually affluent guests milled around eating and drinking and ignoring the band. Doug mentally counted down, like a worker on a time clock, wanting only to have his money and be gone. The bland music felt like the weather, and a sheen of mist glazed his equipment.

Odd—he noticed the man in the brown jacket several numbers before it struck him who he was. Something about seeing him from a distance. He leaned against the bar, occasionally speaking to the bartender, whom he seemed to know. He had gained some weight. Doug hadn't seen him in several months; his band had been on the road. At the end of the set Doug worked his way around to him. Seeing him coming, the man smiled faintly and waited.

Something haunted his manner. The smile lingered. Doug smelled whiskey.

"Crashing your party," he said. "Long as they think you the help, they don't even see you." He gave a little laugh. "That piano player kind of takes off, don't he?"

Doug shrugged.

"I know some things you just give up fighting."

"He's not going to change—he can't."

"I know." Lonnie smiled. "How you been doing?"

"Okay. How about you?"

Lonnie exhaled. "Well, not too good." Doug looked at him, waiting. "Some bad news, man. About Artie."

A cold blade sliced his guts. "What?"

Lonnie shook his head, sniffed. "Man, I knew him all my life. Wasn't nothing in my life he wasn't in on."

"What happened?"

"He was drinking. Out with a woman. Didn't even kill her—the way it always is."

"Who was she?"

"Just somebody—nobody. Car flipped over. Driving way too fast."

Doug shook his head, stunned.

"We were in Chattanooga. They're bringing the body back. Funeral's tomorrow."

Doug stared at the indifferent crowd. He could think of nothing to say.

"Listen—how much longer you got to play?"

"Another set."

"Can you come by my place when you're done?"

Doug shrugged. "Yeah—okay."

"Good man." Lonnie reached out, squeezed his shoulder, and slipped away.

———

Thelma, in hospital whites, was leaving for work. Lonnie and Ray and Fred the bass player sat around the kitchen table.

"He wasn't but twenty-six," she said.

Doug shook his head. "All that talent."

"All that everything—gone now."

"Won't be another one like him," said Fred.

"It a show you about all that drinking and carrying on," said Thelma.

The little circle exchanged glances, Lonnie sighed, but no one responded.

"And some get along just fine without it—wonder how?"

"Ask Doug," said Lonnie.

"That's what I'm talking about."

"I just don't have a taste for it."

"I pray to God you never will." She put on her sweater. "Well—won't nothing bring him back. He was a good, sweet man. I hate it."

She left, and the whiskey bottle came out. They seemed to resume a conversation.

"I ain't never done anything else—don't even know anything else. And neither do you," said Ray.

Lonnie shook his head, scowling.

"Things are going good. People know your name."

"How long you think that last?"

"It don't matter about that. I'm talking about *now*."

Lonnie frowned.

"I tell you one thing—I ain't in the mood to start over."

"The man dead! Don't you understand that?"

"I understand that just as good as you! Artie might as well been my brother."

"I feel like he'd want us to keep playing," said Fred.

"I'm tired."

"You want to know about tired—get you a job where they hand you a shovel."

"I ain't talking about shoveling."

"Then what?"

Lonnie looked up. "I don't know. Maybe it's time to find out."

"You know, the thing that gets me is *you*. *You* were always the one kept pushing, wouldn't give up, wouldn't let it die. *You* the reason we're where we at. *You* the man's name up on the sign. And where are *we* without that?"

Lonnie shook his head with a sigh.

"We got to let 'em know something."

Doug had been listening keenly. Now Lonnie looked over at him. "You figured out what you doing here yet?"

Doug looked back at him expectantly.

"We had to cancel the weekend. But we're still booked..."

"When?"

"Next weekend."

"I'm playing," Doug said.

Lonnie gave a wry laugh. "We figured that." Doug stared at him. "Man, I been right where you at."

"I'm playing—Friday and Saturday," Doug repeated.

"Oh, my man," said Ray. Doug turned to him. "I'm just say this: it's like anything else. Your chance come, you take it. You let it go by, it's gone."

Doug shook his head incredulously. "I don't even know your material."

Ray shrugged it away. "Yeah you do."

"I need some time."

"That's what you ain't got. That's what ain't none of us got. Just Artie the only one got all of that."

"I can't walk out on them," Doug protested.

"Don't want to and can't is two different things."

"Any one of them would do it to you," said Fred.

"It doesn't matter."

"They your friends? You in tight with them? You get down in the gutter any of them come help you out?"

"They're counting on me."

"What'd you get today—" asked Ray, "fifty, sixty dollars?"

Doug gave a noncommittal shrug.

91

"Man, we're a four-man band making six hundred dollars a night. Sometimes more."

"You're playing below yourself," Lonnie added quietly, looking up at him. "Which you already know that. Them old guys, man, playing the same stuff—where you going with them?"

"Aw *man*..." Doug leaned back in his chair miserably.

"They got a week to find somebody—look at it like that."

"You gone tell him about Atlanta?" Fred asked.

"What about it?" said Doug.

Lonnie finished the whiskey in his cup, swallowed it slowly. "If we stay a band," he said, "if we keep going..."

"We *got* to keep going."

"... *if* we keep going, we're booked at a place up there next month. We've played it a bunch of times before. It's a good gig. We have a good time up there. And there's some other stuff too."

"We stay out a while," said Fred.

"How long?"

"Could be two or three months. Maybe longer."

Doug sighed, thinking.

"What you got to hold you here?"

"It's good sometimes when you need to get out of town for a while," said Ray. "Have a change."

Lonnie gave a rueful laugh, and poured a new half cupful.

———

"Say what?" Monroe asked, in a fog.

"We're going to Atlanta."

"Who is?"

"All of us—the band."

Monroe stared at him, then blinked several times. "Atlanta?"

"Yes."

"Where that at? Up north?"

"No—just north of here. Everything's north of here."

Monroe thought this over. "Hm," he snorted.

"That's where my mother is—and my aunt."

"Your mama stay there?"

"Yes."

"What about your daddy?"

Doug shook his head.

"Just your mama—ain't no daddy."

"That's right."

"She ain't married?"

"No."

"Hmm." Monroe thought a moment. "They lots of rich folks in Atlanta?"

"Yeah, I guess."

"Cold there?"

"Colder than here."

"What the po-lice like?"

"I guess like anywhere."

"Hmm."

Doug looked at him sitting there in thought, one scuffed hand cupped in another, and he felt a wave of pity.

"I'm paid up—I'm not keeping the room. You'll be all right, won't you?"

"Oh hell yeah—Monroe be just fine. You ain't got to worry 'bout Monroe. I been studying on dusting the broom. Atlanta do as good as anywhere."

Doug stared at him.

"Long as I got something to sleep on, I be just fine."

———

"Man, you haven't lost a thing," gushed Grube.

"Just my best friend."

"I mean the sound."

Lonnie shook his head, stepping down from the stage. "No."

All day in the Chrysler, towing the trailer. Set-up, sound check. A couple of hours to kill.

"What you gone do?" Lonnie asked Doug. The others stood around the door: a bright rectangle of April afternoon. A couple of women waited outside.

"Just stay around here, I guess," Doug answered.

"You ain't gone see your mama?"

"Ain't got time today."

"You need a ride, just say so."

Doug shook his head. "I'll be all right."

They left. Then Grube bustled away and Doug watched him: a little man, little hands and feet, in a silk shirt.

Then the woman, standing there the entire while—who had the papers, knew what was what—as everything else fell away, emerged.

"I was sure sad about Artie," she said.

"You knew him?"

"Just acquaintance really—from when they would play here."

"Yeah, he was a good guy."

"So happy. He touched everybody around him."

"That's true."

"I'm Alma Lowe." She held out her hand.

"Doug Earley."

"I work for Mr. Grube."

"I had about guessed that. I'm the new drummer."

She laughed. "Well, I had about guessed *that*. Since you was playing them." They stood at the foot of the stage. "We're happy to have you here."

"Thanks." Pause. "You need to be somewhere?"

"Not really."

"Why don't you sit down a minute?"

They sat at a front table.

"He said your mama live here?" she asked.

He nodded.

"Whereabouts?"

"Down in East Point."

"That's nice—you get to see her while you're here."

"Yeah."

"That where you gone stay?"

"I'm not sure."

"Seems like you would."

He made an odd face. "It's a long way."

She smiled. "You must have a lady friend."

He shook his head.

"You ain't got a car?"

"Used to—till it died. We all came up together."

"I can give you a ride."

He nodded, smiled. "Thanks—soon as I figure out someplace to go."

She smiled back, regarded him for a moment. "How long you been down in New Orleans?"

"Be two years in June."

She laughed. "You don't look old enough."

"How old I look?"

"'Bout seventeen."

"I used to be."

"So how old are you?"

"Twenty."

She laughed. "You don't even pose to be in here."

"Anybody wants to know, I'm twenty-one. Maybe even twenty-two."

"Just don't be drinking. They do come in sometimes."

"Ain't got to worry—I don't drink."

She laughed, then stopped. "You serious?"

"Yes, I'm serious."

"Then, honey, you the first."

"How about you?"

"How about me what? Do I drink?"

"No—how old are you?"

"Little bit older than you—and, no, I don't drink. Can't stand it."

"Man, we boring, ain't we?"

She cocked her head. "I don't know about *you*—I ain't boring."

He laughed. "That just about make somebody want to find out what you mean."

"Well—I ain't boring right now, am I?"

"No. What about me?"

"You're not to me."

He nodded his head, smiling. "How long you been working for him?"

"About a year."

"He owns this place?"

"No, he just wants you to think that. He just runs it."

"Lonnie says it's a good crowd."

"Yeah—always is for him. He's about the only one I stay and listen to. I love that song he sings. You know you got to play it—half the people in here waiting to hear it."

"We play it."

"I'll be listening."

"Lonnie says he—" Doug nodded his head toward the side of the room—"what's his name?"

"Grube?"

"Yeah. Says he books us some other jobs too."

"Yeah, we do. For several different ones."

"What's he—Mr. Big Shot?"

"Just thinks he is. I don't worry about none of that. I just do my job and so far he's paid me. And I like it."

"What *is* your job?"

"I'm doing it right now."

"Man, here I was about to decide you liked me, but all you doing is your job."

She laughed. "He brings in a lot of colored entertainment."

Doug gave a little snort, shook his head.

"But I do a lot of things. Mainly take care of the details."
Pause. "And you ain't even gone ask me if I'm married."

"Yeah. Are you?"

"No."

"Then you go get a hamburger with me."

"I don't like hamburgers—but I'll be happy to fix something."

"At your house?"

"My apartment."

"Man, you can't beat that: free ride, free meal, and the company so nice."

She smiled. "You hungry for anything in particular?"

"Everything."

————

Sometime early summer.

"You don't understand what I'm saying. I'm not gone keep this room. I'm not gone stay here. I'm moving out."

"Don't bother me none," said Monroe. "I ain't got to stay in one place."

"No—listen to me. I'm not getting another room. I'm gone move in with somebody else. Won't have just my place anymore. You see what I'm saying? You got to find something else."

Monroe looked at him sternly, blankly. "I ain't listen to all this."

"Monroe, look. Here's what I'm trying to tell you: I'm moving out at the end of this week—done told the man—you understand? Friday the last day. Then I be gone. The man won't let you stay here—you gone have to look for something else."

"Boy, I don't know what all you talking about. I ain't got my sleep out, you standing there talking 'bout something don't make no sense."

Doug sighed. "Friday," he said, at the door. "You better listen to me. Friday the last day."

———

"Get away from that door, Kenny!" Regina called.

Grinning, Kenny backed away and shared a secret glance with Andrew.

"You full of the devil. Y'all both go outside and play."

"I want to go in there where the TV at."

"Well you ain't."

"I want to see Miss Vonceil."

"Where my switch?" She jerked her head around frantically looking; they scattered.

On the other side of the door Vonceil sat rigidly, her hands in her lap and her eyes alternating from the floor to her visitor, punctuating this movement at times with a curious little laugh.

He had put on his best and even shaved somehow, an effort that had taken a few years along with the woolly scraggle from his face. And he had come bearing gifts. On the little table between them sat a hubcap filled with an arrangement of chipped and battered artificial fruit—a good many grapes missing and one end broken off a banana.

"It's pretty," said Vonceil. "I'm bliged to you."

"This here I brought all the way from New Or-leens," Monroe said, reached in his pocket and held up a string of beads from which depended a little plastic baby face.

Vonceil looked at it, smiling, then a transformation came over her features. "Oh," she said, catching her breath.

Monroe studied her. "What's the matter with you? It's just a little charm—come all the way from New Or-leens."

"It scare me a little bit."

"This thing? Ain't nothing but a little charm—come all the way from New Or-leens."

She smiled uneasily.

"You done hurt my feelings now. I just lay it right here," he said, placing it beside the fruit, "and we talk about it later on."

"I…"

"You what?"

"I…nothing."

"You what nothing? Tell me what you trying to say."

"I thought you might like to take off your jacket."

"Oh. Yes ma'am. I believe I will." Monroe rose, took off his jacket, arranged it on the back of his chair, and sat down again. "Yes ma'am—we getting comfortable now."

Vonceil looked away.

"How old is you?"

"Oh, I…" Her brow furrowed. "I can't always remember that."

"You younger than me. I was born in nineteen-aught-seven. Used to have a piece of paper said it on it."

Vonceil looked confused.

"I had me a wife way back yonder. She been dead longer than she was alive. Your husband dead too?"

"I ain't got no husband."

"I know you ain't now. I'm talking about back yonder."

"She wouldn't let me have no husband. She run them all off."

Monroe studied her with a puzzled expression. "Who did?"

"*She* did."

"Who Doug's daddy?"

Her face brightened. "Doug? He was gone a long time, but now he's come back."

"You wasn't married to his daddy?"

The smile decomposed into pained perplexity.

"Well, it don't matter. Now."

"I'm a clean girl."

Monroe nodded. A moment crept by. "You ought to use to see me dance. You ever use to dance?"

"Sometimes."

"I dance ever time I feel like it now."

Vonceil stared at him.

"Your sister seem like a nice lady."

Vonceil nodded.

"She younger than you?"

Her brow furrowed.

"Ne-mine. Let it go. You ever leave the house?"

"I don't know where the house."

"Ain't what I'm axing you, where the house. I'm axing do you ever leave it? Go off somewhere. Shoot—*where* the house ain't hard. The house right here. Anywhere else you is—" he waved his arms around "—ain't the house."

Vonceil's eyes glazed, then suddenly turned bright again as she looked at Monroe directly. "There ain't but just the house," she said decisively.

"Um uh," replied Monroe. He rose. "Maybe I visit again some time."

She smiled at him strangely, wistfully, as he donned his jacket, took his leave, and let himself out the door muttering.

"That woman crazier than I am."

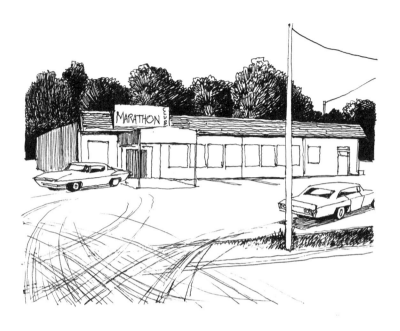

The Trybald Trio

Jimmie Myles

I ran into him one afternoon downtown. I hadn't seen or talked to him for two months. He'd moved back in with Eunice, and of course the band was dead. My old man had pulled some strings and gotten me into college that spring—1970—but I just ended up banging the math teacher and flunking everything else. It was weird to see him because in a way it was like he was a stranger, someone I had never known. Everything we had done felt like centuries ago, and not even us—like it was a movie you'd seen and half forgotten. You couldn't feel it, you couldn't have it anymore. It was over. Of course, it had only been a couple of months, but there was an absolute line between then and now. Looking back, you see that being young is a lifetime all its own—it's got its own story, its own people and places, and then it's gone, leaving the faint scent of Jade East, and it might as well have been somebody's fireside tale.

We never mentioned Louis, never said his name. That's the thing about death—it's so absolute—you can't add anything, and no matter what, people turn away from it. It seems strange at first—the person is dead and the bread trucks and school buses are going by and you have to wait for the train and the village idiot is coming down the sidewalk—life goes on. But that's the way it is. Glenroy told me he was moving to Atlanta. He wanted a band.

What else could he want? But me—good God, the *thought* of going through all that again—Jesus. It's not like he asked me; I don't really remember how it happened. I just remember the feeling I had standing there talking to him: I've got to get the hell out of this rat-hole town. And Glenroy had this look I'd never seen on him before: I guess you'd call it desperation. It really was all he had—I could feel that and it was scary as hell.

He needed me.

It damn near killed Eunice—man, was she bad off. But at least it was her cousin we were going to stay with—that much of a thread to her—a bachelor who had a little house in Decatur. He was a salesman and gone most of the time—he let us stay for free. We put down two mattresses on the floor of his spare bedroom, and bang, Trybald no more. We were living in Atlanta.

Of course we didn't have a dime between us. I got a part-time job in a warehouse and Glenroy did a little painting—just at first, not much. We got around okay—he had left Louis's Plymouth with Eunice, but we had my Camaro. I can't remember what all we did—and that's another thing about Glenroy. He never had but one real problem in his life: what to do when he wasn't playing. I'm sure we must have been bored a lot, but you know how memory is—you forget all that. But I haven't forgotten how poor we were. We ate a lot of macaroni and cheese and tuna fish, a lot of peanut butter. In fact, I can remember a few peanut butter dinners—I mean *just* peanut butter, big spoonfuls of it. Later you'd want to puke. I still can't eat it. Starting on Thursday we'd go out to hear bands and there were some good ones around in those days.

I do believe in destiny. Things happen when they need to. It really wasn't but just a few weeks before we found a band. It was a little place downtown on West Peachtree called the Electric Banana. We went there so much we got to know the owner, a huge red-headed guy with a ponytail and one of these ZZ-Top beards, named Wilson. Wilson did maybe a little too much acid or something—he was a good guy, but every now and then he would just go berserk. To stay in practice, I guess. He was diabetic, and I heard just a couple of years ago they'd had to amputate both his legs and he'd been so depressed he blew his brains out. That building got bulldozed several years ago. Anyway, there were several bands that played there—some all right, some awful—and Glenroy started sitting in with this one group and that was all it took. The drummer was the drummer only because they didn't have one—he was really a guitar player, so he went to bass and there we were. Subway Wizard, we called ourselves, and we started out just playing the Banana for the door, usually for a catatonic crowd of tripping freaks. The other guys in the band were acidheads, but I was through with all that, and so was Glenroy. Wouldn't have worked. There's something about tripping and desperation that don't go together too well. We just smoked a lot of dope, and Glenroy had his juice, but I had become the basic Joe Six-Pack you see before you today.

We were pretty good. For a couple of minutes I remember thinking, hey maybe I can do this again—and even believed it—for those two minutes. But there was no way in hell. *Glenroy.* I don't even know if he'd been playing—but it seems like he was about ten times better. He was on another planet. And I just *thought* he pushed us in the old days. Just being with him wore you out—like playing a football team that wants to win so bad they'd rather die than lose. The other guys were decent musicians but not really serious; they had a big house in Little Five Points—the whole freak show. It reminded me a lot of The Mansion. Too much, actually. And the music—God it was hard, and Glenroy wanted everything to be perfect, but we were just a bunch of jackasses—we'd forget everything from one week to the next. Glenroy was about to blow out a major blood vessel. I couldn't figure out how to get out of it. It was just the Glenroy band anyway; he started playing these long leads that the freaks loved, but I would get so bored sometimes. And the other guys—we didn't even hardly talk to each other—I mean, it wasn't like a band at all: everybody was in their own little world—but they did so many drugs they just kept hanging around out of habit, I think. Or maybe it was the attention we were getting—*we* meaning Glenroy. He developed a following and we started playing in other places. People would show up just to hear him. And—he just poured it all out—everything he had.

But living with him was becoming a problem. He was so frustrated he was in a bad mood all the time. Plus, this little frizzy-headed hippie chick named Tawana had taken up with him and was there all the time like a growth on the couch. I couldn't stand her. F-minus in personal grooming—which doesn't work for me. Finally, the topic of finding a new drummer peeked out into the open. I told him, no hard feelings, but he was uncomfortable talking about it. It was this loyalty thing he had.

But it had to be. One night we were watching a band that had a really good drummer and I said something like, that's what you need, and I'll never forget the look he gave me. It was, like, somehow in that one second we had dealt with it. Funny thing, that was the very night I met Angela. Destiny again. This would have been mid-August or so. We were in the old Marathon Club—what did they put there, apartments?— where we went pretty often. They had great bands there. I could tell from the first minute: she was at a table with two or three girlfriends—there you go—and I kept catching her eye: you know, where you keep trying to check her out without her seeing but she's doing the same thing too, so you keep catching each other? It got to the point where I had to go over there—so I did.

Subway Wizard broke up not long after that. I don't think anything happened—we just didn't play for a couple of weeks, and all of a sudden it was sort of over. Meanwhile, things were going really fast with Angela—it wasn't long before I moved in with her. Just in time: I was so sick of sleeping on the floor in that little house, with Glenroy banging Squeaky Fromme on the next mattress, and her sitting around stoned eating doughnuts and sucking her fingers the rest of the time. Glenroy started going out hearing bands all the time, looking.

I was spending most of my time with Angela—nothing like that early love—but I tried to hang out with him too. Along in there somewhere I remember we went to the Marathon Club to see Lonnie Ray White. We'd never seen him before. It turned out to be quite a memorable night. It was the first time I ever heard Doug Earley.

I remember wondering, right after they started playing— where's the other drummer? I couldn't take my eyes off him the entire night just trying to figure out how he was making the sounds he was making. His kit was pretty basic, about like mine, but of course he had all these other doo-dads hanging around. Jesus, this skinny, math-class-looking kid with glasses sounding like a cross between Buddy Rich and God. He blew me completely away.

The whole band was terrific. They had this real tight show down—zero dicking around—which really impressed Glenroy: and of course Lonnie was incredible. When he sang "This Time Tomorrow" I swear to God there were people crying. We went back to see them at least three or four more times during that stand. Then they left town for a while, and not too long after that—September, I guess—we heard Lonnie was in the hospital. I didn't find out till later he'd almost died. It was the silver spoon and something. Nobody knew at the time how it was with him.

Anyway, after a while we heard that Doug Earley was back at the Marathon Club, and it turned out he was playing with a sort of pick-up R&B group—something kind of like a house band. Horns and all that—they were pretty good. But the personnel wasn't very stable and they had their good nights and their bad nights. But I could have sat there and listened to him forever. I finally went up to talk to him one night, and he turned out to be this nice, quiet kid—just like he looked. It was the first and last time I ever offered to buy him a beer—plus, there was a woman obviously waiting for him, so we just chatted for a few minutes, and he showed me the instruments he had made, with all these weird names: goat drum, hot sticks, water tubes, mojo beads, black snake rattle, dead-man's eyes, and I forget what all. I asked him about Lonnie and he said they'd had to break up for a while. The rest of the guys had gone back to New Orleans, but he'd decided to stay up here. For a while at least, he said. Till Lonnie got back on his feet.

I wasn't seeing Glenroy as much, but he just couldn't get anything going and it was rough. Couldn't find the right music, the right people, nothing. He was like a caged animal. Something had to change, and I've always thought it was funny how it was Angela who started the whole thing, who of course had no idea what she was doing. This was back when she still liked the idea of me playing—those ten minutes—but *nice* music. She'd only heard Subway Wizard once—one of the last times we ever played—and of course hated us, and I can't really blame her, except that she was completely incapable of appreciating Glenroy. She never liked him. I don't think it was just that he was from such a different world—this possessed guitar-playing mill kid, and a northern suburb accountant who shit in stacks—but also what he represented, to her anyway: a force she didn't understand and couldn't control and that had a lot of influence over me. She did everything she could to try to

keep him away from me—we won't go into that—and when
The Decisions thing came up she thought this would be a nice
harmless way for me to indulge this kooky part of myself—
without Glenroy—which she could keep tabs on. Okay, this is
my interpretation.

Anyway, the guy's name was Skip Horton—somebody
she'd gone to high school with who had won all these awards
and had a band. A trumpet player. She talked about him like
he was God's gift—you know, from somebody that knows dick
about music—and always said I should go talk to him, and
I'm thinking for God's sake *why*? and so basically I ignored
her. Then one day she called me all excited from work and
said his drummer was joining the Air Force. For some insane
reason I went—mainly just to shut her up, I guess.

The first thing I found out was that I had to make an
appointment.

He had a house in Smyrna. The front room was an office,
and the day I went, there was a little group of people stuffing
envelopes for a mailing. And the phone kept ringing. All over
the walls were photographs and posters and plaques and awards.
In the photographs it was easy enough to figure out who Horton
was—the one out front with the trumpet looking about twelve.
In some, he *was* about twelve—posing in a sharp little suit and
holding his shiny horn. Somebody went to get him, and while I
waited I picked up a color brochure from the desk titled
"Ladies and Gentlemen—The Decisions!" They had a horn
section, piano, guitar, bass, drums, and a female vocalist. In the
photographs they were in tuxes (and evening dress), trying their
best to look Dynamic.

Finally Horton came out and he was almost exactly what I
was expecting: a brisk, hyper, clean-cut little Napoleonic
shrimp. He asked me what he could do for me.

I hadn't given it much thought. "I was just interested in
seeing what you were up to."

He had the pissy look of someone who considers his time valuable. "Allison gave me the impression you wanted to audition on drums."

"Angela."

"Angela."

The thing is of course, I never had the slightest desire or intention to do any such thing. Like I said, I'm not really sure why I went. But in the ten minutes since I'd come through the door, something had happened to me. I guess it was the atmosphere.

"Well, actually, I represent some musicians," I said.

"Represent musicians? She said you wanted to audition."

"No, not me personally."

He shook his head with a sort of what-kind-of-bullshit-is-this look. "Do you have a card?"

"Not with me."

"Well, just leave your information with the secretary and we'll keep it on file." He turned to leave.

"But you are in need of a drummer, right?" I pressed on.

He stopped. "This minute, no. But we are going to be auditioning over the next few weeks."

"I happen to represent an exceptional drummer. A really exceptional drummer."

"Where have I heard that?"

"I don't know—but this time you can believe it. Also an exceptional guitarist."

"I don't need a guitarist."

"I was thinking, it wouldn't hurt to hear him. He and the drummer both happen to be looking for work at the moment. It's actually a rare opportunity..."

Everybody in the room was listening. "Yeah, yeah," Horton said. "When can they audition?"

"Ah...well, they're both playing this weekend."

"So are we. I thought you said they were looking for work."

"They're both interested in finding something more stable."

"How about tomorrow night?"

"Tomorrow night? Well—I might possibly be able to work out the details."

"They can read music." It was a statement with one little shake of question in it.

"Read music? Well—I know they can both play anything."

He rolled his eyes. "We rehearse at seven."

On the way home I stopped at a printer and ordered some business cards: "Myles Talent and Booking Agency—'Filling the Dixie Night with Stars'—Jimmie Myles, Agent." I put down Angela's phone number and gave the guy five dollars extra for a rush job.

Then I went to find Glenroy.

At first he just laughed. "What have you been taking, Jimmie?"

"Nothing. I don't do that anymore."

He laughed again. "So how do you explain this hallucination?"

"It sort of...*developed*."

"Man, I may be desperate but I draw the line," he said.

"No, you've got the wrong idea."

"Horns?"

"They've got guitar, bass, drums, and piano too."

"So does Lawrence fucking Welk."

"Look, I don't know what kind of stuff they do..."

"*I* do."

"No you don't. And whatever it is, this is what I'm thinking: *you* could take them in a new direction."

He shook his head. "Like this fucker you're telling me about is going to let that happen. It's *his* band, Jimmie. A fucking horn band. I want *my* band."

"Look Glenroy—just listen to me," I said, trying to sound calm and rational. "I can see this—it's really clear to me. When he hears you, he'll see the possibilities."

"No he won't."

"Okay—*maybe* he will. What have you got to lose?"

Glenroy shrugged.

"They play regularly and get paid."

"How much?"

"Well, I haven't gone into that with him yet. Shit, I haven't had time. Anyway, we're not talking about a permanent thing here. We're talking about exposure. Experience. Contacts. It's a stepping stone."

"To what?"

"Well, to…who knows?"

"I think you've gone crazy."

"Look, Glenroy, I've all of a sudden realized this is what I should be doing."

"That's what I thought: *you*."

"No, goddamnit, I'm trying to help you."

He laughed.

"It's hard to get appreciated around here."

He just shook his head, looking at me funny.

"Don't you think I'd be good at it?"

"Yeah," he said, "you probably fucking would."

"Me too. And—actually, there is one other thing."

"Here it comes."

"Goddamn, Glenroy."

"And I'm going to listen to it because I just want to hear what it is."

"Glenroy, how many people in the world are helping you right now?"

His expression changed. "All right," he said.

I took a breath. "What they're actually looking for is a drummer."

"They why in the hell are you bugging me?"

"Because I had an idea about somebody that could play for them, maybe."

"Who?"

"Doug Earley."

The name didn't quite register yet, but for the first time he seemed to listen to me. "You mean the guy at the Marathon Club?"

"Yes."

He was quiet for a moment. "What are you talking about?"

"Just that—he could play for them. He'd be perfect. And he could make some money and I'd have a satisfied client."

He thought. "Okay." He waited. "What's this got to do with me?"

"Well, like I said—it would be an opportunity for you too. And—it would get you two together."

He was silent. Finally he said, "Have you talked to him?"

"Not yet."

He shook his head, frowning. "He won't do it."

"Why not?"

"Jimmie—think."

"I've already thought."

"You're talking about some kind of white country club band, right?"

"So?"

"So forget it."

"No, I'm not going to forget it."

"Did you tell the horn guy?"

"No. Why should I?"

"You know why."

"This is 1970, Glenroy."

He shook his head. "You don't even know if they're any good."

"They are."

"How do you know?"

"They must be."

"Right."

"Why don't you just go find out?"

"Because I don't want to."

"Look, Glenroy—I guarantee you the minute Horton hears Doug he'll want him."

"And I guarantee you the minute he *sees* him, he won't."

"I think you're wrong."

"You want to make a little bet?"

"Yeah, I'll bet you twenty bucks."

"Deal."

"So you'll go?"

Glenroy just shook his head.

———

Late afternoon—I was surprised to find the front door unlocked, but it was, so I walked in. Beyond the foyer the cavernous room stood silent, empty. I angled toward the bar and someone carrying a case of something came through a door behind the stage.

"We're closed," he said.

"I realize that. I was looking for somebody."

He waited.

"Do you know Doug Earley—the guy who plays drums here sometimes?"

"No."

"Is the manager here?"

He started away, gesturing over his shoulder. "He may be in the office."

I'd never noticed it before—but you know how different clubs look in the daytime: a little dim hallway off the side of the room. I followed it to the only door and knocked.

Someone said, "Come in," and the door scraped as I pushed it open. I entered a small, cluttered room. Right away I recognized the woman at the desk—I had seen her with Doug; and standing beside her holding some papers was another dapper little guy—it seemed to be the day for them. He had a goatee and thinning hair up top, strategically combed. "Yes?" he said.

"I was wondering if you could help me find Doug Earley."

"Who is that?" he said, and the woman glanced at him.

"The drummer in the band that plays here."

"A lot of bands play here."

"I mean the house band."

"We don't have a house band."

"Well, it's sort of *like* a house band."

"What do you want with him?"

"I wanted to talk with him."

"About what?"

"It's a personal matter."

"I don't give out information like that," he concluded, and returned his attention to his papers. "Let's look at Thursday, the seventeenth…"

I caught the woman's eye and there was something in her expression.

Whatever it was, it stayed with me as I went back outside. I looked around, then walked over to the little shopping center next door to try to figure out what to do. I went into a drug store and started looking through the magazines. I was trying to cook up some kind of fake phone call, but I couldn't think of anything that wouldn't be obvious. But then, after about ten minutes: destiny struck again. The man, snappy in a porkpie hat, strutted to a silver Corvette and drove away.

I just caught her, gathering her things to leave.

"I hope you don't mind me being a little sneaky," I said with my best smile, "but I saw him leave—and I thought I'd see if maybe you could help me."

"Why do you want to see Doug?" she asked.

"Well—I have a proposition for him."

"About his music?"

"Oh yeah—his music. I'm not—I mean, I'm not an insurance salesman or anything—it's something that might be a pretty good opportunity for him."

"Does he know you?"

"We've talked a couple of times."

She looked me over, sizing me up, for a moment. "All right," she said, "I'll call and see if he's home, and then you can talk to him." She reached for the phone.

"I'd rather talk to him in person."

"He'll be playing Friday."

"Actually, it's kind of important to see him now."

She inspected me some more, then sighed. "All right."

Her car, she said, was languishing in some shop, and she'd been taking the bus, so she let me drive her home. I had already pretty much figured out where he was staying. We talked on the way; she told me a little about herself, and Doug, and her job, and Grube, her boss.

October had come, but it still felt like summer and I remember a window fan was stirring up the muggy air in her apartment as we walked in. It seemed like every light in the place was a forty-watt, and a jazz record was playing.

"Doug," she said at the door, "there's somebody here to see you." He materialized from the couch, sat up, and gave me a startled look. Barefoot, his shirt open, he got to his feet looking at me and fumbled a few buttons together. I couldn't decide if he recognized me or not.

"Hello," I said. "Do you remember me?"

He nodded. "Yeah, man, how you doing?"

"Okay."

"He said he had something important to talk to you about," said Alma.

"It'll only take a few minutes—I'm really sorry to disturb you—it's a proposition, I guess you'd say."

"I'll be out in the kitchen," she added, and disappeared down the hallway.

We sat down—both of us a little stiff.

"I know this must seem like a lot of rigmarole, but it's pretty simple, really. It's an opportunity I found out about. For a drummer. I...thought of you."

He mumbled something.

"I get the feeling the band at the Marathon Club isn't really permanent. If I'm wrong, just tell me."

"Ain't none of it permanent, man."

"I know. But..."

"It's just pick-up, really. One night to the next."

"That's what I thought. So anyway—I know a band that's looking for a drummer. They're holding auditions."

"I'm still playing with Lonnie."

"Yeah, I know—but I had the impression it might be a while before..."

"It might." He waited a second or two. "What kind of band?"

"Horns, piano, female singer."

Some puzzlement came over his features. "Like big band?"

"I guess so. I'm not really sure. Maybe a little more...contemporary. I do know they play a lot. I just thought about you—I thought, if you weren't doing anything else particularly, you might be interested in checking it out."

He nodded. "I appreciate it. I guess I need to find out a little more about it."

"I'm going to be honest with you—that's about all I know. I thought—you could do the audition and find out for yourself. Nothing to lose."

"When?"

"Tomorrow night."

"Where?"

"I can give you the address. It's up in Smyrna. Actually, I was thinking I could take you. Introduce you."

His expression turned quizzical. "Is it a white band?"

"Well," I said, "So far."

He just barely nodded.

"I don't think it will matter," I added.

"It always matters, man."

"Well, it's not like it would be the first time."

"What time?"

"I'd pick you up about six-thirty."

"You're talking about something steady."

"Absolutely."

"What kind of money we talking about?"

"I'll be honest, I don't know. I figured we could find out."

He shook his head with a funny smile. "Man, I appreciate you telling me about it and all that. I'm just trying to figure out..."

I laughed. "About me."

"I was just wondering, man."

"All right. Here's the deal. I'm trying to start a management and booking agency."

He smiled suspiciously. "What's your cut?"

That took me by surprise. "You know—you may not believe me, but I'm not really interested in getting any money out of this. I mean with you. I'm just trying to get my foot in the door—and I know if I had a couple of musicians of your caliber, well..."

"You ain't taking a cut then," he said with a laugh.

"Why don't we say—it's negotiable, and I guarantee you we'll come up with an arrangement you'll be satisfied with."

He just shook his head, still with his funny smile. "Man, what in the world make you want to get in this business?"

"Well, it's just a business, right?"

He shrugged.

"There's something else I want to tell you. I have a friend who's going to audition with you. You met him one night at the Marathon Club—just a couple of seconds, you probably don't remember. He's a guitar player."

"Guy with the sort of red hair?"

"Yeah," I said, surprised.

"Name's Trimble?"

"You must have a photographic memory."

"Naw, I've heard about him."

"You've heard him play?"

"No. Somebody told me he was good."

"He is."

He nodded, thinking. "Only thing—this band don't really sound like his kind of guitar."

"It's not. But he just needs to get something going. I just thought—hell, might as well be playing and making some money while you're looking."

"Yeah," Doug said, nodding a little and thinking.

———

As we walked through the door my first thought was: I've fucked up. It was like I hadn't actually stopped and thought about what I was doing until that minute. I felt like an idiot. And I won't even go into the looks I was getting from Glenroy.

Of course they weren't the right kind of people—but it wasn't like I hadn't known that. But there was one exception— the bass player—and I know if it hadn't been for him we'd have been out of there. He had long straight black hair and a bushy moustache and some kind of Tennessee accent—a complete contrast to the rest of those goof balls clowning around with each other. His name was Alfred and he immediately attached himself to us. We talked—he'd been in a million bands, played every kind of music. This stuff was a lot of work, the gigs pretty boring, he told us—but he'd sure had worse. He was getting paid. We stood off to ourselves, waiting for Horton to show up. I guess I started pacing but the three of them hit it off and were laughing.

Finally His Majesty arrived. I had to remind him who I was—and when I pointed out my clients you should have seen his face. Not just Doug—but Glenroy being there at all. The regular guitar player, one of these heart attack-candidate types, was having a lot of trouble understanding what another guitarist was doing there and had this silent, pissy attitude. God, it was preposterous, the whole thing. But what the hell—I learned a long time ago when you go for something you have to follow through. So I told myself I had to keep acting like whatever it was I was pretending to be.

117

The rehearsal room was the basement, about as far from shabby as you can get—outfitted almost like a professional studio. Had this guy made all this money playing music? I never found out. The singer was out of town, but the rest of them had tuned up and were ready to play. The fucking around pretty much came to an end when Horton got there. They warmed up with some "Grazing in the Grass" type of thing, with their regular people—the pouting guitarist and the Air Force-bound drummer—and the minute they started playing, I felt better—because they weren't nearly as good as I'd thought they'd be. The drummer was mediocre, kind of clunky and cliché. Ditto, the guitar player, who basically didn't seem to do much of anything at all. When his break came, he just played the chords. The rest of them seemed fairly decent, though I'm not the best judge. The bass player at least was funky. But there was no doubt about who the *man* was. I don't know anything about trumpets, but I guarantee you that little dude could play the shit out of his.

They finished and Horton nodded to Doug. The other guy stepped down and Doug got in behind his set. He didn't touch a thing or even look at it. He just sat there waiting. Horton went back and handed him a sheet of music and asked him if he was familiar with such and such (I forget the song). Doug shook his head, took the music, and looked at it.

"We play it up-tempo," Horton warned.

You could see Doug's eyes going down the page; then he just looked up and nodded.

Horton counted it off—there was a little intro, then Doug did a nifty little fill and came in on the money. Within five seconds they were a totally different band. And he wasn't even doing anything, just following along—but it was the *way* he played. And what amazed me was how he caught all the stops and starts, the bumps and shots—he didn't miss a one. It was like he'd been playing that tune all his life, and that was the first time he'd ever heard it. And the *band*—you should have seen them; they kept turning around to look at him and they were rocking. When Horton took his break, Doug went right along with him, punctuating everything he did, just perfect. I know good and well the guy'd never had anybody play behind him like that. Once or twice I caught Glenroy's eye and he just shook his head with a little smile. And the other drummer: *Close your mouth*, I thought. And I'm wondering, how in the hell is this guy going to get back up there? If it was me, I swear to God I'd have slunk out the door. Off into the wild blue yonder.

They got to the end: Doug did a cymbal roll on the last note, choked it, and gave a little bump, and it was over. Everybody turned around to have a look or say something to him. He just sort of nodded. Horton, sweating like a wrestler, his eyes shining like an opium fiend's, put his horn on its stand, wiped his hands, and said, "Okay, that wasn't too bad."

Then, no way around it: it was Glenroy's turn. The regular guy scowled but conceded. "Ed, sit this one out," Horton said, not really going out of his way to spare his feelings, "and let's hear this guy." Ed kept his big black Gretsch on as he walked over to the side of the room like somebody being annoyingly interrupted. Glenroy unpacked his guitar and Horton brought him the chart for the tune.

"You going to play *that*?" he asked, looking at Glenroy's Strat.

Glenroy shrugged. "Yeah."

"Okay." He put the music on the stand. "Think you can handle that?"

Glenroy shrugged again.

Horton exhaled. Ed sneered. "Take the fourth break," Horton instructed. "After the trombone. Ready?"

Glenroy nodded.

As they plunged into it, Glenroy didn't even make a pretense of following the music; he just listened. Then, after one time through, he figured out the basic chords and started playing a little easy rhythm that gradually got stronger until the other players began exchanging glances, and Horton impatiently signaled to him to hold it down. So he did—but then he started throwing in little blues licks. Horton turned around again and gave him a dirty look but didn't stop him. The thing is, in all honesty, I didn't care anymore what Horton thought. Glenroy had the same effect Doug had. They were totally different again. I thought, if Horton can't appreciate that, screw him—and I knew without a doubt I'd done the right thing bringing them there, no matter what happened. They were cooking. I had to laugh to myself; any idiot could have seen the potential. Ah-one and ah-two meets Big Dick guitar. It worked for me.

I had no idea what he would do when his break came, but he just did what he always did. What else could he do? He eased in slowly and started building it toward his trademark eruption, which was like somebody all of a sudden screaming that your house is on fire, then brought it down to a whisper, one last little flare-up, and out—all in thirty-two bars. The expression on Big Ed's face was not to be believed.

Finally, Horton had the last break and it was all about one thing: *nobody* outplayed him. And good God, did he blow the stew out of that horn. Doug was right there, and Glenroy went back to his pile-driving rhythm—and when they got to the end, Horton did this run up into the ozone and Glenroy went right with him, then slid out of it with a long blazing glide. The hair on the back of my neck stood up.

It ended—everybody was sweating and laughing. Horton just said, "Let's take a break," didn't even look at anybody but headed upstairs with a little gesture for me to follow. I passed by Big Ed—who couldn't quite pull off the evil looks anymore and merely looked like what he was: blown away.

"Thanks for the jam session," Horton said upstairs, as I sat down opposite his desk. "It was great fun, but we play from music."

"He's a fast learner."

He gave a contemptuous snort. "You're missing the point—we need someone who can read." He was still shining with sweat.

"Hey," I said. "I know *I've* never heard anything like that." I gestured toward the basement. "Isn't *that* the point?"

Little smile. "No. And I think I know what I do and don't need in my band, thank you."

"I'm sure you do."

"My father is a professional musician, my mother is a professional musician, and I've been a professional musician since I was eight."

Hard ball. I liked this. "I'm not saying..."

"I really don't think I need somebody coming in here and telling me how to run my business, okay?"

"That's not what I'm trying to do."

He took a breath, calmed down a bit, and seemed to be thinking. "Okay, the drummer seems to have a pretty good idea of what we're doing—the only thing is..."

"He's black."

"It's not just that."

"Then what?"

"Look—who are you? What do you know about this band, the kind of places we play, the people I have to deal with? Huh?"

"Okay—nothing. I'm just looking at the potential here. Not only would you have a unique sound—it would give you a reputation as an innovator, a trailblazer."

"I've already got that."

"It would add to it," I argued.

"Okay, forget about him for a minute. The guitar player—in the first place, as you can see, I've already got a guitarist."

"Not like him."

"He doesn't fit."

"Again—look at the potential. You would have a band like no other band in the world. It's an opportunity."

"*Opportunity*," he sneered. "You're talking to *me* about opportunity? Look around you—you think I don't know about opportunity? It's an opportunity to lose our clientele, that's what it is."

"But think of the doors it could open. Maybe a whole new clientele."

He just stared at me with what looked like hatred.

"Why don't you ask the guys downstairs?"

"I make the decisions!"

"Okay, whatever. But just hypothetically—what sort of terms would you offer?"

"I'll let you know. I need to think. Right now we've got a rehearsal to finish and we're wasting time." But he stayed put. I waited. "What if I'm only interested in one of them?" he said at last.

"Well, the thing is—I believe they want to stay together. And look—if it doesn't feel right—you know, whatever—I just need to know something before I decide where to take them next."

He glared at me and took several deep breaths. "Let me make one thing absolutely clear. If I *do* decide to try this— *if*—you need to be aware there's a contract. And I enforce it too. You miss a gig, you're fired. You miss a rehearsal, it's fifty bucks. We rehearse twice a week, we have a dress code, and a no-drinking rule."

"Mm-hmm."

"Give me your card. I'll call you tomorrow."

I handed him one and shook his hand. "We appreciate your time."

"A little piece of advice," he said. "Tell that guitar player to hold it down. And tell him to listen to some Eddie Condon records."

"I'll tell him."

———

Horton's offer was sixty bucks each, per gig—and it was a rare weekend they didn't play twice, he said. I toyed around with the math all day in my head. Not exactly the big money, but the band fetched a pretty good sum evidently—especially if you figured Horton had to make more than anybody else. Angela got over my radical alteration to her design once she got on the scent of the business possibilities. We sat around for several hours trying to figure out how to draw up the contracts. She had a copy of some kind of contract she had gotten from the library, which was no help, and she made about fifty phone calls, but the only thing we found out, which I've found out many times since, was that what we needed to know, nobody tells you.

About all we knew was that agents generally get fifteen percent.

"Of what?" I asked.

"Their salary," said Angela.

"From now on?"

"Well..."

"It's got to be a one-time thing," I said.

She frowned, thinking. "Maybe you just take out a fee."

"How much?"

She contemplated. "I don't know."

"Maybe fifty dollars or something."

"God, Jimmie, if that's all, why waste your time? I think more like five hundred."

"Yeah, right! I'm going to ask Glenroy to give me five hundred dollars." I laughed. "And Doug."

"We said we were going to do this like a business, Jimmie."

"Hey, I'm all for it. But in the first place, the chances of Glenroy giving me five hundred dollars are about the same as that toaster singing the 'Star Spangled Banner.'"

"Okay, then I've got one question: why do it?" She stared at me. "If it's just a favor, that's fine—but I haven't noticed him doing too many favors for *you.*"

"For God's sake, Angela."

"Clients should not be friends. They should be clients."

I thought about it. "Hey—maybe it's Horton who ought to pay."

"He won't," she said.

"I know."

"Anyway, he's already paying something—he's paying them."

I just shook my head, confused.

"The thing is, you're *their* agent. They should pay you."

And so it went. Finally we decided on fifteen percent of their first month's earnings, and Angela typed it all up, throwing in the stuff from the library contract. Feeling pretty good, I took it over to Glenroy.

"You think I'm signing that shit you're out of your fucking mind."

"Come on, Glenroy, it's *standard.* It's just the way it works."

"Not for me."

"We're not talking about a big sum of money here."

"It doesn't matter how much. Anything I make is mine."

"But I'm the one that got you the job."

"Which I don't even want."

"Damn, Glenroy."

"Jimmie, look—if I went out there and heard about a job and told you about it, do you think I'd charge you for it?"

"This is different," I protested.

"How?"

"I'm trying to be your *agent.*"

"I don't need an agent."

"Everybody needs an agent."

"Tell you what: hook me up with Jack Bruce and some of them and we'll talk about it. Mitch Miller doesn't count."

"Oh, come on. The whole point is to get something going while I'm out there trying to find something better for you. Don't you want me to?"

"Yeah, if you want to."

"Well, don't you think I've got to have *some* kind of incentive?"

Glenroy was looking at the contract. "What's this 'subsequent placement' shit anyway? You're telling me I can't even quit this band or get in another one or start my own without you?"

"That's what agents are for."

"And this shit about records? If we make a record, you get a cut?"

"It's standard."

He laughed. "Jimmie, what in the hell has gotten into you?"

"Glenroy, when we first came up here I did my best to take care of you, didn't I? I went around with you, I played with you, I paid for all the gas. I kept something to eat in the house—"

He snorted.

"Okay—but it *was* food, right? More or less."

"More or less."

"I took care of you. Didn't I?"

"All right, Jimmie."

"That's all I'm saying. I'm just trying to get something going here—just like you. That's all."

"Well, can you pick something else? You're talking about the only thing in the world I give a shit about. And I'm still not in the right band, and I haven't noticed time waiting around too much for me to find it—and you're trying to say I can't have control over that? That I've got to pay you if anything good happens for me?"

"That's not the way I look at it," I objected.

"But it's how *I* look at it—it's the only way I can look at it."

"Okay Glenroy—look. How about this?"

———

125

Angela gave me hell about *this*—but what could she do? What could I do? I understood where they were both coming from and they were both right. But I had to do something to keep it alive.

I talked Glenroy into driving over to Doug's with me—I knew he wouldn't have done it without Doug, and I seriously doubted if Doug would have done it without him—and they signed Horton's contract. Then we tore up my contract and had what I believe they call a gentlemen's agreement that they would each pay me fifty dollars at some point, let me say I was their agent, and get head shots made and put them on the wall behind my desk in Angela's apartment.

So, Glenroy and Doug joined The Decisions, and I had about a three-week period where I went out just about every night looking for talent: it took me that long to realize I didn't really know what I was trying to do with it. I wasn't sure how to get to the next step, especially since I had no idea what the next step was. I only caught The Decisions two or three times—the last time at some kind of reception at a hotel downtown, and I actually got embarrassed. This brash, new, innovative band—what a crock. Nobody was listening to them; Doug was on brushes most of the time, and Glenroy did almost nothing, standing there with, I think I can safely say, the most bored look I have ever seen on a human face. They were wearing ruffled shirts with little red bow ties.

I slunk out and never could bring myself to see them again. In my defense—I still think the guy missed a great opportunity, but whatever. At one point I heard they were doing some recording, but I didn't even look into it. I couldn't face either one of them—and I told myself I was trying to figure out something better for them—but nothing came up. Meanwhile, Angela was reading these books and pushing me to get out and "develop the business" and would come up with these ideas that gave me the willies like putting on talent shows and going around to high school bands. Finally one day it just hit me: I didn't have a clue what I was doing and the whole thing was insane. I'm an expert on this moment—the fuck-it moment—and in this case I've still got about four hundred and fifty business cards to prove it. I did keep going out to hear bands, especially to the Marathon Club, where Doug wasn't playing anymore, and I saw some fairly decent groups, some that were awful, and everything in between. But on the few occasions when I tried to get somebody a gig, I couldn't come up with anything they couldn't have done themselves.

Bad time in my life. For some reason Angela didn't kick me out—must have been the chocolate-brown eyes—plus, it was still early enough where she believed she could turn me into something. She used to say I had so many gifts that I just wasn't using, which coming from somebody like her means I wasn't figuring out how to make money. Funny, my mother used to say that too—who *loved* Angela by the way, and so did my old man. We went down to Trybald sometimes and they pretended not to know we were living in sin. I had cut my hair too. We would eat meat loaf and then sit around talking about college and the real estate broker's exam, and percentage points and shit like that—or rather, my old man and Angela would. *They're* the ones that should have gotten married: they'd have made a cute couple.

Anyway, one night in the depths of that dark time we went to the Marathon Club, and the poster said: "Lance Tomorrow and the Knights" and had something about their hit single "If You Want To Be With Me." I had never heard of the band or the song.

Weird night. We had hardly gotten inside before I ran into an old buddy of mine from Trybald—a guy I'd started out in kindergarten with named Larry Speake. I hadn't seen him since high school; I'd heard he'd been somewhere in Florida doing something. He had been—but was back in Atlanta now with his new girlfriend named Kandy. Fiancée, actually. They had a table and when Larry saw me he stood up and made a big deal out of pulling chairs over for us and all that. We sat down and about the time the dust settled I realized there was someone else there. She always had that quality—the ability to dissolve into the surroundings and become invisible, like an animal blending into its cover. The only problem was, once you *did* notice her she stayed with you, like a dream you remember, or a tune you can't get out of your head.

The introductions went around, and we learned that her name was Rainy and she was a friend of Kandy's who had followed her here and was staying for a while—a "while," I found out later, a period of time that had already lasted some months, with its termination not yet in sight. I guess I kept looking at her because I could feel Angela watching me like a hawk—but it was mostly out of curiosity. She was undergoing an amazing metamorphosis: from trailer park queen with greasy jet black hair, frumpy clothes, battered glasses with a rubber band wound around the side to she's not bad looking to she's actually pretty to *goddamn*, what *is* it about this girl? It was her eyes—big dark eyes with long lashes—and *something* in there. I kept feeling her looking at me, and when I would turn and catch her eye, it was like, *Jesus.*

Talk about awkward. She never said a word, and after a few painful attempts nobody said anything to her, so she just existed. Angela felt like a wound spring, Kandy never made it past dull, and Larry and I eventually bled our repertoire of old times dry. At last, thank God, the band came on, and we finally had something else to do besides look at each other.

Lance Tomorrow and the Knights—brand new in town. According to the announcer they were originally from Jacksonville, and as for their "hit" single—well, it's a relative term. They had made a record and some radio station had played it. They got a good response from the crowd; we were actually catching their third or fourth night, it turned out, and they had already made some fans. They were good, but it didn't take long to realize that the band was basically one guy—the lead singer with the skin-tight leather pants, the unbuttoned shirt, and the big hair—who pretty much had to be Lance Tomorrow, right? I'd been thinking, with a name like that it could go either way—but in spite of all the prancing and humping he was good enough that he finally just won you over. Great voice. Most of the time he played bass—real fast and flashy—but they swapped around some and he played everything else, I guess just to show he could, which he could. They did quite a bit of original stuff—too much, because it was a whole bunch of the same thing—either slow like the "hit," a list of his requirements in a woman that about halfway through went into an insane fast part, then out of nowhere back to slow—or hyperfast with a slow part in the middle. Or even, on some of them, five or six completely different things so it kept stopping on a dime and going into something else—like he had all these ideas but couldn't decide which one to use so he used them all. They had obviously worked hard learning it all, and I was impressed—not that it was *that* tight—but it got pretty exhausting after a while. You pretty much had to be able to see past all the bullshit, which my disgusted Angela couldn't do. What did he care—he had his own little fan club of moonies crowded adoringly around the stage—one of which had a camera and took pictures of him all night.

We left early. Guess why.

"It's just his act," I explained. "Rock'n'roll is show business. He's good enough he can get away with it."

"I don't like prissy men," she glowered.

"But you've got to admit, he could sing."

"It was too loud."

"It's rock'n'roll," I said. "It's supposed to be loud."

She snorted and we drove for a while in silence. "You never knew that girl before," she half said, half asked.

"What girl?"

She just gave me a look.

"You mean that friend of Larry's girlfriend?"

"You know who I mean."

"You know I never met her before."

She exhaled and didn't say anything for a minute. "Is that all she can do—just sit there and stare at everybody?"

"How would I know?"

"How boring can you get?"

"I didn't think she was boring."

"Oh no, she was so mysterious and fascinating."

"I didn't say that. I just didn't think she was *boring*—I'm not saying she was not-boring or anything you would be instead of boring, I'm just saying…"

"I see right through her," Angela said.

"What are you talking about?"

"Nothing."

"For God's sake, Angela, what the hell have you got against her? All she did was sit there."

"I *know*."

"She didn't do anything to you."

"You sure are *defending* her."

"I'm not defending her—Jesus, I didn't even bring it up. You did."

She wasn't listening. "What an act."

I just laughed and shook my head.

She cut her eyes to me. "You sure looked at her enough."

"What do you mean I looked at her? How could you not look at her? She was sitting right there. Everybody looked at her."

Angela turned back, staring straight ahead.

"What the hell are you talking about—I looked at her?"

"Just drop it."

"God, you brought it up. I don't know what's eating you."

"She's just trouble, that's all."

"Trouble?"

"*Trouble.*"

"What does *that* mean?"

"It means just what it says."

"What kind of trouble?"

"Just trouble," she said with finality, and the car fell silent.

———

During the following week I kept seeing Lance Tomorrow in my head, and about Wednesday I called the Marathon Club and found out that they would be playing again that weekend. When I told Angela I wanted to go back, she just laughed—at first—but on Friday mysteriously changed her mind.

I had hardly thought of Larry and his exciting wife-to-be at all during the interim, and the impression left by Rainy had smoldered away to a coal, so I was surprised when we found the odd little threesome there again. We went through the table rigmarole all over again, this time down front, and it was all like a repeat of the last weekend, except that once we got settled in, Rainy seemed a little more open. She talked a little—even, amazingly, to Angela, who had commandeered the seat between us. They actually began to carry on a conversation, and even laughed, and after a while I realized they were disemboweling Lance Tomorrow, about whom they seemed to have the same opinion. As for me, I tried to keep my distance, I really did, but sometimes I could feel the strange girl's eyes like ray guns, burning holes in me. I tried my best to concentrate on the band, I swear.

Sometimes when you see a band for the first time and think they're good, you find out when you hear them again that something got exaggerated in your head, but this didn't happen with Lance Tomorrow. The sidemen were so-so, but he was really good. I had all kind of thoughts running through my head.

After their last set, Larry wanted to go get something to eat. I figured Angela would try to wriggle out of it, but she didn't—so I told them I needed fifteen minutes. Actually, it took about that long for me to hack my way through the adulation. But I finally did, and just went up and introduced myself, told him how much I enjoyed the show, and praised the original stuff, which, of course, was all his. His weak spot—he laughed, and seemed like the nicest guy you ever met—still rushing, of course, from being on stage. The first thing I found out was that Lance Tomorrow was not his real name. Gasp. It was Donny Dartt.

"You're from Jacksonville?" I asked him, while the girl with the camera circled around taking shots.

"Oh God, I'm from everywhere," he laughed.

"You work out of there?"

"Actually, we've pretty much moved up here. I think we're going to stay around a while and see what happens."

I smiled. "You're having a good run."

"Man," he said, shaking his head, "it's just been unbelievable."

"I guess you've got somebody handling you."

"Yeah, it looks like we've gotten into a pretty good arrangement—we'll just have to see how it goes."

"That's good," I said, nodding. "I handle a few acts myself. I thought I'd just leave a card with you—you know, in case anything should change down the road. I'd love to work with you."

"Thanks," he said, and took the card.

"Hey, no soliciting on the premises," a voice said. I turned; Grube had materialized out of nowhere, slid up in my blind spot. There was a glint in his eyes, but I couldn't tell if he remembered me or not.

"We're just talking," I said.

"Well, talk somewhere else."

His look had the transient contempt of someone who doesn't really take you seriously—and then he slid away.

"Is he your manager?"

"We're just seeing what happens. No long-term commitments—that's my policy." He laughed.

I laughed too.

"What we're most interested in is getting back in the studio. That's what we want."

"I hope he can help you. Where could a guy get a hold of your record?"

"Our *records*? We've got two." He laughed. "I believe they're on sale out front." But he wasn't looking at me. I followed his line of sight. "You know—I was wondering. You were sitting at that table, weren't you?"

I looked. "Yeah."

He gave a funny little laugh. "I count one extra member of the opposite sex."

I was just a tad slow. "Oh," I said. "Yeah, I guess there is."

"So who's the odd man out? Or odd chick out, I should say." He laughed. "The girl with the glasses, right?"

"Ah...I guess so."

"What's the deal?"

"Well—I really don't know."

He turned back to me with a surprised look. The whole table was watching us.

"I just met her, really. The guy's an old friend of mine—and that's his girlfriend in the green. The other one is..."

"With you. So, like I said..." The girl with the camera came in close and Donny Dartt said, without even looking at her, "Hey Tune, I'm busy—go find something to do." She hesitated wistfully, then drifted a few yards away. "This is the third or fourth night she's been here." Meaning Rainy.

"Oh, I didn't realize that."

"I'm very observant," he said with a laugh. "I'll trade you a round of beer for an introduction."

"Well, I don't really *know* her."

"You know her better than me."

It didn't work. There's only so impressed you can be—especially when you know what the guy's up to—and not only was the supposed target not responding, she was waging a campaign of sly smiles and snickers with Angela that I'm sure he didn't notice. He just turned on the juice: the big smile, the laugh, the hair. But no worship was taking place, and you could tell it was pissing him off. Finally he offered an invitation to us all to visit him at his lake cabin in Trybald the next afternoon. Apparently the band was staying in some cabin their more-or-less manager Grube had on Lake Moon, down on Black Snake Creek. Dartt drew a map on a napkin and left.

It didn't take a genius to see what he was after. We all said we'd love to and all that, but the next day, Sunday, the women backed out, and I had to talk Larry into going with me. Because it was pretty absurd now—but I was still thinking, if I could just get *in* with this guy.

We turned at Allred's Gas and Groc., and then got lost in the maze of dirt roads—I didn't know that end of the lake too well—Jernigan mill land—but eventually we lucked onto it. Talk about remote—hidden, more like it, alongside a narrow, secluded finger of water: you came around a curve and down a little hill, and there it sat: a weathered cabin in a clearing that could be called a yard, but shady and damp-looking with mushroom rings, and a sheen of green moss on the buckled roof, and a rundown, vaguely foul-smelling feel to the whole affair. The woods loomed on every side. The back end of the slough had become a catch basin for the lake's aimless floating junk, but the front opened into a vista of broad water. October had slipped up on us, and I remember the dogwoods everywhere, just turning red.

We pulled in beside the two vehicles parked out back—a van with a fringe of baby blue shag carpet around a porthole and a beat-up Falcon. The air, barely cool with an odor of musty leaves, felt good, and we started around the side of the house toward the high steps of the screened-in front porch—but we didn't quite make it that far. The sight—the spectacle—of Donny Dartt down at the waterfront by the sagging dock interrupted us: standing in leopard-skin swimming briefs, his mane in a head-band, gleaming with sweat, lifting weights—while the girl from the club, a short, voluptuous redhead oozing out of cut-off jeans and a halter top, circled around him taking photographs. When he saw us he finished his set of reps, then gave us a grin.

"Hey—no fair. Where's you friend?"

We gave him the disappointing news. An angry look flashed over his face, but he got over it.

Snap, snap went the redhead to whom we finally got introduced. Her name was Datha Quirk. "But I call her Moon Tuna, don't I, Tune?" She smiled and blushed. She looked like the Pillsbury Dough Boy about to bust her costume.

"Nice to see you," I said.

Dartt, our unapologetic Tarzan, then gave us a little tour, though beyond the lonely seclusion itself, and the view, there weren't many points of interest: the yard, a rotting picnic table, the propane tank, a slime-filled bathtub by the edge of the lagoon, all under the gaze of the looming house.

"Grube never comes down here, but he lets us use it. Or me, that is—the other guys pretty much stay in Atlanta."

"Grube," I said.

"Yeah. And I love it. Great vibe. I've written I don't know how many tunes here. And they're good too."

"Grube owns the place?"

He shrugged. "I guess."

Then he offered us a beer and we went up to the house. The front porch ran the length of it and was probably half the size of the cabin itself, though heaps of junk choked off all but a narrow passageway and a clearing on one end with a swing, a table and some chairs, and an emperor's view, at that height, of the cove and lake.

The cabin had one big open room, with a kitchen area on one end, and four little bedrooms around the side and back. Amps, guitars, microphones, wires, and all sorts of equipment cluttered the place. A wagon-wheel light fixture with football helmets daring you to walk under it set the tone of the decor: everything in the place, from the spiky furniture and cheap paneling to the sea-shell encrusted picture frames and pilot-wheel lamps, gave you that great feeling you get just about anywhere in Louisiana. Middle of nowhere. God, I was thinking, you could do some nasty stuff here.

Except for one little problem. The more you looked around, the more you realized how many photographs there were in the place of Donny Dartt. They just kept turning up: on the walls, the furniture, the floor—propped, taped, tacked, leaning, lying. Donny Dartt, Donny Dartt, Donny Dartt. In water, on land, smiling, frowning, glistening, brooding, oiled, working out, performing, lying in bed. Oh God, Angela would have loved this. But the grand prize went to the one in the main bedroom—enlarged almost to poster size, over the bed: an orange-streaked sunset shot of the silhouetted but unmistakable subject emerging wetly and nude from the water, his hair curling argonaut-like around his neck.

"Ta-da," said Dartt. "That's a shot Tune took right out there." He gazed admiringly at it.

"Mmm," I said.

"Well," said Larry, "it's something."

We went back out to the porch and sat down and talked for a while—no, make that listened a while as Donny Dartt talked. And the topic was—ta-da: Donny Dartt. His plans, his ambitions, his dreams—which were not small. He had laid out for himself something I guess you'd call a Star Training Program and charted his progress in a notebook—not that we actually saw it. He had two more years to reach his ultimate goal of becoming The Greatest Star in the History of All Time by age twenty-three.

"Wow," I said.

"Do you really think you'll do it?" or something like that Larry made the mistake of asking.

The jaw jutted out, the nostrils flared, the leonine mane tilted proudly back. Okay, never mind.

One could only wonder what Moon Tuna thought about it all. She'd no doubt heard it before—but still just watched Dartt with an adoring expression as though she'd been ordered, no matter what, not to stop looking at him. I schemed madly for a way to open up the topic of my managerial expertise, but since it didn't actually exist, the moment never came. *Fuck it*, I thought, and we just sat on the porch having a little toke and a couple of beers, looking at the autumnal lake, and listening.

"Tell Rainy I don't give up easy," Dartt said with a weird high-pitched laugh as we left. At least he had the decency to do it out of Moon Tuna's hearing. "Tell her she gets a rain check, and I don't really give out a lot of those."

"I'll tell her," I said, but I was already thinking I'd probably never see her again.

———

Wrong.

About a week after our little excursion into the Kingdom of Dartt, I got a call from Larry. He talked about nothing for a couple of minutes and I was thinking, *what the hell does he want?*

"This is going to sound strange, man," he said at last, "but do you remember that girl who was with us at the Marathon Club—Kandy's friend?"

"Ah, yeah."

"Well—she's...I mean, there's nothing wrong with her—but she's sort of insecure a little, I guess."

"I got that feeling."

"But she's really...I mean, there's nothing wrong with her."

"Okay."

"Anyway, the Rock Star has been calling and bothering her—I don't know how he got this number."

"*I* didn't give it to him."

"No, I didn't mean...it's just—she's kind of got herself worked up a little."

"Mm."

"She says he makes her flesh crawl."

"Sounds familiar," I said.

"Yeah."

"I don't think there's a lot of future in it."

"You could say that."

"Well—tell him to stop."

"I did—but he calls when I'm not here."

"Tell her not to answer the phone."

"Well, I did, but she's got this paranoid thing about the phone ringing. She always thinks it's going to be her mother attempting suicide."

"What?"

"Oh—never mind," Larry said. "Look, here's the thing. She needs—I mean, she *really* needs to get away somewhere for a while. She needs to get away from *us*. She's been here since *June*, man."

"Why doesn't she just go back home?" I asked.

"She doesn't really have anywhere."

"What about her mother?"

"Well, that's just it. She's in the hospital. She's *always* in the hospital. And she has tried, you know. Several times, actually."

"Jesus."

"For that matter, so has Rainy."

"What? Tried to kill herself?"

"That's what Kandy told me."

"Well, that's a waste."

"Yeah, I know. That's the thing: she's really pretty cool, she's just been through all this shit."

"I hate that."

"Yeah, I do too. Because she's really not bad-looking."

"No—she's not," I agreed.

"I know she could get something going if she wanted to."

"Sure," I said.

"It's like—she can't get a break."

"Doesn't she have some other friends somewhere?"

"Says she doesn't."

"Hmm."

"I guess that's why I was calling," Larry said.

"What do you mean?"

"Look, Jimmie, this is going to sound weird. But just listen, okay? I'm just asking—you don't have to do it."

"Do what?"

"Well—she talks about you and Angela all the time."

"She does?"

"For some reason she likes you."

"She doesn't even know us."

"Well—she talks about you."

"Hmm."

"I mean—she trusts you." Pause. "We were just wondering if you'd mind letting her stay with you for a few days. Just to give her a change. All she does is sit on the couch and watch TV all day. I mean, she's been here a *long* time, man."

"Did she say she wanted to?"

"Well, yeah, sort of."

It was one of those situations where you need about a week to think about something, but you've got three seconds. I should be saying no along about now—shouldn't I? I couldn't decide—I couldn't think fast enough. "Well—I'd have to talk to Angela."

"Yeah, I know."

"And I don't think she's going to be too crazy about it."

"I'm just asking—that's all. Do you think you could talk to her tonight and call me back?"

"Well—I could, yeah," I said. "But I think I know what she'll say."

———

Wrong again.

After I hung up, I decided I wouldn't mention it to her at all, and then call Larry back tomorrow and lie. But for some reason...I guess it was me. I don't know.

139

I was prepared to duck, just in case. But it was one of those moments you have with women sometimes when they do the exact opposite of what you expected. Some kind of preemptive strike, or some bizarre protectiveness—or something. I didn't even try to figure it out. I just thought: okay, this is going to be weird.

The next evening Larry showed up with Rainy at our door. He stayed about as long as a parent dropping off a kid at camp would and then left us alone with our new houseguest.

Awkward, yes—but not uncomfortably. Just kind of wacky. There we were, there she was—and nobody was saying anything about why she was there, how long she would stay, what she would do, or any of that. She just thanked us for having her, then went in the den and started looking at Angela's magazines while we made dinner. After about a half hour it didn't even feel awkward anymore—just sort of routinely absurd—Rainyesque.

We ate, and she didn't, and then we sat down with her in the den and she opened up a little. We talked about Donny Dartt, which was a good way to start because it got Angela going and got them both laughing, and then about Larry and Kandy, which took about a minute and used up everything we had in common—and then, as we worked our way back into her life she closed up more and more so that we only got a vague impression of a bizarre, lonely, outrageous young life in Florida, with the specter of the neurotic and suicidal mother floating through the tale and hints of trashy men and boys like smudges in her memory. Her past was a minefield, and any time she got close to a mine, she just went out of focus.

Which didn't leave much to talk about. She wasn't exactly up on the news and, as Larry had warned us, didn't seem to be interested in too much except watching TV. That first night she took a bath, after Angela made sure to leave the shampoo handy, and then we fixed up the spare bedroom for her, hooking up an old portable black and white TV I had. Almost immediately she just blended in with the surroundings and

140

needed almost nothing. She had very strange eating habits: she didn't take meals, but nibbled on odd things throughout the day. You might come in and find her eating out of a box of Trix on the couch, watching The Dating Game, or with a cache of about twenty Slim Jims she had gotten from the Seven-Eleven on the corner with the pocket change she always seemed to have, eating them systematically, drinking a Yoo-Hoo. Or eating straight out of a can of tuna fish, the jagged lid sticking up, chasing it with Hi-C. Never would you come in and not find her. Except for the Seven-Eleven, as far as I knew, she never went anywhere.

A "few days" passed—then a few more. Nobody said anything. No word from Larry. Rainy was just there and that's how it was. Angela went to work in the mornings, and I was working temporarily for some guy she had found out about, dismantling shelves and fixtures in grocery stores that had gone out of business and loading them on a truck. Godawful work, but the money was good—plus it got me out of the apartment, which was the best thing all around.

One afternoon, after she had been with us about a week, I came home early and, as always, found her on the couch. I fixed something to eat and sat down on the other end. The TV droned, but I didn't even notice it because it had become perpetual—a part of the walls and the floor and the air. Sort of like Rainy herself—who had melted into our lives—but edgily, like eyes following you from under a rock.

"Want a sandwich?" I asked.

She shook her head

"How're you making it?"

She nodded and smiled. "You're both so nice to me."

"Well—we're glad to have you."

She gave a self-deprecating laugh.

"What's the matter?"

"You'll get tired of me," she said.

I almost protested, but hesitated. "Rainy, what do you want to do?"

Her eyebrows rose. "Now?"

"No—not now. I mean, with your life."

She shrugged.

"You don't like to think about it."

She shrugged again.

"I don't either, to be honest. That's why I'm with Angela—she does the thinking."

"That'd be good—to have somebody to do the thinking. You could just ask them every morning what to think that day."

I laughed. "I do. Because, besides working, thinking is the only part of life I don't really care for."

"You think I should work."

Taken aback, I just laughed. "I didn't say that."

"No—but you think I should."

"I don't think anything—I already told you."

"But if you did, that's what you would think."

I laughed. "Why do you say that?"

"Because you think I should get out."

"Well—yeah, I guess I do think that."

"See?"

"I mean for you own good."

"I know."

"Well, think about it, Rainy. I don't care if you stay here forever, but what good is it going to do you?" And I could hear myself sounding like the Voice she'd heard a thousand times her expression told me I was sounding like—which I didn't want to sound like, but I couldn't help it. "You don't know your own worth."

She shrugged dismissively.

"Because if you did, you wouldn't be sitting here watching *Gilligan's Island.*"

"People underestimate *Gilligan's Island.*"

I looked at her and she looked back at me with her strange, bright eyes. I laughed. "It *is* excellent," I said.

"You think nobody will find me here."

"I...well, they won't actually." I thought about that. "Are you wanting somebody to find you?"

"That's what you think I want."

"How do you know what I think you want?"

"I just do."

"Well—*is* that what you want?"

"Only if they'd do all the thinking. Are you going to marry her?"

"Who—Ginger?"

"No—Mary Anne."

I smiled at her smiling at me. "Well—maybe. If she doesn't throw me out first—and as long as she keeps doing the thinking."

"I like her, but in a way I can't really talk to her," Rainy said.

"In a way, I can't either."

"She tries to sometimes."

"Well—I think she wants to help you."

"I could never be like her."

"Why would you want to be?"

"She's so smart—she has everything—and she's not afraid."

"Not afraid? Of what?"

"Of whatever."

"Are you?"

She looked at me as though amazed I could ask that. "*Yes.*"

I just shook my head. "She doesn't have everything, Rainy. She could never be like *you.* Look at it like that."

"Why would she want to be?"

"Because you're smart, and not some boring person in an office, and there's no one else in the world like you. You're one of a kind."

She gave a little laugh.

"A rare orchid," I said.

"In the desert."

I smiled.

"I never met a guy like you," she said.

"I hate to tell you—I'm a dime a dozen."

"Well, *I* never have."

"I could give you a list of people who'd tell you how lucky you are."

She was looking at me in that strange way she had—not staring, just looking. "Are you going to have children?" she asked.

"I haven't really thought about it," I answered.

"*She* wants to."

"Ah, well, most women do, don't they?"

"I don't."

"Why not?"

"Well," she said, "maybe I do. Except I'd be horrible at it."

"I think you'd be good."

"Do you think I'm a loser?"

"Jesus, Rainy, don't say that."

"Do you think I'm crazy?"

"Crazy—what do you mean?"

"Psychotic."

"No. I don't think that."

"Demented?"

"No."

"Disturbed?"

"Hell, *I'm* that."

"Maybe just dippy. Or dotty. No, that's for old people." She shook her head. "I never know what to check on the form."

"I'd say, stay away from forms."

"If only they had better words. Capricious. Fey. Mercurial." She sighed. "But I guess it's all just crazy, really."

"I think people underestimate crazy."

She smiled.

———

Not long after that, like the first hints of fall in the air, Angela finally started making little remarks about the situation and asking me about Larry and Kandy. We hadn't heard a word. I didn't quite call him because I didn't quite know what to say. Of course he should have called, but he didn't, so we found ourselves penned in the absurd position where anything we did would seem like rejection, so we did nothing. A few more days went by, and then at last one night Angela plunged in.

"Rainy, have Kandy and Larry said anything about you coming back?"

A black cloud passed over the sun. She looked down. "They don't want me back."

"Oh, I don't believe that," Angela said.

"Larry doesn't want me there."

"Did he say something?"

She shrugged. "He got mad."

Angela studied her. "He didn't..."

"I'm sure if he said anything he didn't mean it," I inserted.

"No. He meant it."

"What did he say?"

She shook her head decisively. No going there.

"I was just wondering, that's all," said Angela, not sounding like herself. "I didn't mean to..."

But doom had fallen. Rainy retreated wounded to her room, and we hardly saw her face for three days. We tiptoed around the apartment, whispering, and dared not raise the subject again. The days slipped by.

A month at least had passed since I'd seen Glenroy, but it seemed like longer—like I'd lost touch with him. Of course I felt like a fool and didn't have the guts to face him—or Doug. The whole thing gave me the willies. Angela had even quit bugging me about it, but only because I was working.

So it was completely a wild hair—the day I turned down his street in Decatur. I just happened to be driving down Ponce

145

de Leon—and turned. I didn't even think about it. Tawana answered the door, looking like she had just woken up. She hadn't—she just looked like that all the time. A record was playing and the room reeked of that old smell of cannabis and incense. She wasn't sure where Glenroy was, she said—out back somewhere; I found him ankle-deep in pecan leaves with a knife and some little contraption.

I crunched my way toward him. "Hey, what's been happening?"

"A lotta nada," he answered without looking up.

"How're The Decisions going?"

"I wouldn't know."

"What happened?"

At last he looked up at me. "You really want to hear it?"

"No."

He nodded and turned back. "We recorded some stuff. Or *tried* to anyway."

"Never mind. How about Doug?"

"I think he's driving a taxi."

"What?"

"He was, anyway."

"That's ridiculous."

"He said he made pretty good."

"Yeah, but *Jesus*. The man's a musician."

"Yeah, they're everywhere."

"Not like him," I said. I thought a minute. "What we need to do is all get together some night and go out."

"Yeah," Glenroy nodded. "We could."

I sighed. "You know—I'm glad you never actually gave me any money."

He looked at me again. "You know—I am too."

"Of course, you *do* owe me twenty bucks."

"How you figure?"

"Horton hired Doug." I smiled. "But I tell you what I'm gonna do..."

Glenroy laughed. "You're amazing."

"Okay, what I want to know is—are you going to hold any of this against me?"

"What the fuck—right? Nobody made me do anything."

"What about Doug?"

"It's not a big thing, Jimmie. It was just something that happened—it was no big deal." He paused. "As long as you don't stop and think about it."

I laughed. "Well, look—we'll get together and go out, okay?"

"Oh yeah," he said. "Let's do it."

———

But we didn't. At least not right away. God, what a weird time. If I find out when I die I've got to do all this again, I'm going to see if I can skip those couple of months. Nothing clear, nothing hopeful, all these loose ends floating around. The whole world stuck in a rut.

I came home one afternoon and the second I walked in the door something felt wrong. I stood there for a minute and then I realized it was the quiet. No TV. No nothing. Just this empty silence. I walked past the kitchen and into the den.

"Rainy?" I called.

I didn't hear anything. I could see that her bedroom door was cracked open, so I walked to it and stopped.

"Rainy?"

No answer. An icy feeling went through me.

"*Rainy?*" With a surge of panic I shoved the door open.

She was standing there, by the bed, looking at me. There was no surprise on her face, and not a stitch on her body. She just stood there, looking perfectly relaxed. She didn't do anything—nothing. She didn't gasp or reach for something to cover herself up, or anything. In fact, I don't think I've ever seen anybody more at ease in her own skin—like someone who walks around the house without clothes all day. She wasn't wearing her glasses either—it was maybe the second time I had seen her without them—which made her look like a completely different person. God, those big black eyes! For a second I thought, she's on something—but I knew how scared she was of anything like that. And where would she get it anyway? She just stood there, pale white like one who never sees the sun, myopic, looking at me with unfathomable nonchalance.

"Hi," she said.

———

When I finally called Glenroy, I still didn't quite see the whole picture. Just intuitive, I guess you'd say.

"There's somebody I think you need to hear," I said.

"What—a polka band?"

"Come on, Glenroy."

"Well?"

"This is different."

"How much are you going to charge me?"

"I thought we agreed to forget that."

He sighed. "Okay."

"Look, I'm going to call Doug too. He's not playing either—this is ridiculous."

"What have you got?"

"Just a guy. In a band."

"Too many cooks again."

"Look Glenroy, what do you think the chances are of finding somebody any good who isn't already playing? And how would you find them if they weren't? You've got this idea in your head of some magical band full of people who don't have egos..."

"The guy has an ego problem, in other words."

"I didn't say that."

"Yes you did."

"Okay—he does. But he's also real good."

"I'll pass."

"Glenroy, all I'm asking you to do is to hear him. What else have you got to do?"

"Nothing."

"All right then. Let's go hear him."

He was quiet for a moment. "You're calling Doug?"

"Yeah, I'm calling Doug."

He hesitated. "I'll go if he will."

"It's a deal."

———

Thank God, the women weren't interested. I didn't need all that. We just needed to hear the band without any crap going on.

Calling Doug took some nuts, but I did it, and instead of the hostility I was half expecting all I got was a feeling of boredom. He said he'd go if Glenroy would. I picked up Glenroy first and then we ran down and got him. We got to the club in time to have a beer before the band came on. Doug just sat there, looking around.

We hadn't been sitting long before I noticed Grube, on the far side of the room.

"There's your old friend," I said to Doug, but I could tell he had already seen him. He just gave me a shrug—hardly even a shrug.

And then I saw Larry and Kandy. They were with some people I didn't know a few tables over. I watched Larry for a few minutes, until our eyes met. He looked away; it was quick enough he could have pretended not to see me, which is what I expected, and half wished, but a couple of minutes later he came over. Just him.

It was great to see me, etc., etc. Glenroy provided the perfect smokescreen—someone he had never really known, nor would have, but knew of, in the way of small town contemporaries. The pleasantries took a few minutes—the whole business incredibly awkward. Finally, when every possible irrelevant thing had been exhausted, he said, "How's Rainy doing?"

"Okay."

"What's she up to?"

"Same old thing."

"Well—tell her to come back if she wants to."

"I'll tell her."

And that was it. He took the first opportunity to exit, and then I didn't see him or Kandy anymore that night. Come to think of it—ever.

"Who was he talking about?" asked Glenroy.

"It's a long story. I'll tell you some time."

Finally the band came on stage and started getting ready to play. From that moment on we all sort of sank into our own little holes. The lights went down, somebody announced, "Lance Tomorrow and the Knights!" and none of us said a word for the entire first set. We hardly even looked at each other. When the lights came up and they took their break, I at last turned to Glenroy.

"Well?"

He had slid into a slump in his chair and at my voice bestirred himself. He sat up a little, took a drink of beer.

"You're right," he said, "he can sing."

"I told you."

"He's a good bass player too."

"I know."

"But all this swapping up shit—they ought to leave that out."

"I agree."

"And the rest of the band—I don't know."

"That's what I was trying to tell you." I turned to Doug. "What'd you think?"

He gave his indecipherable little shrug. "They're all right."

And it was just about then that I realized the man himself had seen me and was coming our way.

"You're back," Dartt said with a laugh.

"Just can't stay away."

"Where's your friend?"

"Well," I said, "I'm not sure what she's doing."

"She's hiding."

"No—just trying to get her bearings, I think."

"I could help her do that. I know all about bearings." He gave a laugh. "Tell her I'm not a monster."

"Well, I will—if I see her."

"You wouldn't have a phone number, would you?"

"No—I'm sorry."

He laughed again—that weird, high laugh. "Why do I get the feeling you're trying to protect her?"

"Man, I don't even know her."

He regarded me suspiciously.

"Hey," I said, "let me introduce you to some musician friends of mine. Glenroy Trimble and Doug Early. I brought them to hear you."

At last Dartt seemed to notice them.

"Oh yeah? What do you play?" he asked Glenroy.

"Guitar."

He cut his eyes to Doug.

"Percussion."

"Around here?"

"Sometimes," said Glenroy.

"You ever let anybody sit in?" I asked abruptly.

He gave a dismissive expression. "No—it's gotten where people come to see *us*."

"Well—I was just wondering. It might be kind of interesting."

"Jimmie," said Glenroy.

"Yeah?" Dartt said. "How so?"

"Well—they're both sort of out of the ordinary."

"Jimmie, shut up."

"Is that right?"

"Yeah," I said, nodding. "Way out of the ordinary."

"What sort of stuff do you play?" he asked, looking at Glenroy.

"Anything," I offered.

The nostrils flared. He gazed down at Glenroy, who hadn't moved.

"And this guy," I said, looking at Doug, "plays with Lonnie Ray White."

"For real?"

"Oh yeah. In fact, he's played here a lot. And Glenroy too."

"Jimmie."

"Well," said Dartt, "like I said, we usually stick with our sets. It's what people expect."

"I was just asking. Because I'm sort of seeing something— you know, like nobody's ever heard before."

Dartt laughed, glanced again at Glenroy and Doug—then back at me. "You tell your friend I asked about her, okay?"

"If I see her."

"Get me a phone number."

I half nodded, half shrugged.

Then, leaving, he nodded toward Glenroy and Doug, not really looking at them, and walked away.

Across the room I caught a glimpse of Grube, watching us.

"Jimmie," said Glenroy, when Dartt was gone. "What in the fuck are you doing?"

I shrugged. "What?"

"You want to crash his act so bad, why don't you squeeze your own ass up there?"

"Me? Are you crazy?"

"And who was he talking about?"

"Just a girl. I told you, it's a long story."

"The same one?"

"Yeah, the same one."

They played their second set and we quit talking again. At the end the band took their break and this time we didn't see any of them.

"You've got to admit one thing," I said. "He's way better than the band."

"He can play some bass," said Doug.

"Yeah," said Glenroy, making a face, "but good God almighty."

"Well—I warned you."

"You girls mind if I take my shirt off?" he mocked.

I laughed. Even Doug smiled and emitted a little chuckle—practically a guffaw for him.

"And what's with this crap they play—is it his?"

"Yeah, it is."

Glenroy scowled.

They came back for their last set and played a couple of songs. It was the time of night when the energy began to shift in the club—when you start to feel the raw edge of why people are really there. I've always liked that—the squares clear out, people let their guard down, weird things happen.

Out of the blue, Dartt made an announcement. "I understand there's some guys—some musicians—in the house tonight some of you may know," he said, and for a second I wasn't sure what I was hearing. It came out of nowhere. He shielded his eyes from the lights and looked our way. "Where are you, guys? Want to come up and help us out on a couple of numbers?"

You could tell it was a total surprise to the band. They glanced at each other and shifted around.

I put my fingers in my mouth and whistled. Somewhere across the room someone whistled back. I stood up and clapped my hands, which drew a sympathetic little smattering of applause from around the room, though of course nobody had any idea what they were applauding for.

Yet.

"What do you say, guys?"

I whistled again and the applause picked up a little. I knew, knowing Glenroy, there was no way out now. As I stood there I saw Grube across the room, but I ignored him. Glenroy

153

reluctantly stood up; the applause grew louder—mostly out of curiosity, no doubt, and the scent of new blood in the tedium of the waning night—but there were obviously some people who recognized him. I gave Doug an encouraging nod and he stood up too.

"All right," said Dartt. "Come help us out."

"First Lawrence Welk, now this. I'm going to fucking kill you," said Glenroy.

They made their way to the foot of the low stage, where Dartt's little harem of admirers had their camp. I'm not saying it was thunderous applause or anything—probably only about half the room was even paying attention, if that—but there were some people clapping, just waiting to see what was going to happen. The Knights stood droopingly as Dartt bent down and talked for a second with Glenroy. Then he turned back to his guitar player and said something, and the guy made a strange expression and unstrapped his guitar. Glenroy came up, looking apologetic, and said something to him; they smiled, at least, and the guy handed it over. Then Dartt and Glenroy coaxed Doug up, and Dartt signaled to the drummer who stood up and offered his sticks with an odd little flourish. He took them and sat down—I remembered this part: he touched nothing, looked at nothing, just sat there waiting. Meanwhile Glenroy familiarized himself with the new guitar— a Strat, like his—and the two displaced guys disappeared, leaving only the keyboard player. The four of them had a little confabulation in front of the drums and seemed to reach some agreement. I looked across the room and Grube stood in the same spot, watching. A moment later I looked in his direction again—and this time his eyes cut a laser path across the room to me.

I'm a player, I said to myself.

It's one of those things you can say you were there for, if you were—maybe even if you weren't—and of all the people who were, who has forgotten it? I haven't—but it's been two things to me for a long time: something not real, like a myth;

and something I remember exactly, in every detail, like it happened just a few weekends ago. Instead of—what?—nine years.

I had my suspicions at the time about Dartt's motives—especially when, before they'd hardly gotten on stage, he came out of nowhere with this blazing, in-your-face riff. If his mission was banishment, you could say that backfired. Or did his sixth sense whisper something else? Who knows? Both, probably—not that it mattered. Because the minute Doug came in, the old time ended and the new time began.

Like an explosion—the kind where everybody jerks their head and looks. No handle, no center, just an avalanche tumbling down a mountainside out of control—until with one pop he slid into Dartt's groove and sat there working like some crazy funky engine. Dartt, his shirt at least back on if not buttoned, hunkered down and turned to him with a grin, and they just played to each other like bloody murder for a couple of minutes. People all over the room were stomping their feet and whistling; it felt like someone had injected the entire place with a massive dose of adrenaline.

Glenroy moved his head with the rhythm and just listened, waiting.

Then, from way underneath he started scratching out a rhythm, punctuating it with little high notes, and it was cooking so good they just did that for a while—people stomping and clapping. Gradually they started building it up—people began to get to their feet—and there they were, this amazing triangle, already within three minutes the best band I'd ever heard in my life. I say triangle, because the keyboard guy, on the end, after trying to find a place in it for a while, gave up and evaporated. And then Glenroy just left the earth, screaming this thing he had to tell: amazing that gift he had, that made you look, made you listen, like the center of gravity, everything falling into him. He looked up, their eyes met, and they took it down—simmered a while—then another eruption, people yelling, whistling. Then down again—a little bass and drum duo—then

Doug took a solo. People screaming—they built it back up; Glenroy left the earth again, then finally after twenty or twenty-five minutes, they brought it home big. I was exhausted.

Glenroy took off the guitar, shook Dartt's hand—then Doug came around and did too. They said a few words, gestured to the screaming crowd, but you could tell it was over, for then, complete.

People swarmed the stage, but I just stayed at the table, waiting. No Knights anywhere to be seen. All kinds of ideas flashed through my head, and I didn't see him—only felt the air behind me become a person. I turned and Grube sat down in Glenroy's vacant chair.

"I just want to explain something to you," he said. "These are my guys."

And I saw immediately that he was the kind who missed nothing, forgot nothing. "I'd say they're their own guys—they're whosever guys they want to be."

He smiled. "Not exactly. See, I brought the drummer here, and I brought Lance Tomorrow here. I'm the one that's paid them. This is my place. The guitar player is just moving in. But I can deal with that. Anything that happens in here is mine. Understand?"

I tried to look nonchalant. "I don't know what the hell you're talking about."

"Then I'll make it clear for you: if you want something on your hands you can't handle, just try to move in on me."

I laughed. "What makes you think I can't handle you?"

"Because you don't know how, and you can't afford it."

"Afford it?"

"Yes—afford it. Have you got fifty thousand dollars? Because that's a *minimum* of what you'll need just to get started. And then you'll have about a one percent chance of succeeding." He stood up. "I'm just telling you, friend. I know what you are and I've pushed people like you out of my way before. So do yourself a favor and go back to whatever it is you do because you can't do this."

"Fuck you."

He nodded snidely and smiled—held my eye a moment, then casually turned and walked away. I was about one inch from tackling him from behind and pounding his face.

But I didn't.

———

I had only one more encounter with him, about a week later.

They had started practicing down at Grube's lake cabin in Trybald—supposedly this big secret, but of course Glenroy had told me about it. I drove down there one afternoon. It was December by then; the lake was down, the trees bare, leaves blown in deep drifts around the house.

The day, I remember, was cold and breezy, the sky clear blue, and smoke curling from the chimney as I drove up. Several cars, including the silver Corvette, sat around at all angles; and out by one of them, a blue van, a little encounter was taking place. I parked, got out—the air throbbed with muffled music from within the cabin—and walked over.

"You're trespassing," said Grube. "I'm going to tell you one more time—all of you—" he gestured towards the other three guys, the unsaddled Knights—"get off this property or I'll call the cops."

"We just want to talk to Donny," one of them said.

"He's busy."

"Bullshit. He can't fuck us over like this."

"He's not fucking anybody over, so just get out of here."

"What do you call it then?"

"I don't have to call it anything. Now *go*." He looked at me. "You too. I don't have anything to say to you."

"You little fucking prick."

"Get the hell out of here!" he screamed, turning crimson and the tendons standing out on his neck. "You're trespassing!" He turned and stalked across the yard and up the steps and disappeared onto the porch. The throbbing music, oblivious, never wavered.

One of the guys, the guitar player, shook his head disgustedly. "I think we ought to beat the shit out of him," he said.

"Who?" replied the drummer, sarcastically.

They laughed.

"You're the guy that started the whole thing," the keyboard guy said to me.

I shrugged.

"Fuck it—let's go," said the drummer, and looking at me like you would a snake, they got into the van and drove away. Dumped by the bitch.

I stood there for a moment, alone, listening, thinking about the scene I had intended to make, and suddenly knew I wouldn't. They were together, playing; I was nothing.

I could hear Glenroy saying, "One thing you can say for the guy, even if he is a little dickhead—he's done it before. He can promote us, get us in the studio."

"So was I," I had protested.

Glenroy just shook his head. "Well—when?"

And Angela—she had washed her hands of the whole thing. And Grube—like something out of a comic book. I had believed, for a while, I was meant to do this. I didn't believe it now. Punt.

The next weekend The Trybald Trio opened at the Marathon Club.

Rainy

Outside, the fragrant witchery of an April twilight: an aromatic quality timeless and reminiscent stealing through the open doors—as much the breath of something lost as the promise of something that might be, but both.

Inside, smells from the kitchen, bangs, clinks, scrapes, the bright explosion of a broken glass, people crossing the empty room on errands: all swirling in a medley as the club awoke for another night. On stage the band tumbled through a new piece, like three people trapped in a runaway car, astonished. Suddenly around a hairpin curve a short drum solo appeared, built a bridge back to the accelerated vocal; then with a punctuating comment from the guitar it ended dramatically, like somebody's last movement.

"Jesus!" cried euphoric Dartt. "Where the *hell* did that come from?"

They were laughing. Glenroy ran his hands through his sweaty hair, caught Doug's eye—the culprit who had goosed the motley ballad. They had simply jumped in behind him.

"Would you mind telling me where you got that?" Dartt asked.

"It just came on me," said Doug.

"Beats the last time something came on me."

"Came on me the last time I beat it too," added Glenroy.

"Hey," said Grube, with a fatherly laugh, as he walked up, "save something for the show."

"Hey, don't worry about the show—we got the show," said Dartt.

"What was that anyway?"

"Something that came on us."

"What's it called?"

"Well," said Dartt with a laugh, "it's called 'That's Just Who I Am'—I *thought* it was a song I wrote."

"It got a little carried away," said Glenroy.

"You going to play it?" Grube asked.

"Hell yeah," said Dartt.

"Like that?"

"I think we can safely say that was a one-time thing," Dartt replied. He laughed.

"Hell—I kind of liked it fast," said Glenroy.

"Aw, come on."

Not that they hadn't often discovered another of the multiple personalities of songs this way—covers mostly, though they were doing fewer and fewer of those, just a handful of eccentric survivors now—but their own material too, old and new, should the fancy strike: trusted some abrupt whim, followed a random riff passing though the head of one of the three, often Doug who could lay out an intricate rhythm like a hundred-pronged hat-rack—spontaneous compositions, sometimes even the lyrics, improvised by Dartt on the spot, never improved upon, the titles sly like secret jokes: "No Fucking Way," "Eleventy Mo' Dozen," "Where's the Moolah?" "Do the Dirty Turkey," "This May Stink a Little."

"Why not?" Glenroy asked.

"Because it happens to be a good song, and it's not how it goes," Dartt returned.

"Yeah, but it really got moving—didn't you think, Doug?"

Doug shook his head, the humor having evaporated from his face. "Hey man, whatever."

"You didn't think it got cooking?"

"Yeah, it got cooking."

"Okay," said Dartt. "Agreed. It was fun." He paused. "But it's *my* song." His nostrils flared; something ticked at his jaw hinges. "It happens to have something to say."

"I didn't say it didn't—and it doesn't matter, we'll do it, whatever," said Glenroy.

"Come on, guys," said Grube.

Dartt looked around the faces. "I mean—what? You don't like my song? Wouldn't it be easier just to say so?"

Glenroy exhaled. "I'm not saying I don't like it."

"That's what I'm *hearing*." Dartt gestured toward his ear.

"I'm not saying anything—about the song or anything. I'm just saying I thought it worked—what we did. Worked for me—that's all."

"It's *my* song."

"I know it's your song. I said we'd do it the way you want to, so forget it. It was just a passing thought."

Dartt snorted a laugh, cocked his head in ironic reflection, looking at nothing in particular. "Wait a second—forget it? It's like, hey, Donny's written a good song—let's make sure he knows we think it sucks and then just *forget* it and go ahead and do it." He laughed. "Yeah, I feel good about that."

"Come on, man—it's not like that at all."

"Yeah?"

"It's bullshit. It worked—that's all I'm saying. Like we've done a million times when we're jamming and something works—it doesn't matter whose fucking song it is or anything else."

"What? Some bullshit up-tempo thing? We could do that with any song. Any fucking song at all."

"You're right—like we have a million times."

"Except not your brother's songs."

"Oh come on, we've changed a lot of his songs."

"I mean like this—totally change the whole concept."

Glenroy sighed. "Look—it doesn't make any difference. We'll do it the way you want to. It doesn't matter to me—I'm serious—I don't care. It's not worth arguing about."

Dartt nodded, his lips tightly together, chewing somewhere. "O-*kay*. I guess we settled *that*." He unshouldered his bass in a practiced fluid swoop, plopped it against his amp with a resounding thud. "Did you even listen to the words? Do you have any idea what the song's about?" He shook his head, stalked halfway across the vacant room, turned and called out "No!" then disappeared out the front door.

Grube frowned at him, but didn't say anything.

Glenroy let out a long breath, took off his guitar. Doug cluttered his sticks onto his bass drum and stood up.

Outside, dusk crept towards them and someone began shutting doors.

———

At twelve minutes past eight, by the backstage clock, Donny Dartt, dressed for show, made his re-entry.

His revenge was gasoline poured on smoldering coals, and they went into "Jeez Louise" like rival demons. *This is nuts*, Glenroy thought somewhere in the back of his mind, a righteous but a dull place, and they just got better. The music fell like ripe fruit into the hand.

At the break they didn't speak or even make eye contact. Dartt, shadowed lately by a tall, silent, ironic, long brown cigarette-smoking girl, just disappeared, and Jimmie Myles materialized from the faceless crowd at the foot of the stage.

"Ah, ah, ah—don't you slip away," he said, half singing the last two words. "Come on over for a beer—we've got an announcement. You too, Doug."

"Let me find Alma."

Glenroy followed him to a cluttered table near the center of the room. Angela sat there in green, some people Glenroy didn't know, and a half hidden girl.

"Pull some chairs over," said Jimmie, and poured a beer for Glenroy. "Where's Doug?"

"He's coming, I think."

"You've been practicing, I see."

"Some," said Glenroy.

The unknown people around the table couldn't help staring at him. He drank his beer, kept his eyes away.

"And I knew you when." Half singing again.

"Ha," Glenroy snorted.

Then Doug and Alma picked their way through the tables—they came up a chair short; another was sought and found—and at last they all converged more or less around a central point. Jimmie held up a glass.

"To the Trio."

"Hear, hear!"

"A pretty fair little band. They could have had me—but they let me get away, and look what happened."

Laughter.

"There's still time," he said, appealing to Glenroy and Doug. "Tambourine and lead cute boy. How about it?"

They laughed.

"How about the announcement?" said somebody.

"It's coming," Jimmie said, nodding, "don't worry. Just be patient."

Somebody else said: "You don't think somebody that spent their whole life trying to be the center of attention is going to rush through it, do you?"

Some laughs.

Jimmie turned to the table. "I wanted these guys to be here—my old pals. And everybody." He took a breath. "The thing is—Angela has come to the predictable realization that life without me would be unthinkable—and so, preferring a thinkable life, she has decided to relinquish her status as maiden and fate as probable spinster and take on the rewarding task of honoring, cherishing, and obeying my lovable, brown-eyed self until she..."

"Throws up," somebody suggested.

"No—*dies*, I think it is."

Angela gave him a comic sock on the arm. "I don't know about your *wording*, James."

"Oh, it's only wording, dear. To put it concisely: we are betrothed."

A chorus of applause and congratulation went up; then someone offered a toast. They drank, ordered another round, and just about the time Doug and Alma excused themselves and retreated, Glenroy became aware of the eyes—the dark eyes peering like somebody's imaginary companion. She looked back at him with some indecipherable wonder or fear.

Then Grube, from the side of the room, like somebody's angry wife, was making annoying gestures, and she melted back into her obscurity, leaving him as he returned to the stage not with thoughts of Jimmie or Angela or their world, but only with those beguiling and lingering eyes.

As the power of the music repossessed him, not even that could quite displace the touch. It might have been the cool remnant of a dream, or a scent-haunted memory, and he tried to say what he had to say exactly, imagining a listener.

When the set ended he went back, and this time made sure of the introduction. And as her name took form, only an instant after his realization or recollection that she somehow *was* her name and that she had been alluded to in the indistinct past and that she was someone—why was this so?—not mentioned, not part of the commerce of daily talk, like the sibling gazing ghostlike through a forgotten back window, he looked at her and she ventured an uncertain smile.

Rainy.

———

When Glenroy had packed up his guitar for the night, he headed back once more to Jimmie's table. That bad time of night when everything died around him, leaving him alone—he went imagining the eyes and was almost surprised to find them still there, as though one might have expected them to vanish at the chiming of the hour.

"Who's up for something?" he said.

Angela sighed dreamily and nestled against Jimmie.

"What you got in mind?" Jimmie asked.

"*Jimmie*," Angela protested.

"Come on, baby—it's early."

"It's *not* early, Jimmie."

"I don't know," said Glenroy. "Get something to eat?"

"Why don't you come over to the apartment and we'll find something," Jimmie said. "Then get into the liquor."

"I'm going to *bed*, Jimmie," said Angela.

Jimmie gave Glenroy a helpless look.

"I guess we'll head on," said one of the unknown guys.

"Well, I'm going to get a cheeseburger," Glenroy said. "Nobody wants to come?"

"We've been eating all night," replied someone with an apologetic laugh.

He looked at Rainy, sitting there uncertainly with an expression of brewing panic.

"I don't see why we couldn't go out for just..." Jimmie started to say.

"*Jimmie*."

Glenroy looked into the eyes, looking back at him.

"Rainy?" he said, and the sound of her name seemed to hang in the air, "How about it? It's on me. Blue plate special—you name it."

She smiled, then in her little-used contralto voice said, "I'm not very hungry. I mean, I'm not any hungry."

"Well, there's always coffee," Glenroy proposed. She glanced at Jimmie, then Angela, then back to Glenroy. "Don't worry—I'll get you home," he said.

She shrugged, then ventured an almost imperceptible nod.

He smiled at her. "Let me go get my guitar."

———

Passing forlorn Moon Tuna haunting the front tables, Glenroy made his way to the little backstage room. Doug sat in a stuffed chair looking tired, and Dartt, the tall girl with him, stood with his things, ready to go. A look passed between them. Neither spoke. The tall girl wore a permanent half smile that looked snide.

Then Grube came in. It was Saturday and he had three envelopes. "Good crowd, good crowd," he said, handing them around. "Let's keep an eye on those breaks, though—all right? I'm not paying you to socialize." With his little smile he turned to Glenroy. "Are you staying at the cabin tonight?"

"I don't know."

"Well, if you do, take these, please." He handed him a box of fuses. "And don't forget to lock it."

"I always lock it," Glenroy said.

"No you don't."

"Man, it doesn't make any difference, if somebody wanted in there."

"Just lock it, okay? Make it a habit."

They dispersed. At the foyer Glenroy, with Rainy and Jimmie and Angela, turned and caught the eye of Dartt on the far side of the room, with his girl—holding his bass, watching.

Then they stepped into the cool April night.

———

Glenroy had remobilized Louis's old car—the Valiant, powder-blue.

"Where you want to go?" he asked.

Rainy shrugged. "I don't know."

They headed for the all-night Denny's out Buford Highway. The Valiant, long in need of a muffler, growled along spewing an acrid trail of smoke. Rainy tried to close the glove compartment door but it kept flopping open. She laughed.

"I think it's broken," said Glenroy.

"I think it is too."

A half-full pint of low-grade vodka sloshed atop the clutter there. She reached for it, barely touched it, then withdrew.

"Want some?" Glenroy asked.

She made a face and shook her head.

"You don't like it?"

She shook her head again, one nostril slightly curling.

They arrived, and something fell out and hit the parking lot with a clank and rolled under the car as she opened the door. She laughed again.

Inside, they lucked into a corner booth. "Offer's still open," Glenroy said. "Anything you want."

She shook her head. "Just some coffee, I guess."

The waitress took their order.

"Does it keep you awake?" Glenroy asked.

"Nothing keeps me awake," she replied, yawning.

He studied her with amusement. "Nothing?"

"Well—almost nothing. I guess if there was a war or something…come to think of it, I lived in an apartment one time where the couple next door had these horrible fights, and it *did* keep me awake—but only because I wanted to listen."

Glenroy laughed. "What did they fight about?"

"Oh—everything. She would lose the keys or something and he would go into this screaming fit. I'm pretty sure she would do it on purpose. He had an artificial leg."

"She lost that?"

"No, I mean he was just real mad about everything—except when you saw him outside he was nice. So was she. I think when they went inside they drank an evil potion."

"An evil potion?"

"Isn't that what it is?" she said, searching for the word.

"I don't know. Where was that?"

"In Florida."

"You lived in Florida?"

She nodded.

"Where?"

"It's kind of near Tampa."

The waitress brought the coffee and Glenroy watched with great interest as Rainy stirred in five sugars and three creams.

"My goodness," he said.

"I don't actually like coffee," she explained. "In fact, I can't stand it."

He laughed. "Well, get something else."

"Nah," she said.

He shrugged. "Is Rainy your real name?"

"I guess so."

"I mean, what they named you."

"It was my mother's maiden name. It's what everybody has always called me."

"What's your real name?"

"Ugly."

"Aw, come on."

"It is. I hate it."

"What is it?"

She made a face.

"Are you going to tell me?"

"No."

"Please."

She let out her breath. "Mary Ellen."

"What's so ugly about that?"

"It just is. It sounds like somebody with big stupid shoes."
Glenroy laughed.

"I don't like it. I don't like Rainy either."

"I do," Glenroy said. "I don't know anybody else named
that."

"Yeah, there's a reason."

"I like it."

"It's too sad."

"Sad?"

"Don't you think? It sounds like somebody waiting in a
bus station."

He laughed again and shook his head.

She raised her brimming cup wobbly to her lips and
slurped. It was very loud; Glenroy laughed, and she sputtered in
laughter, spraying coffee and spilling half the cup.

"I'm sorry," said Glenroy, and started pulling out napkins
from the dispenser. They spent a minute or two mopping up.

"You want some more?" he asked.

She shook her head. "I can't really drink it."

"No wonder you put all that stuff in there."

"I tried M&M's once. It wasn't *that* bad. But I guess i t
didn't work."

He made a distasteful face. "No kidding."

"I really don't have a favorite beverage."

Glenroy smiled. "So how do you know Jimmie and
Angela?"

"Oh, it's a long story. How do you know them?"

"Well, I *don't* know Angela," Glenroy answered. "But
Jimmie I've known all my life."

"I bet he had a million girlfriends."

"He did."

"He's funny," Rainy said.

"Yeah, he is. Are you staying with them?"

She shrugged and an odd expression crossed her face.

"Okay—it's none of my business. I was just wondering."

"I *was*. But I guess not anymore."

"I'm sorry—I won't ask anything else. Except just—what brought you here from Florida?"

"I came to see some friends—and didn't go back," she said.

"Yet?"

She shrugged.

The waitress arrived with Glenroy's cheeseburger platter.

"You sure you don't want anything?" he asked.

She nodded. Quite sure.

"It won't bother you to watch me eat?"

She shook her head. "You know they make that out of lips and everything."

"I know."

"I used to work in a place like this," she observed.

"You did?"

"Well, for two days."

"Probably longer than I would have. They say if you work in one of these places you'll never eat there again."

"There used to be a place in Tampa that ground up stray dogs."

"I think there's one of those in every town."

"I don't know if it was true. Do you like playing in a band?"

"Yeah, most of the time."

"What's it like?" she asked.

"I don't know. I've never done anything else. Right now it's pretty good. But sort of weird."

"Why?"

"I guess maybe just the way you feel when something finally happens."

"I've never had anything finally happen so I wouldn't know."

"Like it's not what you thought."

"I thought that was how everything felt."

Glenroy smiled. "Yeah—maybe not *everything.*"

"I haven't done that much, so I don't know how much of everything I've got left," she said.

"Probably a good bit. Do you ever take your glasses off?"

"When I'm asleep." She paused. "Half my life."

"You don't really sleep that much."

"Yeah. I do."

"How about when you take a bath?"

"How about when I take a bath what?"

"Do you take them off?"

"My clothes?"

"No, your glasses."

"Usually."

"Would you take them off now?"

"In front of all these people?"

"Your glasses."

"Why?"

"Because you have beautiful eyes and I want to see them."

"My glasses?"

"No, your eyes."

"I can't see without them."

"Your eyes?"

"My glasses."

"Well, what's there to see in here anyway?"

"All these people," she said, but reached up and, handling the wobbly things carefully, took off her glasses and laid them on the table. She looked up at Glenroy, squinted, then relaxed and gave a little smile.

He just looked at her a moment admiringly. Dark, beautiful, secret, myopic eyes—rich black eyebrows, long curling lashes: it was like someone taking off a disguise. She was a different person.

"You know something?" he said. "You shouldn't wear those."

"I can't see without them."

"Get contact lenses."

"I hate them."

"You have really, really pretty eyes."

"I like *your* eyes—except I can't see them right now," she said with a squint.

"Mine?"

"Yeah. They're a different color."

Glenroy shrugged. "Brown, aren't they?"

"Sort of a reddish brown."

He shrugged again.

"I always wished I had blue eyes," she said.

"God, why?"

"I just like them. I mean the real blue kind."

"Believe me, you're better off the way you are."

"Does anybody in your family have blue eyes?" she asked.

"Mama does. My brother did."

Rainy looked puzzled.

"He's dead," said Glenroy.

She hesitated. "A long time ago?"

"No—just last year."

"Oh."

An interlude of silence neither quite broke.

"What about you? Do you have any brothers or sisters?"

She shook her head. "Just a crazy mother."

Now he looked inquiring.

"Don't ask," she said.

"Does she live in Florida?"

Rainy nodded.

"No daddy?"

She shook her head curtly. "I don't remember him."

"I was twelve when mine died," said Glenroy, but the mood was veering in the wrong direction. He laughed. "Hey, let's talk about something *good*."

"What's something good?"

"I don't know. What do you think?"

"Good—or funny?" she asked.

"Funny."

She put her glasses back on and looked across the room. "That couple at the cash register."

He turned and looked over his shoulder. She was obese, wheezing and peeling off bills from a roll; he skeletal, cigarette in one side of his mouth, toothpick in the other, waiting.

Glenroy turned back with a laugh. "You want to talk about *them*?"

She shrugged. "What do you think their names are?"

He looked again—they were on the way out now. "Well, I'd have to go with Sally."

"Sally?"

"You know—everybody calls her Big Sal."

Rainy considered. "I think it'd be something like Crystal or Trixie."

"What about the guy?"

"Same thing," she said. "You know, Buster or something. She probably calls him Daddy."

They laughed. A moment passed.

"You must like it here better than Florida," said Glenroy.

She shrugged. "I think I would like anywhere better than Florida. Well, maybe not Biafra."

"Biafra?" he repeated, studying her amused. "What's so bad about Florida?"

Her lip curled in a sneer. "It's boring."

"Did you grow up there?"

"I went to high school there. There were other places before that—I don't remember them."

Glenroy considered her for a second. "You don't like to remember them," he half asked.

"No, I don't *remember* them."

"At all?"

She shook her head.

"You must remember something."

173

"I sort of remember junior high school, I guess. I don't remember where it was. I can't remember anything before that."

Astonished, Glenroy studied her wondering if it could be true.

"Do you?" she asked.

"What? Remember..."

"Anything."

"Well, yeah. I remember being a kid," he said. "I think about it all the time."

She had turned contemplative. "I must not have ever been one."

"Aw, come on."

She shrugged.

Glenroy felt a sudden and unexpected surge of pity for her. He looked at her, moved and preoccupied with the extraordinary idea.

"Well," he said. "Did you like it?"

"What?"

"School."

"No, I hated it," she replied with a scowl.

"That's funny—so did I." He paused. "I never finished." She looked at him. "You're hanging around with a drop-out."

"I would have been. I just didn't have the nerve." She thought for a moment. "Does your mother live here?"

"Mama? No, she lives in Trybald."

"Where's that?"

"Oh, about twenty-five miles south of here. Mill town. On a lake."

"What does she do?" Rainy asked.

"Works in the mill."

"Does she like it?"

Glenroy shrugged. "I don't think she thinks about whether she likes it or not. She just does it. Always has."

"Like you playing in a band."

"Yeah, sort of."

"Your band is good, isn't it?" He gave her an amused look.
"Well, I'm not the best judge," she apologized.

"I think so."

"Do you think you'll be famous?"

"Hell, we're already famous," he said, laughing, then shrugged. "Who knows? Maybe if we're lucky. The main thing is just to be able to keep doing it."

She considered that. "What was your brother's name?"

"Louis."

"Was he older than you?"

"No, younger. A year younger."

"Do you have any other brothers or sisters?"

"Nope. Just Louis."

She reflected. "I wish I'd had a brother. Or at least a sister—except we'd have probably fought all the time."

"Maybe not," he said and, done with his food, pushed his plate away. He looked at her and smiled. She smiled back.

"You're..." He just shook his head.

"What?"

"I don't know. Something."

"Well, I'm glad I'm something."

A chord he'd never heard before. "Want to get out of here and take a ride?" he proposed.

———

"What are you doing?" she asked as he turned into a darkened Gulf station.

"Getting a drink," he answered, and pulled alongside a dimly-lit Coke machine between the lube bays. "You want one?"

She shook her head. He got out, the Valiant rumbling, and put in a quarter; a Big Orange came tumbling noisily out. He opened it, came back to the car and sat down leaving the door ajar. The night had grown chilly, and the heater was blowing, rustling something at Rainy's feet. She had found a jacket in the back seat and wrapped it around her.

She watching interestedly, he poured out about a third of the orange drink, made it up with the vodka from the glove compartment, and gave it a couple of shakes.

He smiled and offered it to her; she declined with the curled lip but kept watching. He gurgled down a long swallow and she kept her eyes on him, absorbed, in silence. They groaned back out into the sparse traffic.

"You got anywhere you want to go?" he asked.

She shook her head with a shrug, like one ignorant of the options.

"You sleepy?"

She watched the world drift by. "Not as much as I thought I'd be."

"I had an idea," he said, thinking maybe she likes it, just being out, moving around, "—we could drive down to Trybald, see the lake. It'd be something to do."

She glanced at him, didn't immediately reply.

"Just to go somewhere, you know. If you're tired, I'll take you back to Jimmie's."

"I'm okay."

"It's just—I'm wide awake—as always. I've got to do something. And I like talking to you."

"What would you do if I wasn't here?"

"Talk to myself. I like that too. Don't I? Yes I do."

She glanced at him.

"Nah—same thing, probably. Sometimes I just drive around. Not really going anywhere."

"I never learned how to drive."

"You ought to. That way, you could drive around nowhere too—some time if you didn't have anything better—like me."

"I'm too scared. I'm scared I'd have a wreck."

"Just get you some old piece of junk like this and go slow. They'll go around you and have their wreck up the road with somebody else."

She smiled.

"How about it? Want to ride down to the lake?"

"Well—Jimmie and Angela..."

"They know you're with me. I'll get you back in one piece, I promise. Besides, they're celebrating."

She gave a little grunt, looking out the window. "I guess we could."

As they passed through downtown, Rainy sat watching the night skyline in silence. Once past the stadium, Glenroy opened the ashtray and fished out a roach. Rainy watched. Swerving a bit he felt around the floorboard and came up with a lighter.

"Want a hit?" he asked.

She shook her head and watched him light it with practiced awkwardness, draw in a deep toke, and hold it. After a few seconds he blew out a stream of smoke.

"Do you like doing that?" she asked, watching him like a curious child.

"Yeah."

"Why?"

"I don't know, it just kind of takes the edge off things," he replied, and took a swallow of his cocktail. "You don't smoke?"

She shook her head.

"Never did?"

She briefly contorted her features. "I sort of did, once."

"You must not have liked it."

She shook her head.

"Some people don't." He took another toke.

The car, its radio long kaput, fell silent after that; the air whistling at Glenroy's just-cracked window, the blowing heater, and the hum of the tires together made a sort of dreamy rhythm. Rainy huddled under the jacket, taking in the sights impassively. They cleared the airport and the city began to recede behind them. Soon they funneled onto a two-lane highway, the traffic intermittent. Fleeting spring fragrances spiced the night air. The sky, brilliantly clear, burned with stars.

Eventually, their movement lulled to a drone, the road widened to a four-lane. "Now you can say you've seen Trybald," Glenroy said. "Not that there's anything to see."

Quiet and sleeping: a sprawling junkyard, Ray's Nursery, a strip motel, its turquoise competitor, a cemetery of appliances, three car lots, an AM radio station, the Rodeo club, paint store, flooring company, drive-in burger joint, and some filling stations drifted by the windows like a surreal film. Rainy watched it all float past, silently.

"There's a little college here. Jimmie even went there for a while—I think one semester. And the mills. The lake." He looked at her. "And of course—the Trimble birthplace."

She gave a sleepy laugh.

"Actually, I was born in the hospital, if you can believe that. But there's the house. Same old house. Mama's still there."

"Is it far from here?"

"Nothing's far from here in this town."

"Can we see it?"

"Why?"

"Just to see it."

"If it wasn't so late we'd go say hi to Mama."

"No..."

"Don't worry. I wouldn't do that. Even though I bet you five dollars she's up."

Glenroy turned off the main drag, wound through the gameboard neighborhoods, at last turned down a dark street, and slowed. The muffler's menacing growl set the neighborhood dogs barking.

"That's it," he said, pointing to a small frame house with white awnings, below street level, half digested by unruly shrubbery, shadowed by a canopy of trees, barely visible in the weak streetlight. Sure enough, a light burned somewhere in the back, filtering into the front room and spraying a ghostly wash of light over the low end of the driveway where a white Pinto huddled under a rickety aluminum shelter.

"That's where you were a kid?" asked Rainy.

"There—and about three square miles around here," he answered, sweeping his arm.

They lingered a moment, at least ten dogs barking now, then Glenroy eased slowly away.

"Jimmie lived a few blocks that way," he said, gesturing.

She turned her head in the darkness, briefly, then seemed to sink into herself. They drove for a while, and Glenroy began to wonder if she had fallen asleep.

But she said, "I remember some sticker bushes with long pointed stickers. And a girl next door. She was two-faced."

"Where was that?" Glenroy asked.

"I'm not sure."

A new moon had begun its ghostly climb over the eastern horizon as they reached the lake. Glenroy pulled into a little picnic area, deserted, on Whitetail Creek, where they had a widespread view across the water: the opposing shoreline lights, a little circle of yellow from a night-fisherman's boat, the Highway 9 bridge, the wide, starry sky, and the sharp little lunar sliver.

"When's the last time you watched the sun rise?" Glenroy asked, feeling around in the ashtray for the roach.

"I guess never."

"Never?"

"Except one time, but I wasn't actually *watching*."

"I come out here sometimes when I can't sleep. There's something about seeing the sun come up that's always made me tired." He laughed.

"You're backwards."

"I know. Ass backwards."

"A night owl."

"Yeah. I get it from Mama. She worked third shift all those years and she'd just stay up on her off-nights too. When we were kids. I can still hear her going around the house in the middle of the night singing. I wish I had a tape of it some of these nights I can't sleep. After she went to first shift she never got used to it. Still hasn't. But she's one of these that can get by on just three or four hours."

"I go to bed sometimes when there's nothing else to do," Rainy said.

"Now see, that's a waste. That's why you sleep so much: you've gotten in the habit."

"I know. But it doesn't matter."

"Except for what you're missing. You ought to go out and watch the sun rise or something."

She shrugged. A moment slipped by. "Is it a long time?"

"What?"

"Till the sun rises."

"I'd say it's about four o'clock—it comes up about six—so it's a couple of hours."

"I don't think I can make it," she said.

Glenroy looked at her and saw she was telling the truth. "Well, we can do it another time. We'll stay up all night and bring a picnic and do it right."

"A picnic in the morning?"

"Why not?"

She smiled. "But I remember—I didn't really like it."

"What?"

"Staying up all night."

"Why?"

"It was like you were doing something wrong. Like you were seeing something you shouldn't see. If they caught you, you'd be in trouble."

"Well," Glenroy laughed, "that's the beauty of it."

"And it was just a few hours—like daytime. I was disappointed."

"What'd you expect?"

"I don't know. Like it'd be a lot longer. And different. Not just the same thing in the dark."

"Yeah, the Same Thing. I hate it too," said Glenroy. "I wish there was something that wasn't."

"So do I."

The conversation lapsed. Glenroy sat reflectively, gazing out the window. He fired up the roach, took a last toke.

"You ready to go back?" he asked.

She hesitated. "Yeah. I guess."

"What's the matter?"

"Nothing."

"Well..."

"No, it's okay."

Glenroy thought a minute. "You know, what we could do—if you want to—Grube's cabin—he's our manager—is sort of that way." He pointed northwest into the darkness. "I mean, actually it's way around on the other side of the lake, but it's not that far to drive. I've been staying there about half the time. Other people have stayed there too, but nobody really is anymore, except me. Matter of fact, I'd probably just come back down here after I took you back anyway."

She looked at him. "It's too far."

"Nah, I'm wide awake—I do it all the time. I'm used to it. But if you wanted to, we could head over there and you could crash—there's several beds. And it's got a shower and all that. We could call Jimmie in a little bit—there's a little store at the end of the road."

She shrugged, thinking about it.

"Either way. Whatever you want to do."

"I hate to wake them up," said Rainy.

———

The cabin, remote, pitch-dark, and deserted, had the half-real look of a discovered sunken ship as the headlights swept over it from the ridge. Glenroy rumbled into the clearing behind the house, turned off the motor, and silence flooded in.

"It looks cold," said Rainy.

"I'll get some heat going."

The opening and closing of the car doors jarred the air, then all sound sank once more into the dank, mossy silence as they made their way, Rainy holding Glenroy's arm, towards the porch. The air met them coolly, carrying a dozen suggestive scents, and one pervasively foul.

"What's that smell?" Rainy asked with a grimace.

"The septic tank. You get used to it."

They dodged through the obstacle course of the screened front porch—around furniture, boxes, a busted refrigerator, bench with barbell—to the door at the far end where a swing and some chairs and table circumscribed a little clearing. Glenroy felt under the mat for the key.

"It's ridiculous—Grube makes us use the key, but all you have to do is pick a window—any window."

"Who'd you say he was?" Rainy asked.

"Our manager. It's his place."

Glenroy unlocked and shoved open the reluctant door and they entered the tomb-like room still smelling of smoke from the winter's fires. Familiar with the territory, Glenroy felt his way to the nearest lamp and turned it on. The low-watt bulb brought the wide, cluttered room into dreamlike view.

"Hmm," said Rainy, looking around.

"This is a pretty good heater," Glenroy said at the big brown space heater across the room. "It takes it a few minutes, but it'll warm the room up. And I'll make a big fire." He nodded towards one of the bedrooms. "That's the best bed in there. You'll be warm once you get snuggled in."

"Are you going to bed now?"

"Oh, shortly." His eyes indicated the couch. "I usually sleep out here."

"Why?"

"I don't know—I just like it."

She walked slowly and appraisingly through the room, still holding the jacket around her. Near the opposite side she stopped and made a funny sound.

"What?"

"These *pictures*."

Glenroy half reared up from lighting the heater and looked. "Oh yeah," he said. "Forgot about those." They had been taken down from display but left in a trove leaning and stacked against the wall. "And that's not even all of them."

She made a face and turned away. Glenroy laughed.

"Hey—he likes pictures of himself," he said.

"He likes *himself*," Rainy replied.

"He can't help it—he's never found anybody else as wonderful."

"All of the guys I've ever known in bands were stuck on themselves," she said.

"Me too?"

"Well, maybe you're sort of different. Why do you play with him?"

"Because he's good."

"Is he?"

"Afraid so."

She yawned.

Glenroy rose from lighting the heater. "Want to sleep in there?" he asked.

She shrugged and followed him in. He turned on a driftwood lamp by the bed.

"Oh my God," she moaned.

"Whoops—forgot about that," said Glenroy. It was leaning against the wall—the sunset poster. Glenroy picked it up and disappeared with it.

Rainy took in the room—its one or two pieces of furniture and what looked to be a comfortable bed—tousled with quilts and pillows. She yawned again.

"Need anything?" said Glenroy just outside the door.

"Where's the bathroom?"

"Over there," Glenroy pointed.

A brief glance passed between them at the threshold as she returned. She closed the door, and a moment later Glenroy heard the squeak of bedsprings, then went outside to get some firewood.

The sky, he saw, was beginning to lighten. A little later than he had thought. He moved slowly, at last beginning to feel the possibility of fatigue himself, finding some familiar pleasure in the cool morning air, the solitude. He gathered the wood and some kindling, went back inside, and laid out a monumental pyre in the broad fireplace. As the fire began to crackle into life, he went out to the kitchen and took a half-full jug of his special orange juice from the near-barren refrigerator and took it back to the couch. He reached with the certainty of a blind man just under the dust flap beneath him and brought out an old green cookie tin.

He had a toke, sipped from the jug, and sat watching the fire rise as the gray morning made dim rectangles of the windows. Amazing thing, fire. Utterly itself, irreducible. Not like anything—everything had to be like it. His mouth slightly open, he marveled for a while at fire, then felt his thoughts bending behind him to her. Was she possible? She seemed more like something imagined or remembered or wished for than real. Her eyes lingered in his mind.

He went out for a walk and now the profile of the far shore stood out distinctly. Mist rose ghost-like from the water. An outboard motor rasped in the distance. A jet hissed overhead while the enterprising clamor of birds swelled with the light. The lake was on the rise, but still low in its banks—sandy, rocky, littered with old bottles and rusty cans, orange fishing floats, and pieces of Styrofoam as he walked beyond the slough to the main shoreline. He found a flat rock, sat down, and waited for the sun. It came, a burning shard of brilliant orange across the water, steadily rising, searing the treetops above him, finally clearing the horizon and hanging in the sky.

End of show. Glenroy yawned and headed back, thinking of Louis.

He stoked up the fire, pulled a quilt over him on the couch, and dozed off.

———

Its early promise forgotten, the day was slipping toward late afternoon, the shadows said, and precisely a Sunday afternoon, as Glenroy, who had been up about an hour sitting on the porch, thought he heard a rustle, a creak, followed by a gentle thump. He half turned his head. So—it was real.

As her door creaked open and she shyly emerged, drenched with sleep, he smiled. Something slightly touched her expression in return. Cross-armed, she came out to the porch.

"Afternoon," he said. The mere proximity of a night had eased the strangeness.

"What time is it?" she asked.

"I don't know exactly."

"It *is* the same day?"

"Well," he replied, "I don't guess there's any way to prove it."

"Did you sleep?" she wondered.

"Oh yeah," Glenroy said, "I slept fine. How about you?"

She nodded with some emphasis. "Have you been up long?"

"Nah, not very long. Are you hungry?"

She nodded.

"We'll run up to Allred's and get some stuff. We'll finally have our picnic."

"I need to call Jimmie and Angela," she said, vaguely anxious.

"We'll do that too."

————

Shrewdly situated where County Road 91 teed into Whitechurch Road, sprawling around the end of a long inlet called Rabbit Creek, Allred's Gas and Groc. had that piece of the lake covered. The empire included a boat launch, a battered dock with a marine gas pump, an eyeless bus being digested by the sloughscape, at least half a dozen smaller vehicles in the same fix, more nameless ramshackle structures than one could or might care to count, a few trailers, and of course the store itself, a malconstructed beehive with some overpriced, out-of-date version of every merchandise conceivable, that smelled of crickets.

The drive, up the vein-like maze of dirt roads from the cabin, was about a mile. They rumbled up inconspicuously—loud mufflers turning no heads here—displacing only an old, maybe young, hound who lumbered a few yards away and recollapsed, and parked between a beached party boat listing on one pontoon and a Dodge van with a sign in the front window: "$450—Needs Moter."

The dogwoods had aged beyond their glory, mere trees now, but azaleas still blazed—including one particularly impressive Pride of Mobile just behind the mired van.

"God," said Rainy as they got out, and walked over to it. "What is it?"

"Just an azalea."

"It's pretty."

"You don't have azaleas in Florida?" he asked.

She shrugged. "I guess."

Inside, Big Steve Allred sat behind his checkout counter half watching a basketball game. He peered from his Chap-Stick, Slim Jim, Yellow Bole, Kool-Ray, nail clipper surrounded cubicle like a carnival barker among his prizes. He recognized Glenroy. "Come on in here. What you need this afternoon?"

"A little of everything," said Glenroy.

Big Steve laughed.

They got bread, ham and cheese, Cheetoes, Oreos, milk, and a six-pack of beer. Everything cost half as much again as it would anywhere else, except the beer, which, it being Sunday, was double—but as Big Steve himself might have reminded you—anywhere else was a good ways off.

Then Glenroy placed the call at the pay phone outside.

"Yes, I'll accept," said Jimmie.

186

"Hey, it's me," said Glenroy.

"Where are you? We were just about to get the law out after you. You got Rainy with you?"

"Yeah, she's here."

"Where are you?"

"We're down at the lake. We spent the night here."

"Oh-h."

"No—she was tired. She slept in the Dartt room."

"You've got to be kidding."

"We had to fumigate it."

Jimmie laughed. "You heading back today?"

"Yeah, I guess. We haven't been up long. We're up at Allred's getting some stuff to eat."

"Take your time, take your time."

As they left, Rainy broke off a small branch from the azalea bush. "Do you think he'll mind?"

Glenroy shook his head. "Who says he's got to know?"

In a vase, it reigned as the centerpiece of the little porch table. The fragrant afternoon passed easily, the air neither warm nor cool, water lapping softly at the bank, birds, boats out on the open lake, music from the record player inside. The cabin had a few azaleas of its own that Rainy had discovered with gentle delight. They ate their sandwiches and lingered over the Oreos, Rainy drinking milk, Glenroy the costly beer.

"I can't believe you drink that with Oreos," Rainy frowned.

"I think they go together good. You've got some milk on your lip," he pointed out. A white glaze on the soft dark down.

She wiped it off. "I hate beer."

"You hate all the bad stuff, don't you?"

"I used to steal pills from my mother. Only a few times, really. I sort of liked it—then I didn't. It scared me. I think I have an addictive personality, probably."

"I think I have too."

"Does it scare you?"

He shrugged. "Nah, I wouldn't say it *scares* me."

"Does anything scare you?" she asked.

He regarded her with surprise. "Sure."

"Like what?"

"Well—water moccasins, cop cars behind me, mad dogs, Mama dying, getting my hand chewed up…"

She laughed. "What?"

"You know, in a machine or something—so I couldn't play anymore."

"Oh."

"Ending up alone—of course, everybody's scared of that—not that I ever think about it. And I'm always a little scared when I play in front of people."

"Really?" she said, surprised.

"Yeah—a little."

"Why?"

"Well, you just are. I think you need to be—a little. Maybe scared's not the word. Playing music is funny. It's not the same every time. Some nights it works and some nights it doesn't. You don't know why, it just doesn't, and then you start thinking about it."

"Is that bad?" she asked.

"Kiss of death."

"Hmm," Rainy reflected.

"You just have to tell yourself it's like that sometimes. How about you?"

"Everything scares me," she said.

"Everything?"

"Just about. You're scared of being alone?"

"Ending *up* alone."

"What's the difference?"

He thought about it. "It's whether you want to be or not."

She considered that.

"Do you like being alone?" he asked her.

She shrugged. "Yeah."

"All the time?"

"No. Not all the time. Do you ever think about what it will be like when you die?"

"No. Yes."

"Maybe you're alone all the time. It's just you."

"That would suck," he said.

"You know what I think the worst thing would be?"

"What?"

"If you died, and it was just like this."

Glenroy laughed. "Maybe we did."

"Do you like playing with that colored guy?"

"Yeah, I do."

"What's he like?"

"I don't know, just a guy. Kind of quiet," Glenroy said.

Rainy listened with interest.

"I don't claim to really know him. He stays pretty much inside himself."

"What does he do?"

He looked at her. "What do you mean what does he do?"

"I mean, is he just a regular person..."

Glenroy laughed. "What do you think?"

"I just wondered."

"He's just a guy, like any other guy, except he's kind of quiet. He's like me—he only does one thing. He happens to be extremely good at it, and if he ever picks something else I'll be up shit creek."

"Why?"

"You've heard him."

"But I don't know anything about it."

"Take my word for it."

"Is he better than Jimmie was?"

Glenroy shook his head. "You can't compare them."

"Why not?"

"You just can't." Rainy looked puzzled. "Jimmie would tell you the same thing."

"Hmm," said Rainy.

189

"It's nothing against Jimmie." Rainy seemed to be trying to digest it all. "He's kind of taken care of you, hasn't he?"

"They've been nice to me."

"I guess you're staying with them for a while?" Glenroy asked.

She nodded. "I was." She fell quiet. "I was wondering…"

"What?"

"Oh, nothing."

"What?"

She hesitated. "This place."

"Yeah?"

"I mean—I was just thinking. That guy that owns it…"

"Grube?"

"You said nobody really lives here…"

"Ah!" Glenroy suddenly exclaimed.

"I was just wondering."

Again the pity, the protectiveness, or whatever it was, passed over him.

"Does he come down here much?" she asked.

"Grube? Never."

"I just thought…"

He smiled at her. "I'll take care of it," he said.

She lowered her eyes, crossed her arms around her.

"Cold?" he asked.

She nodded. "A little."

The day, of which their slice had been so small, was dying; shadows dripped over the lost place like honey down the sides of a jar.

She sat watching from the couch as he scraped away the old ashes and laid out a new fire. When the flames caught and began to rise he came and sat beside her. He pulled out the cookie tin; as he opened it she peered in and made a disagreeable face. "Do you have to do that?" There was not censure, but a plea, in her tone.

"No," he said, replacing it. "I don't *have* to." He sat back, raised his arm in invitation, and she leaned against him. They kissed a while.

Then, that having run its course, her head in the hollow of his shoulder, she said, "You said there was a shower?"

The gene for hurry made no appearance in her code. She emerged in her own time from the steamy bathroom re-dressed in her clothes, combing her wet hair. Glenroy meanwhile had fetched more wood and involved himself in the fire.

"Ah, that's nice," she said.

"You look happier."

"I am."

"I'm going to give it a half hour and get one myself. You want to pick out some records?"

She nodded.

A considerable, manhandled collection crowded the planks on concrete blocks by the stereo, and after combing out her hair she went over and started flipping through them.

Later, Hawaiian music, like a thick cheap perfume, softly filled the room as he came out from the bathroom, wet-haired himself and in new clothes.

"Mmm," he said. "What is it?"

"*Adventures in Paradise.* I liked the picture."

She was standing before the fire, holding the quilt from the couch around her. "You must be cold," he said.

"Not now."

She had taken off her glasses, he saw, and then he became aware of her bare lower legs and feet, below the quilt, and his gaze moved to the couch where he noticed the brown pants, the baggy flannel shirt in a heap, and he looked back at her.

They stood there. Then she relaxed the grip of her fingers holding the makeshift garment at her neck and it fell around her into a tumble about her feet.

He neither moved, spoke, nor breathed. Some slow seconds passed. Then at last his lips parted and he began to breathe again, in a quick shallow rhythm, matching his racing heart. The light of day had all but died, and the fire behind her haloed the smooth contours of her body and her glistening hair with an aura of orange light. He looked into her eyes, mystified. Then with the attentiveness of a man trying to memorize something for eternity he moved his eyes almost like physical touch over her body: the faint down disappearing in delicate points along her cheeks, the gentle curve where her neck became her shoulders, her smooth arms, her breasts, the guitar-shaped curve of her waist and hips, the dark wispy trail following the curve of her belly from her navel to the jet-black triangle below.

He undressed slowly and approached her. As she ever so slightly moved her arms invitingly away from her sides, the fuzz on her body shimmered in the firelight, and he slid his hands up the outer sides of her legs, over the swell of her hips, to the fire-warmed small of her back. Then he pulled her to him.

He ached, rich pain spiking through him; and when on the floor in the rumpled quilt before the fire in the frog-croaking, insect-twittering, many-smelled, middle of nowhere twilight he pressed himself against her, for a moment all the questions had their answers.

———

They had set up camp in Macon—the Thursday of a long weekend stand. They had traveled separately, Dartt, the tall girl with him, arriving almost exactly at nine.

That afternoon Grube had sent somebody; they had set up, run sound check, gone to eat, and come back. And when nine o'clock came, the club manager pacing, it was not an arrival, but an entrance—the newcomers creating somehow the impression of an entourage. The tall girl took a seat against the wall and lit a long brown cigarette, as Dartt unpacked his instrument.

"Let's open with 'Come When I Do' tonight," he said abruptly.

192

Taken aback, Glenroy turned to him. "What?"

"Come on, don't act like I just landed from Mars—I want to try it as an opener."

"'Jeez Louise' is our opener."

"Is there some law that says it has to be—always, forever?"

"There's no law—just that it's our opener."

"It *has* to be?"

"I don't guess it *has* to be. It just is."

"And that can't change," Dartt said.

Glenroy shrugged. "People come to hear us, that's what they expect—that's what they want."

"So that's what we're about here—giving people what they expect?" Dartt said.

Glenroy reflected. "Well, yeah, in some things."

"You're afraid of trying something different? Shaking them up?"

"I'm not afraid of it. I just don't see any reason to change something that works."

"Works for everybody?"

"I thought it did."

Dartt exhaled. "We can't even *try* it?"

Glenroy shook his head, perplexed. "As an *opener?*"

"Why not?"

"Well, for one thing, it's slow."

"It's not just slow."

"That's another thing."

"What?"

"What you said—it's more than one thing."

Dartt gave an astonished laugh. "Is there supposed to be something *wrong* with that?"

"I'm not saying there's anything wrong with it—I'm just saying an opener needs to grab people—it needs to rock."

Dartt laughed. "And of course none of my songs do *that*."

"That's not what I'm saying."

"You ever heard of variation? Dynamics?"

"Yeah, we've got all night for that."

The manager appeared in the door. "Guys—it's after nine o'clock."

"Okay," replied Glenroy, shortly. *Just like Dartt,* he thought, *bringing it up two minutes before we play.*

"You do something enough times," Dartt argued, "it's a cliché. I want to send a message to people: don't get comfortable out there, folks, don't sit there thinking you know where we're coming from, that you've got us pegged. Don't put us in a box."

"I thought we already did that."

"No—we're predictable."

"Predictable in a good way, maybe."

Dartt shook his head. "It's just another word for boring."

"*I'm* not bored," Glenroy insisted.

"Look, I'm not saying we don't make good music. I'm just saying I want to try some different things. If you don't like the song, just say so."

Glenroy sighed. "It has nothing to do with liking the song."

"Then *what?*"

"'Jeez Louise' is one of our best songs…"

"That's a matter of opinion, but whatever."

"What? You don't think it is?"

"I just said it was a matter of opinion, that's all."

"It's our trademark."

"Oh, our trademark."

"Well, it is."

"A hundred songs could be."

"But this one *is.*"

"Why couldn't it be something different every time? Like those airplanes they paint different colors."

"I can't understand why you're bringing it up now. We're supposed to be playing fifteen minutes ago. There're people out there waiting for us."

Dartt laughed and shook his head. "When *do* you want me to bring it up? What difference does it make? You're not even listening to what I'm saying." The tall girl, listening but not looking, blew out a stream of smoke and crushed out her cigarette. A smile played on her face. Dartt laughed again. "There's no way in hell you're going to mess with your brother's songs, are you?"

"It's not that, goddammit," Glenroy said.

"Oh no." Dartt shook his head. "You know what's confusing for me sometimes? You're not consistent—you contradict yourself. You say you want to be so different and original—and then you've got this formula thing."

"It's not a formula."

"It's not?"

"No."

"And why have you got all this energy when it's one of your things, or one of your brother's, but if it's *mine*, then all of a sudden it's nope, can't do that, it's new and different—got to stay with the old shit, give them what they expect?"

Glenroy exhaled impatiently and turned to Doug.

"Hey, I don't care," Doug said. "Let's just play."

"Don't you think 'Jeez Louise' is a good opener?"

He shrugged. "Yeah. Has been."

"Hey, this is different: two against one."

"It's not two against one," Glenroy said.

"That was a close one. For a minute there we almost tried something new. Something *Donny* did. But that's all right—let's just go dig up some more of your brother's songs instead."

"Just leave my brother out of it! What's your goddamn problem anyway? We do a ton of your songs. I'm just saying I personally don't want to open with this one."

"And so that's it. Decision made. No further discussion. What way do we do it? The same old way—case closed."

"Guys, it's twenty-five after," complained the manager, listening at the door. "Can't you work this out later?"

"Let's go," Glenroy grumbled.

——

Dartt played it crazy, teaching them all a lesson, and the insane energy electrified the room. The first set left a smoking battlefield.

At the break they sat backstage. Someone handed them beers, Doug a ginger ale.

"I guess you heard," said Dartt.

"Heard what?" Glenroy said.

"You haven't talked to Grube?"

"Not lately."

"Yeah. Well, it looks like we're going in the studio."

"No shit?"

"Looks like it."

"What, like to do an album?"

"Eventually, I think. A single for now."

"No shit. Grube said that?"

"Yeah," Dartt nodded.

"When?" asked Glenroy.

"I don't know—a few days ago. He said we needed to get something on the radio."

"Well—he's right."

"Yeah." Dartt nodded for a few seconds. "The question is what."

Glenroy nodded.

"The tune, I mean."

"Yeah, I know."

"I guess we need to see if we can agree on something."

Glenroy slowly nodded. "What's Grube say?"

"He hasn't said anything."

"Hm," Glenroy snorted.

Dartt rose, holding his beer. The tall girl seemed to be waiting for him across the room, though not looking at anything, smoking a long brown cigarette.

"So—what? You're staying down at the lake now, I guess."

Glenroy shrugged. "Some. Still at my cousin's some too."

Dartt nodded, still just standing there. "I enjoyed it—when I was there. For a while. Then it got boring."

"It's not boring yet," Glenroy said, looking at him.

Dartt nodded, took a drink of beer, started away. "Good. I'm happy. Just be careful you don't catch something."

The tall girl took a fragrant puff.

———

The second set picked up the momentum of the first, leaving hardly a trace in the memory, as though it had burned itself cleanly away. Glenroy, sweating, lightheaded, stepped out back for a toke, then returned and joined Doug backstage for the rest of the break and drank another beer. They said a total of seventeen words. Dartt and his slinky shadow were nowhere.

The last set loomed wearily. Glenroy wished he could leave now. But he couldn't, so when they resumed playing, his thoughts left the room, prowling.

They flitted past Grube's waiting cheap motel rooms, then soared over the moon-soaked rolling pine hills to the shimmering slice of silvered water, then down to the ridge, the drive, the yard, floating slowly through the cool fragrances of the night, pausing here or there simply to gaze, at last hunting along the borders and corners and turning toward the center, the heart, knowing she would be there.

Not even an hour away.

———

It was a smell that lingered—or rather, a complex of many delicate smells: her hair, the woodsmoke still clinging faintly to her clothes, the milky fragrance of her skin, her breath, the wisteria, the new grass conjuring of childhood, the vague, almost reassuring stench of the septic tank—all haunting him like a half-remembered song.

197

She was a profound sleeper—a drowsy spirit by nature who could sleep unnaturally long hours at a stretch, any time of day, who seemed to reach some deeper morphean cavern than most and dwell there like one to whom the waking world is far the stranger place. And dreams—wondrous strange companions so odd they beguiled the soul like a drug—cohabited her mind with daytime thoughts, always intruding, fading, never expressible. She didn't awaken easily, and Glenroy sometimes thought about her vulnerability there alone, but didn't know what to do about it. When he came, he tried not to frighten her and usually just slipped into the bed beside her, and she only felt, didn't know till morning—but there were times, like tonight, when something in the music had been too good.

He turned on a light in the den and put on a record, softly.

The cabin showed signs of her presence now—light touches as though she, like a flower in a pavement crack, dared not reach far or deep, fearing that something in the shadows behind her might at any time re-congeal into nightmare; and one, seeing these effects of her, felt touched by the mere fact that they spoke of her, ephemeral footprints of a spirit who scarcely thought to leave more in her wake than a breeze leaves blowing through a room: magazines, stacks of them, more than the few he brought her and that she got he knew not where, and never asked; some glossy pages—landscapes, gardens, flowers, a bird—she had cut out and taped here and there on the walls; a plate, glass, cup, fork and spoon in the drain board by the kitchen sink; an afghan-draped hollow on the end of the couch before the ancient TV that received two channels, on rare days three, requiring a trip outside to turn the antenna to change from one to the other; a roll of toilet tissue on the end table; toothbrush in the bathroom but few of the usual lotions and tubes and jars that accrue around a woman; another roll of tissue beside the bed; and then, in the tiny closet, her clothes: the two or three flannel shirts, no blue jeans, just the brown pants, the other brown pants, and then the tan ones—that she washed, occasionally, at Allred's.

She made periodic visits there—a long walk, but she liked walks—and he wondered about the regulars seeing her on the road, curious, sizing her up, stopping maybe, engaging her. Or maybe not. Maybe like almost everything else about her, this lived solely in her mythical privacy. She might have been the last surviving human being.

Or so he fancied her. In fact, he didn't know and didn't want to know. She was the Other Thing in his life; she came into existence when he topped the ridge—as, he suspected, did he for her, and his mind shied from imagining her before or after, and they rarely talked of his music, as though they were both instinctively aware that the one way to destroy any of this improbable dream was to recognize it. They had their things they did talk about, but those only, and sometimes they didn't even talk at all—two wordless people at ease in the long spring afternoons. Often he quietly played his acoustic guitar. He brought her things: the magazines, puzzle books, food and drink, truck-stop souvenirs from the towns where they played, and always left some money in a ceramic turtle on the kitchen counter—another subject they never discussed. She spent it at Allred's, he supposed—where else?—and whatever was left she kept in the same place so that an evolving combination of bills and coins came and went there, which nobody ever saw anybody touch.

The hour had crept past two. He had a toke, a drink, and when he heard her stir he turned the record off, put out the light, took off his clothes in the cool morning air and slid in beside her warm body.

———

Wisteria snaking through the tall pine trees around the cabin purpled the woods and filled the air with fragrance. When Glenroy woke up, the morning had aged. In spite of the open windows, the dark-paneled room closed in warmly. He opened his eyes and lay for a while gazing through the bedroom door, across the center room to the porch where the living picture of late morning looked too real to be real. He could see the lake in mosaic, shining through the trees. Birds sang in full chorus and the inevitable outboard motors buzzed distantly over the water. He lay, idly replaying the scenes of the previous night like a film in his mind, and when Rainy turned over and half opened her eyes, he returned to the present.

"You woke me up last night," she said.

"I'm sorry—I couldn't help it."

She smiled groggily, closed her eyes again. He raised himself on an elbow.

"It's hot," she exclaimed, and pushed the covers away from her, raised her knees and kicked them in a wad to the end of the bed. "Ah-h," she said.

And there she lay smiling, like a hidden treasure.

———

They drove up to Allred's for food, came back and had lunch on the porch, then fell idle. At last Rainy decided to take a shower, and as she did Glenroy got out the cookie tin. When she was finished, and drying off in the bedroom, he came in and was upon her again, entwining her and pushing her back gently onto the bed.

"Good God," she said.

Later, loafing on the porch with his guitar, hearing ideas randomly, he luxuriated in nothingness. The fleeting riffs came too casually, too many to worry over—maybe they would never come back, probably they would. The sun's going to burn out one day—who cares?

She came out with tea and a magazine and sat down.

"We're going to cut a single," he said, violating the unspoken rule.

She frowned slightly. "What?"

"We're going to make a record," he repeated.

"Is that good?" she asked.

He looked at her.

"I guess it is," she said.

"Why wouldn't it be?"

"I don't know. I guess it would be good."

"I think most bands would say so."

She nodded, gazing at something.

"Get on the radio maybe."

"That'd be fun," she allowed.

He nodded, observed her momentarily, then looked away across the lake. "We've just got to decide on which tune." He reflected. "We've got a ton of stuff—I know a lot of bands wish they had our problem."

"There's a hummingbird," she said.

He looked, and there was: emerald green, ruby-throated, vibrating under the eaves of the porch, visiting the red blooms of a coiling trumpet vine. "That's cool," he said.

"I see them all the time. I counted thirty-two one day. Not all at the same time."

"I'm just thinking about Dartt," said Glenroy.

"What about him?"

"Just—how we're not going to agree."

"On what?"

"On the song."

"The song for your record?"

He glanced at her. "Yeah. For our record."

She was watching the hummingbird again, then it was gone. "I had a dream about Hitler last night."

"Hitler?"

"Isn't that bizarre?"

"Yeah, that's bizarre." He thought about it, shook his head. "Why the hell Hitler? What do you know about Hitler?"

"Just that he's Hitler." She frowned, recollecting. "He was real pasty and pudgy and he was acting nice but he wasn't really. He would look at you and it would give you this horrible feeling because you knew he did things to you in secret you couldn't do anything about."

"Jesus, Rainy."

"Maybe I'll cook tonight," she said.

"Cook?"

"I was thinking about it."

"Well—I've got to play, remember."

"Oh yeah."

"Maybe Sunday."

"Yeah."

"What are you going to cook?" he asked.

"I was thinking about lasagna."

"You know how to make lasagna?"

"Angela sort of showed me."

"Mama used to make it sometimes," he said. "She thought it was real exotic."

"There's another hummingbird."

"It's the same one."

"Uh-uh—it's two of them."

He looked, watching the pair until they chased each other out of sight. He shook his head and gave a little laugh. "We finally get in the studio...shit, I can predict the whole damn thing."

———

They were on their feet cheering, the entire crammed-full place.

"Lake Trash" had never sounded like that before, never been that song. He caught Dartt's eye, saw an expression he hardly saw there anymore, and was trying to remember, to understand what had happened before the moment passed. But that was the thing about moments these days: they were always just gone, swallowed into the haze, and even the sense of how maddening that was was only another moment, swallowed. And now, all he could do was react to what Doug was doing. Good God, the man was a universe all himself of sound, seemingly but not at all erratic, like three people, all feet and

202

arms, his left hand catching the bell of a cymbal in a steady 1-2-3-4, offering the key into the maze. What was the song? The playlist went out of focus in his mind. Did it even matter? But then Dartt was on it, the familiar bass line of "Mother Roach," fitting into the intricate open spaces of the rhythm—and then he remembered and knew where he was and what to do.

An extraordinary night, one to remember—though he wouldn't—not really—only the swollen place in the blur it would become. All a voracious, accelerating, exhausting, ecstatic rush. And like a man tumbling down rapids he just rode and didn't have time to care.

———

"Where's Ace?" Grube demanded.

"He's on a project out of town. I'll be working with you."

Grube rolled his eyes and let out a breath. "David said we'd have Ace. That was part of the deal."

"Well, Ace isn't going to be back for a couple of months. But trust me, I'll get the sound you're looking for." He seemed sure of himself. Grube looked at him, big nose and thick glasses.

"What's your name?"

"Boyd."

"All right, Boyd, look. We came in here to make a hit record. You make us a hit record and we won't worry about it. Even if it is breach of contract. You don't make us a hit record and David and I are going to have a problem—which I'm sure means David and *you* are going to have a problem."

Boyd made a distasteful face, almost said something, but didn't.

"Hey, don't worry about my guys, okay? We wouldn't be here if we weren't ready."

Boyd shrugged.

Tomorrow Studio hid in the basement of an office building in Doraville, built into a hill so that the offices up top faced the street, the studio accessible only from the back. One drove down the steep drive and parked in a little privet-choked clearing. The door, battered and scratched from the outside, like the door to any studio was a portal to a surreal environment without day or night, without time, its own world.

Once they had brought in their instruments, through the anteroom with the cluttered desk and compact refrigerator and head-shot covered walls and into the padded inner sanctum, Dartt said, "Okay, what's the plan here?"

"The plan?" said Grube. "I've already told you. To make a hit record."

"Yeah, yeah. I mean, *what* hit record?"

"All right," said Grube. "My thinking is this. We've got the facility, and our expert engineer—"

"Boyd."

"—Boyd, for three days. I want to do as much as we can in that time."

"But what song?" Dartt persisted.

"That's what I'm saying. As many as we can do in three days."

"Aw, come on. I've done plenty of recording—we'll be doing good to get one tune in three days," said Dartt.

"I guess I've got more confidence in you than you have in yourself. I'd like to do seven or eight songs at least. Ideally, ten."

"Come on," Dartt protested impatiently.

"Why not?"

"Why?"

"Because we might as well get something done while we're in here. You never know—down the road. And who knows when we'll get back?"

"I would think if we produce something good—and we are—we'll be back a lot."

Grube shrugged.

"Look, let me ask it like this," Dartt said, "what's the *main* song we're working on here?"

"I don't know yet. Whichever comes out the best."

Dartt exhaled. "Why don't we decide that first, then put all our time on it? Get it right."

"Because I believe you guys are at the point where you don't need to be taking three days for one song. Now, I'm spending a good bit of money here and I want to get something out of it."

Dartt shook his head. "Whatever. It doesn't make any sense, but whatever. Can you at least tell me *what* songs we're going to do? I mean, I've got some ideas, but I don't recall anybody asking my opinion yet."

"'Jeez Louise,'" said Glenroy.

"God, haven't we about beaten that poor song to death?"

"If we're making a record…"

"All right, guys. Now listen," Grube cut in. "We're not going to stand here burning up our time arguing about songs. I'm spending *money* here and I'll decide. We'll start out with 'Jeez Louise' and go from there."

"I'm not sure I can play it," Dartt complained.

"You're a professional musician, aren't you?"

"I thought I was. I want to do 'Till Something Better Comes Along.'"

"We'll do it," said Grube.

"I think it's got hit potential."

"It may."

"Also 'Come When I Do,' 'You Can Go Now,' 'That's Just Who I Am,' maybe even 'Once You Get to Know Me.' They're all good tunes. They'd all work on the air."

"Yeah, we'll get to them. And there's something else I wanted to tell you. I wanted to wait until I had it finalized, and it's close. It's going to happen."

"What's going to happen?" asked Dartt.

"You're booked in the Auditorium in November. You and two, maybe three other bands."

"No shit?"

"No shit. So you see why I want something on the air—at least by summer. We need to fill that place up."

"What other bands?" Dartt asked.

"It's not final yet."

"Who's top billing?"

"You, I hope."

"You hope?"

"I guess a lot of that depends on what happens here. Plus, I'm dealing with several people. It's complicated. If we get a record out of this and it does like I hope it will, then it'll be your show."

"What label anyway?" asked Dartt.

"You don't have to worry about any of that. I've got it taken care of."

"Why's it a secret?"

"It's not a secret. We're still working out the details. It's David's label essentially. A new label."

"Homegrown kind of thing."

"You don't need to worry about it. I'm working out a deal with a distributor—you make a good song, I'll get it on the air, okay? The right people will know about it. You just play the music."

"We can play the fucking music," Dartt said.

"Good," Grube replied.

———

Boyd Ange proved meticulous in his preparations. He spent an hour miking the drums. The rest of them sat in the control booth listening as Doug played countless runs, filling the room with crash and thunder. Back and forth Boyd bounced with frisky energy from Doug to the board, adjusting the mikes, tracking down every vibration and ring, tweaking each track with the care of a surgeon, perpetually on the edge of his chair.

"Not your ordinary drummer, is he?"

"No."

When they were almost done, Glenroy went out to the bathroom. Grube, who had disappeared, now lurked in the hall.

"Look," he said. "I wanted to tell you something. The reason we're here is to do 'Jeez Louise,' okay? That's our tune—you know it, I know it."

Glenroy nodded uncertainly.

"And we'll take one of his for the B-side. The best one. Okay?"

Glenroy nodded.

And then he slipped away.

Boyd labored equally over the bass and guitar and then the band did a little warm-up jam. In the booth, Boyd attended obsessively to every detail, emerging periodically to check this or that, and finally after ten minutes or so he came through their headphones.

"Okay, I think we're pretty close."

They gathered around the board and he rewound the tape. When the rich sound came over the speakers, they just looked at each other. Scot-free in the ultimate candy store.

"Not too bad," said Boyd, his hands flickering over the controls.

It was four o'clock by then, and they started on 'Jeez Louise,' Dartt singing a scratch vocal. They false-started several times, bailed out a couple more, then finally made it through. They listened and squirmed—then played it a couple more times—then finally, about halfway through a take, fell into the groove. The veil parted—all distractions evaporated—the music played them. They had it on the fourth take.

"What do you want to do?" asked Boyd. "Knock off? Keep going? Do the vocal? Actually, I'd rather save all the vocals."

"Let's keep going," said Grube, having reappeared.

No arguments.

By midnight they had, in addition to 'Jeez Louise,' three keepers—all Dartt songs. Dartt scowled malcontented, but let them stand. Everybody sensed they weren't likely to get them any better. Fatigue settled in.

Dartt left, then Grube. "We're flying," said Boyd. "Have another beer."

Glenroy opened a beer and Doug didn't seem in a hurry. Boyd took a half-joint from an ashtray on his console, lit it, and handed it to Glenroy.

"This can't be your first time in a studio," he said.

"It is in a real one—for me," said Glenroy.

"The Decisions," reminded Doug.

"Well yeah," Glenroy laughed. "Except for that. Doug did some stuff with Lonnie Ray White."

Boyd turned to him in surprise. "You played with Lonnie Ray White?"

"Yeah, for a while."

"I'll be damned. Man, that was sad about him."

"Yeah."

"I always heard he was a good guy."

"He was. Good-hearted guy," said Doug.

Boyd shook his head. "How come I've never heard you guys before?"

"I don't know," Glenroy smiled. "Where you been?"

"In my hole."

"You ought to come out and hear us."

"I will. Who does your sound?"

"Hah," said Glenroy. "Us, basically. Grube's PA—he sends a guy when we set up."

"I'd be interested in that. This guy—your manager—has he said anything about an album?" Boyd asked.

"Nothing definite."

"Well, *usually*—you get an album ready, then take the best cut from it for the single. Then they go out and buy the album."

"Maybe that's what he *is* doing," suggested Doug.

"I'm not sure he *knows* what he's doing," Glenroy said.

"Well, keep me in mind. I'd be really interested in working with you."

"Thanks."

"I'm serious. He said something—I mean, I get the impression you've got a good bit of other material."

"We do—we've got a lot," said Glenroy.

"Like your bass player's stuff or what?"

"No, not that."

"More like the first song," said Boyd.

"Yeah."

"I'd like to hear it."

"You need to come check us out sometime."

Boyd nodded. "I'll definitely be doing that."

———

The next day they laid down five more rhythm tracks—another Dartt, then "Lake Trash," and three of Louis's songs. They listened to the playbacks until they couldn't anymore—a disheartening experience of diminishing returns as each time took something more from what was good, ultimately leaving only the weaknesses, the could have been betters, the mistakes, like exposed wounds—got something to eat, and still felt like playing.

"Let's try this," said Glenroy, and started one of his riffs. They jammed on it for a while, then did another one, tape running—finally growing tired all together.

"You ready to sing tomorrow?" Grube asked Dartt.

"Big time ready."

They didn't know yet what they were in for. Dartt doing vocals was like a woman getting ready for the night of her life. It transcended perfectionism. There wasn't a molecule of his heart, body, and soul he didn't pour into it, and he had the temperament all day of a pissed-off cat. But it was worth it—even if Dartt himself seemed to hate every note of it. They did "Jeez Louise" first—then he and Glenroy did the backgrounds. They gathered in the booth and Boyd played the rough mix back. He grinned. "That's a wiener," he said.

Dartt just glowered.

They continued, Glenroy and Doug idling the time away in the booth until it was time for Glenroy to sing, while Grube increasingly had to take on the task of keeping up the pace. It was their last day, after all; Dartt might otherwise have worked on the songs into eternity, asking for punches, more grease, doing phrases, sections, verses over, growing all the while increasingly dissatisfied. Luckily he kept his voice, and somehow the tracks went down. At about one a.m. they had a wrap. Nine songs—four of them his.

Grube laid out the coming schedule—a week off, then a weekend gig in Raleigh.

They were tired of each other and needed some distance.

Glenroy stepped into the spring evening like a returning time traveler. He hadn't been to the lake for a week, and now, feeling the cool night air on his face—something good behind him, something good to go to—he had a sad premonition.

He knew it would never be this good again.

——

When he woke up a little before noon he found himself alone in the bed, with a bright May morning waiting outside. A breeze blew through the open house, billowing the curtains just beside him.

As he came into the den he didn't see her, nor was she on the porch. He stood by the swing, gazing over the yard to the lagoon and waterfront beyond. The scent of honeysuckle filled the air and the woods rang with birds. But no sign of Rainy. Suddenly a hummingbird darted into view under the porch eaves, visiting a red feeder hanging precariously there now. He smiled to himself.

Back inside he paused, surveying the room. There seemed to be candles everywhere now, and thumbtacked on the wall in a few places pale watercolors of the woods, the lake, things in bloom. He walked over to have a closer look at a couple of them and they struck him as faint but rather good. He ran the tap water to maximum hot, made some instant coffee, went back out to the porch and sat down.

Forty-five idle minutes passed before he saw her, carrying something and picking her way along the path on the far side of the slough. She obviously wasn't aware of him, and he realized that he'd never seen her like this, unguarded, from a distance, before. He watched her.

She might have been a perfect stranger, a random person moving in a world he knew nothing about. Oddly, she didn't match the person who lived a ghostly life in his mind; she looked heavier, the proportions different. He looked away, until she had come around the junky back of the slough into the yard, and then called her name.

She started, seemed for an awkward second to want to hide her things, then continued up the steps, across the porch. The closer she came, the less alien she seemed.

"How you been?" he asked.

"Okay."

"It's pretty, isn't it?"

She nodded.

"What you been doing?"

"Nothing."

"Aw, come on. You don't have to be shy. I'd like to see what you're doing."

She shook her head, frowning. "No."

"I saw the ones inside," he said.

"They're not any good."

"I thought they were."

"They're not."

She passed by him with her sketchpad and paint and went inside. He sat down again and in a moment she returned, empty-handed.

"I like it," he said. "I wish you'd let me look."

"Not now."

"Everything going okay?"

211

She nodded.

"We made a record."

"Good."

"I think it's pretty good. I want you to hear it."

"I'd like to."

He reflected back over the experience. "God, it was great."

"I'm glad," she said.

"I love that place. I'm going back Tuesday when the guy does the final mix. You can come if you want to."

"Yeah, maybe."

"And guess what?" he added.

She raised her eyebrows.

"We're playing in the Auditorium in November. Can you believe it?"

"That's good," she said.

"And listen, I want you to be there, okay? I really mean it— for this one. I want you to be there."

She nodded.

"Do you promise?"

"Um uh."

"Have you eaten?" he asked.

"Not really. I'm not very hungry," she answered with a little frown.

"It doesn't look like there's much here."

"There's not."

"You want to ride and get something?"

"We could."

"I wish you'd let me see what you've been drawing."

"I will later. It's not any good. That girl came."

"What girl?"

"The one that took all the pictures. She got all the rest of them and said she was going to Texas."

Glenroy squinted his eyes. "Moon Tuna?"

"I don't know. I felt sorry for her."

"Ah, she'll get over it."

"It's pretty weird me being here, isn't it?"

"What do you mean?"

"Me staying here."

"It's not weird. I don't know what you're talking about."

She made an odd face, but didn't say anything.

———

Excalibur Records.

That summer, through the southeast, thundered with "Jeez Louise." It preceded them wherever they went and they stayed constantly on the road. The venues grew bigger—concerts, outdoor festivals—and always an audience waited for them. Dartt still traveled separately and had his own ways. Usually the tall girl lurked somewhere, but now and then others took her place. The flip side, "Come When I Do," went nowhere, and Dartt relentlessly nagged Grube to promote it or one of his others, but without success. As for "Jeez Louise," they had yet to see any money from it, but as Grube explained, they had no idea the kind of expenses he had.

Doug and Glenroy fell into roughly the same routine—the gig, a couple of days with Alma/Rainy—then the next gig. Life became a film running too fast and the studio session fell into the past like a receding buoy.

Sometimes Glenroy, feeling himself dissolving in the blur, wanted to scream "stop!" but he knew better. He toked up early afternoon, started on his personal concoction about three, and had himself in the right state of mind by nine, though he was so used to it now it didn't seem like a state.

The more out of focus his life became, the better the music grew, and the more responsive the audience—though its devouring embrace felt more and more like a stranglehold. And as Dartt's songs failed to make it to the air and played like weak sisters in performance, something in his attitude festered, and that insane, resentment-laden tension that had always been their secret perverse cohesive force, grew even stronger.

From that voracious world to the placid, changeless lake, where the resident spirit seemed to haunt rather than live, he lived his pendulum life.

One day, as he drove along Highway 91, he realized that Labor Day had come and gone. The water had fallen, and everywhere the cabins looked locked and cold, boats covered in the yards or stored away, no curling smoke from barbeque grills, no children, no boaters, only the occasional solitary fisherman. That old sad song.

The Auditorium loomed just two months away—the promotion was well begun—but Dartt had long since been hammering at his own campaign. It wasn't argument because no one seemed to have the stomach for argument, only a struggle of visions: his, a show heavy on the Dartt, nothing instrumental vs. theirs, because he *was* outnumbered, a set of crowd-pleasers with a couple of their trademark jams. Dartt lost, stormed out a number of times from a number of places, but always came back—wounded and moody.

––––

The sensation—as though they had spent the preceding months just beyond the sandbar, thinking the water deep—was of the bottom suddenly dropping away.

From the wings the cavernous sold-out hall sent back a deep echo one felt in the stomach. The sensation of that many people exerted an almost unbearable pressure, like something physically weighing down upon one that one must hold up or be crushed. They had no parallel in their experience for this. Pure adrenalin flowed in their veins, and they glanced at each other, looking for something that could be found in themselves or nowhere. The first two bands had tilled up a good mood—and now, the restless audience throbbed with expectant energy. Grube pranced about in a white suit, flower in his lapel. Rainy, supposedly, was out there somewhere with Jimmie and Angela and a few of their crowd; she, or the idea of her, came and went in pulses through Glenroy's thoughts.

"Man, it's just like playing anywhere else," Doug said. "Same thing—just bigger."

He might have been standing on a street corner, waiting for a light to change, he looked so unflappable. *The guy you'd want in the foxhole with you*, Glenroy thought.

As for Dartt, he seemed on the threshold of the trip of his life, and catching his fiendish eye Glenroy knew he'd be all right. *Got to worry about me*, he thought, knowing they had to do more than just get through it. Way more.

As they came out onto the low-lit stage, the crowd sensed their presence and the electricity in the arena went up a level. Glenroy felt a surge within himself in response; he looked around and Doug and Dartt seemed so separate and far away they were like three frogs on lily pads. Then Dartt smiled, and all at once the oppressive feeling became the sensation of energy flooding into him from out *there*.

They're here because they like you. They want you to be good.

From the introduction, the rising of the lights, the roar that came upon them like a heroin rush, time began to accelerate. The first few seconds of "Jeez Louise" were panicky—they couldn't hear, the parts seemed to wallow separately—then they fell together, comprehending at once the new, alien dynamics. And the second they saw they could do it, the fear vanished. They got better with every song. Finally, in a climactic rush as though no time had passed, they reached the end.

It all seemed like something that had taken place in a capsule.

The rush, backstage, was overwhelming. They waited, listening to the feet rocking the bleachers, looking in amazement at each other. Dartt said, "'That's Just Who I Am.'"

Glenroy's expression changed. "I thought we said 'Mother Roach.'"

"'Mother Roach,'" said Grube.

Dartt looked straight ahead. "I'm playing 'That's Just Who I Am.' You can play whatever you want to."

He wasn't kidding. They returned to a swelling roar, and he didn't let the noise abate before he plunged into the opening—and they had no choice, they plunged with him. The audience grew quiet.

Doug didn't plan it, any more than he ever had. But a moment came—and he could no more resist the moment than he could resist breathing. He socked the song with a million volts. Now it was Dartt who had no choice.

The crowd surged to its feet like a force of nature. When the final drum solo came, they roared and whistled and cheered, until the band released them with a dramatic ending. The bleachers rocked.

"Should we go back?" Glenroy asked backstage.

"No," said Grube, shaking his head. "Leave them just like that."

Not that they had a choice. Dartt had already stormed away.

———

It took Jimmie thirty minutes to talk his way backstage, even though everything had been supposedly arranged.

A throng surrounded Glenroy—everybody wanted something of whatever it was he had. They pressed themselves on him like relentless aunts, and he endured it, still rushing. A bar and buffet table stood across the room and Grube slid among the crowd like a politician.

She looked excruciatingly out of place, like a bad bruise, and shrank mousily into a chair along the wall beside upright, purse-holding Angela. Glenroy would catch her eye, but she would look away. She didn't eat or drink. It took him ten minutes to work his way to her. He offered to bring her something; she didn't want it. She wanted only to leave. He could almost smell the panic.

Then at last Jimmie, who kept running into people he knew, reached him.

Big hug. "God almighty—I don't know if the world can *handle* you, man." Then the wave took him away.

Glenroy had imagined the moment otherwise, never envisioned it as an experience alone. The sight, the feeling of her oppressed his spirit. No part of it—nothing to take or give. Nothing to say. A cornered rat. People continued to approach and recede, and then he looked over and saw them making their way out. Jimmie stopped by.

"Come on over when you get done here," he said. "We'll be partying."

Glenroy nodded.

He didn't even try to catch her eye; he turned his back to the hole where they bled away and began to drink.

When Doug and Alma left he felt completely alone and then realized how the crowd had dwindled. No sign of Grube even. The old, old inevitable moment was hunting him down.

Precisely then he became aware of her. He had already seen her, even talked to her briefly, but now, being among the things remaining she was more conspicuous. And she was looking at him, had been looking at him, with a look he understood. She had a friend—they were standing together—but it wasn't the friend, it was her.

He walked over.

———

He didn't realize until he got outside how drunk he was, yet he felt at the same time the sobering effect of the cold November night.

"I've got a car," she said. The friend had evaporated.

They drove and he wanted to slide his hands under her clothes. He pressed against her and tried clumsily to nuzzle her neck, running his hands along her legs.

"I'm going to have a wreck," she laughed.

He hardly knew where she took him. Some shady block in Little Five Points, a big house. Some people sat around downstairs talking and drinking. "It's a Beautiful Day" played on the stereo, and the smell of cannabis threatened to make him sick, but the feeling passed as she led him to a room up the cold stairs. As soon as she closed the door he came after her. Laughing, she pushed him away and lit candles and incense and put on some music. He waited, gazing vacantly around the room at the posters on the walls, books on a homemade shelf, a big mattress on the floor.

"When did you first learn to play guitar?" she asked.

"Last week," he answered, and pulled her down onto the mattress.

———

He awoke with a headache, and a burning need to piss. He got up and couldn't see her well, huddled on the far side of the mattress. She didn't stir at his movement and re-snuggle herself, as Rainy would have. He couldn't remember exactly what she looked like, but felt a strange revulsion. Dull light filtered through the tall, half-covered windows. Very early morning. He pulled on his pants and went to find a bathroom.

When he came back the room felt alien and cold. He put on the rest of his clothes and stole out of the room. No one appeared awake anywhere in the chilly house. Downstairs a big dog sleeping on a rug looked up cautiously but seemed used to strangers. Somebody snored on the couch, maybe two people. Beer, Boone's Farm bottles on the table. Hash pipe in the ashtray.

Something about the gloominess of the November morning, among people who didn't concern him, gave him an odd sense of relief. *I need a BC,* he thought, *and something to drink, and I'll be all right.* He started walking. Rainy permeated his thoughts like an injury. After only a couple of blocks a guy in a van pulled over and asked him if he needed a ride.

Sheer luck. One, the guy didn't recognize him, and two, he was headed across town, by the Auditorium, to work. Not until Glenroy directed him to the woeful Valiant huddled in the back shadows of the building did he ask any questions.

"My band played here last night," Glenroy explained, though he could hardly reconcile the memory with the impervious facade of the silent building.

"No kidding?"

"I got sidetracked. Thanks for the lift, man."

The act of getting into the cold car, again, was curiously reassuring—just him, a familiar sensation, a simple act stretching back through the years.

He had the heater blowing by the time he found a Seven-Eleven. He got a Big Orange and some BC's and headed out of town. The morning had advanced by then into something humid, overcast, not much warmer, and altogether dull. He felt very tired, as though those few hours of sleep in that strange bed hadn't happened at all. Gradually, as he drove, his headache eased, while his heart thumped from the caffeine in the powder.

As he came over the ridge it suddenly hit home: she's not here, she spent the night at Jimmie's. The place looked barren and lonely and frigid. Inside, he lit the heater and got into the icy bed. He drifted away to a familiar scent and didn't want to see the world for a long time.

——

When he woke up, sometime mid-afternoon, it was raining. Thunder rumbled gently and he could hear the rain tapping on the roof and splattering off the eaves into puddles just behind his head. He lingered in bed, finally got up, and looked for something to drink, but there wasn't anything so he drank a glass of tap water, then went to stand at the front windows and gaze upon the hopeless day. He thought of building a fire, but the wood would be wet and the exertion seemed overwhelming. He needed something to eat, to drink, but the red-clay roads would be muddy. So he just sat down and did nothing as the old, old day dripped all around him.

Feels like it's raining all over the world.

————

The pace, already mad, now doubled. "Mother Roach" took life on the radio. He began taking his first toke right after he woke up, sometimes without even getting out of bed, and started on the juice shortly after. He went down to the lake one Sunday afternoon in mid-December and Rainy had packed her few things. He had a moment of panic.

"I'm going to see my mother," she said.

"For how long?" he asked, a surprising urgency in his voice.

"Just for a while."

"For Christmas?"

"Yeah."

"Then you're coming back?"

She shrugged. "Can you take me to the bus station?"

————

Christmas came and went, then New Years. January settled in like a toothache.

He didn't know how to get in touch with her. He started to understand what was happening, that she wouldn't be back, but he couldn't handle the thought and tried to drink and play it away—and the music got better.

It happened somewhere in South Carolina the first time. He took her back to the motel room and after he was done with her made her leave, pushed her whining out into the cold. The next weekend it happened again, then the next weekend. The taste of strange was strong—and it was easy; a certain type just flew to the light like moths.

"Man, you Mister Tomcat, ain't you?" said Doug one day. They sat listlessly in a Waffle House with a couple of hours to kill.

"Oh yeah," Glenroy replied.

"What you hear from your lady?"

Glenroy shook his head. "Nothing."

"She said she'd be back?"

"Yeah. Said it. So far she hasn't done it."

"She will—don't you think, man?"

Glenroy shrugged. "I wish I knew."

"Aw, she will."

"I don't know," Glenroy said.

Doug was studying him. "You want her to?"

"God," Glenroy laughed. "Yeah," he said. "Yeah, I want her to."

"She will, man."

He let out his breath. "But it's not like I didn't always know it."

"Know what?"

"That it would happen—sooner or later. Just a matter of time."

Doug watched him, listening.

"I always knew it. Just, you know—not *yet*."

"She got *inside* you, man."

"Yeah," Glenroy said. "I mean, she's got some stuff, now—some stuff to work out."

"Yeah," Doug said. "Who doesn't?"

"I'm just saying she does. And there's a lot of things I can't give her—I can't solve her problems. I can't even solve mine. But I know one thing—I'm not going to see one like her again."

"Aw man, there'll be other ones," said Doug.

"Not like her. I don't think. I'm just being honest."

"Y'all ever talk about getting married?"

"No."

"She ain't like Alma then."

"Getting married isn't the answer. That'd just ruin it."

"You're probably right."

"I am. It's like everything else. It comes along, then it's gone. You have it while it's here, then you don't."

"Like us?"

"Yeah—like us."

"How far you think we'll go?" Doug said.

"I don't know. What do you think?"

"I don't know, man. Looks like we might go a long way."

"Do you want to?" Glenroy asked.

Doug laughed. "I already know about the other, man. Might as well see what it's like."

"Shit, I already see what it's like. It's like everything else."

"Naw—it's different, man."

"Look at Elvis."

"That dude just need to go on a *diet*," Doug said.

Glenroy laughed.

"You think Grube can get us to the top?" asked Doug.

Glenroy scowled. "Deep down in my heart? No."

"You think he's fucking us over?"

"Probably, but I'm not smart enough to know how or what to do about it."

"Alma talking all the time about getting somebody else."

"Yeah, she doesn't trust him," said Glenroy. "Neither do I."

"He won't let her see the books," Doug said. "Alma says there *ain't* any books. He just putting that money in his pocket."

Glenroy frowned. "Well—he pays us."

"Yeah, but man, he don't give us shit. Think about that record—how many you think we sold?"

"I have no idea," Glenroy answered.

"They *still* out there buying it. Say it was ten or fifteen thousand, which ain't really that much. Dollar apiece, that's fifteen thousand dollars. What if it was fifty thousand? The studio time was about fifteen hundred dollars—Alma found that out—and it was, I don't know, maybe twenty-five cents apiece it cost to make them. Where the rest of it gone?"

"I don't think there's any way in hell it sold that many," Glenroy said.

"How come he ain't told us?"

"Because he's Grube. And because we haven't stopped long enough."

"That's another thing. And think about when we do an album. Think about all that work—it ain't him, it's us. He already got three or four songs he can use—think about it, man. We might sell a lot of records and I bet you we won't see a dime out of it."

"We need to make sure we sign something this time," Glenroy said.

"I'm telling you. And you better look into getting your brother's songs published."

"How do you do that?"

"I don't know. Talk to Alma."

"Does she talk about getting married, really?"

"All the time, man."

"You going to do it?"

Doug frowned and shook his head. "I don't know."

"Man, you're lucky. Got a good woman like that. Takes care of you. Ain't got to worry about all this skanky trash running around."

"Yeah, I know. I ain't saying she ain't a good lady. Just—sometimes she's *too* good."

"Aw, come on," Glenroy said.

Doug just shook his head. "Anyway, I can't think about it—seems like everything else going wrong."

"Like what?"

"Well, you know my mama's staying at my aunt's. You know about my mama," said Doug.

Glenroy nodded.

"Well, now they're saying my aunt got cancer."

"Cancer?"

"Yeah. Something happen to her, man, I don't know what I'm going to do."

"You mean about your mama."

"Yeah."

Glenroy was silent. "Something'll work out."

Doug gave a rueful laugh. "I'd like to know what it's going to be." He shook his head. "Man, if I didn't have this band..."

"I know."

"Feel like everything kind of closing in."

"Well, at least we've got Dartt—look at it like that."

"You a *big* help," said Doug.

———

One gray Monday afternoon, somewhere in January, he drove down to the lake and she was back. He didn't even wonder how she got there.

She was just standing in the room as he walked in, looking as though she wasn't sure what to do next.

"Rainy!" he cried. "Jesus, Rainy!" He rushed to her and held her like a lost child, found. "Rainy, Rainy." Tears welled in his eyes.

"The girl with nowhere to go," she said. "It could be the new sitcom."

"Don't say that."

He built a big fire and they drove up to Allred's. He enjoyed the uncomplicated act of buying food and drink. They came back and ate on the couch, hardly speaking. Mention of the missing month was forbidden.

The winter day died early. As she grew sleepy, the moment, the feeling, or something wasn't there, and after drifting away on the couch before the fire several times she went to bed. He stayed up a long time, watching the fire, his mind restless—but that one place, that wound, at least for now, relieved.

The girl with nowhere to go.

———

Their schedule remained relentless. In February they played twenty dates. Glenroy made it to the cabin three times, invariably finding a listless, bored, housebound, TV-watching Rainy mired in depression. He himself—the half of his life that bloomed into fiendish energy at nine o'clock increasingly at odds with the drab and self-absorbed other half—spiraled toward exhaustion.

Signs of the end of winter helped, but after a few spring-like feints, the late cold fronts of March dragged on tediously. Then finally, toward the end of the month, a long stretch of mild spring days set in, and they had a two-week stand at the Marathon Club. It felt like a vacation.

They set up on Thursday. Mid-afternoon, everyone was there, even Dartt, and for once they had plenty of time.

Boyd Ange had volunteered his services and was setting up his board. Glenroy sat with his guitar at one of the front tables, waiting for sound check, and turned at the clamor of an argument behind him. Boyd and Grube and someone he'd never seen before were having a discussion toward the back of the room.

"No way, man," from Boyd was about all he could make out. Then the other guy left.

"Who was that?" asked Dartt as Grube returned to the front.

"Ace Sanders," Grube replied.

"Ace Sanders? Shit, man. What did he want?"

"He wants to work with you."

"Let's get him," Dartt said, excited.

"We've got an engineer; we don't need two," Grube replied.

"Yeah, but I've heard about him. Let's get him."

"Too many strings attached."

"What strings?"

"It's not your problem."

"What—money? Who cares?" Dartt said.

Grube gave a snide laugh.

Dartt laughed too. "I guess you're right. Why do we need anybody, the way we're going?"

Grube glared at him with contempt. Dartt glared back. "As a matter of fact—" Grube gestured to Glenroy and Doug—"I wanted to talk to you about that."

"What—the studio?" asked Dartt.

"Yes, the studio. I've just about got it worked out with David..."

"Oh God, I've heard this before."

"Why don't you keep your pissy little comments to yourself? You're going back to Tomorrow Studio at the end of next month to record an album. We're looking at several possibilities with the label."

"We need a major label," Dartt said.

"Possibly. I've communicated with every one of them. I can't say I'm all that crazy about their terms. There's nothing wrong with the label we've started."

"Except we'll never get anywhere with it."

"I'd say you're getting somewhere just fine."

"Oh yeah."

"Anyway, it's not true, it's been done plenty of times. And it's not your problem."

Dartt laughed. "Oh no. Our career, our future is not our problem. When are we supposed to have this record anyway?"

"Early summer. Then, if...everything goes all right, you'll be the top act at a festival in Piedmont Park on Labor Day. And don't say no shit, because it is no shit."

"No shit. I say we get Ace. This is no time to be cheap," Dartt persisted.

"We don't need Ace," Glenroy cut in. "We've already got somebody as good or better—there's nothing cheap about it. We'll stick with what we've got." Boyd, a few yards away, didn't look like he was, but he was, listening.

"Oh, is that right?" Dartt countered. "What the fuck happened to what's best for the band?"

"He *is* what's best for the band," Glenroy shot back. "We're using him."

"Whoa. Listen to Mr. Big Dick..."

"Would you fucking stop it?" cried Grube. "Do you want to make a goddamn album or not?"

"Yeah, I want to make a goddamn album," Dartt said, "and I know exactly the goddamn album I want to make."

"I just want to stop playing every night," said Glenroy.

"Tell you what—sell a half million records and we'll make some adjustments," Grube replied.

"What'll happen if we do?" Glenroy asked.

"What do you mean?" Grube returned, glaring at him.

"I mean how much money will we get if we sell half a million records?"

"A lot."

"I want to see it in writing."

"Oh, you want to see it in writing. See *what* in writing? How about this? You put up the fucking money, you work out all the shit, and do all the promotion, and keep you guys from pulling knives on each other, and keep this act together and out there playing, and then you can do whatever the fuck you want to, okay?"

"What are you doing with all our money?" Glenroy demanded.

"All your money? What fucking money? Do I pay you or not? You don't have any idea of the expenses in this business. No conception. You want to run the show yourself, you're welcome to it. It's yours. Just say the word. But as long as I'm running it, you're working for *me*."

He turned, walked a few steps, stopped. His face burned redly. "Just remember you wouldn't be jack-shit without me. *Remember* that." He stalked away.

"Somebody needs to put a fist through his face," said Dartt.

"Somebody will," said Glenroy.

"I tell you one thing," Dartt went on, "I'm not going to fight over the fucking engineer, but I *am* going to have some control over this record, or I'm through. This bullshit is getting on my nerves."

He made his own indignant exit.

Glenroy didn't move. He had a feeling almost like physical pain.

Boyd ventured a little nervous laugh. "He doesn't give up, does he?"

"Never."

Alma appeared. "Y'all need to get *away* from that man."

―――

Glenroy woke up about noon on Sunday and lay in bed for a long time. His cousin was on a trip; he had the house to himself. He remembered that he had four days to do nothing and the thought was like finding a dropped pillow in the night. Light speared the cracks around the window shades and he could hear birds outside: a decent day, the sort to take one's time, yet something troubled him. He lay searching through his thoughts, but couldn't find the source. Habit assumed a drive to the lake, but he pushed the idea away with a private scowl. He pushed everything away, in fact, and lingering there in bed came to realize that his uneasiness was not a feeling—rather, no longer a feeling—but a tune.

Melancholy and minor, moving, familiar, nagging like a jingle, the ghostly sliver of music haunted his mind, and he tried for a while to puzzle it out. Louis's maybe? No. Then what? He couldn't remember. At last, in frustration, he commanded it to leave his mind.

Like trying to make a smell go away.

It grew stronger, adding parts to itself as one reconstructs a memory. He wished he had someone to ask, though he wasn't sure what he would ask; when he tried to hum it he couldn't exactly. He reached, again and again, the same point where something spooky and indeterminate lurked. It teased like a riddle—what *was* that? As he showered, got dressed, and found himself on the highway mid-afternoon, it still played through his head. At times it seemed indistinguishable from the early spring afternoon itself: the rolling fields, the gray woods pocked with redbuds like pink shell-bursts, a pecan orchard skeletal over the last of the daffodils, a flock of blackbirds rising instantaneously like a million souls as he passed, the houses, random, peaceful, the drab yards splattered with forsythia, some people mowing already, the air rich with the oniony smell of new-mown grass, a single plum tree by a mailbox in full white bloom with a presiding cardinal; and then at other times the fragmentary air returned like a guilty thought, elusive and maddening. He wanted his guitar.

The first thing he saw as he slowed for the turn at Allred's was an obese woman in a tutu-style bathing suit atop one of the trailers, sweeping; the second was a car parked out front that looked both out of place and familiar. He hadn't planned to stop, but did, and as he walked toward the store he met Angela coming out.

"Have you seen Jimmie?" she asked.

He shook his head. "You mean lately..."

"Today."

He shook his head again, mystified.

She was pissed off and didn't even try to hide it. She screeched away spraying gravel; he didn't go inside but returned to his car and drove to the cabin, uneasy.

At least it never changed—always the same remote, impervious, shabby, placid place. The windows and doors stood wide open and the warm afternoon infiltrated the cool rooms. Several vases, standing in little puddles of fallen blooms, spilled out jasmine vines or withering daffodils. He couldn't feel her and assumed, relieved, that she was absent, then had a jolt as she appeared in the bedroom door.

He just pressed his lips tightly together in a sort of greeting. She didn't say anything.

"What you doing?" he asked.

"Nothing."

He nodded. "It looks like it."

She didn't meet his eye. Her expression betrayed the damaged child, but he didn't see it. He turned and went into the kitchen. She slipped out and a few minutes later he saw her disappearing along the waterfront path.

He wasn't worrying too much about anybody's feelings, he just wanted to think. In his mind played the image of his arms pushing the world away from him, opening up some space. He got his acoustic guitar and sat down on the porch. He lit a fat half-joint he had left in the can, guzzled some of his juice, and gazed for a while over the timeworn scene, like a painting. The tune, which had never really left, was back, and as he began trying to lure the mysterious chords from his guitar, he at last understood that he couldn't hear it all because it wasn't made yet, though it was old, came from precisely here, and was his.

I guess I made up it, he thought.

Or was making it up. His heart beat faster as he discovered the chords and the new parts found their places, rushing at him now, his only anxiety that he couldn't keep up. He finished each segment, devised a hasty bridge, then did the next. He was completely absorbed, had no consciousness of himself. Twenty intense minutes passed. It was done.

He could hear the band in his head, and the mad thought of driving back to Atlanta this very moment flashed through him—but no, of course it must wait. He went back to the beginning, played it through. Then again. Then a third time, fixing it forever. He relaxed, took a few more tokes, swigged his juice, and thought about it. Then he played it again.

When he finished he thought, *damn, that's pretty.* And sadness overwhelmed him.

He thought of her, hurt. Her dark eyes, still mysterious, incurably lonely—her long eyelashes, those absurd glasses, her coma-like sleeping habits, the dreamy mornings when he awoke beside her—her dark wit, a window into an intelligence he still couldn't fathom. He remembered the first night, long ago, laughing at people—her ridiculous eating habits, her television addiction—the glossy garden photographs she cut from magazines and taped on the walls, reminding him of his mother's heaven prints—her pale watercolors, her diffidence—her bargain-basement clothes, her lone toothbrush in the bathroom, and her pale green Tupperware cup—the way she took the money he left and put the change back like some odd little night animal—the comfortable feeling of sitting beside her in silence for an hour or two—their easy lovemaking—and her walks, like now, out there alone—but wasn't she always alone?—thinking, feeling, remembering, hoping God only knew what—like a stranger, like a fleeced lamb. All of her. Tears scalded his eyes.

She was a song now.

Lake Moon

"Yeah, that's nice," Doug said, narrowing his eyes, listening somewhere. Around them the familiar atmosphere of the Marathon Club enclosed them like home.

"I don't know—I was thinking something like this," he said, and started an unexpected rhythm. Glenroy listened back, scowling, then tried to lay his melody on it. For a few minutes it refused to work, until groping toward each other in the dark they stumbled right into it. A jolt passed through Glenroy and his expression relaxed.

When Dartt arrived carrying his instrument, Glenroy might have been fourteen: the old surge in the stomach of the bass player walking through the door. Dartt crossed the room listening, a bemused smile on his face, and unpacked his bass, which came gleaming and dangerous out of the case like a cobra. He strapped it on and plugged in with an electronic rasp, turned to them moving his head with the rhythm, then let himself in. Suddenly it had a bottom. A soul. *Music.*

Laughter.

The mood was broken by Alma, who came from the office carrying a file and wearing an expression like she smelled something.

"Hey, boss," said Dartt, "What's up?"

"Y'all listen to me, now. I'm supposed to bring these to you, but I want you to really think about it, you promise me you will?"

"What is it?" said Glenroy.

"Contracts."

"For what?"

"For your record."

"What record—the album?"

Alma nodded.

"He's got a contract?" She nodded again. "The little bastard put something in writing?"

"Yeah, but you better think twice about what that something is," she warned.

"Tell us," said Glenroy.

She exhaled. "He wants to give y'all each a thousand dollars." They looked at her, waiting.

"A thousand dollars each?" Glenroy repeated.

"You understand what I'm saying? Just that. Period."

They glanced uncertainly at each other, feeling possibly affronted but not sure how.

"And royalties," said Glenroy.

Alma shook her head. "It don't say nothing about no royalties."

He frowned, taken aback. "He can't do that, can he?"

"He can do whatever he can get you to sign."

"Yeah, what if it sells a million copies?"

"Then I guess for three thousand dollars you made him a millionaire. And I can tell you exactly what he'll say: what if it don't."

"No way I'm signing that," Glenroy declared.

Dartt frowned, thinking, and said nothing.

Doug shook his head. "Uh uh," he said.

———

This called for Grube himself, whose effort at composure cost him in blood pressure and raised the pitch of his voice one full step, who came across the room with the same file a few moments later. He slapped it down onto a front table.

"Okay, here's what's going to happen," he said with a little quiver.

They looked at him, Glenroy and Dartt standing there, Doug sitting—off balance, in silence.

"Of course there will be no record, that goes without saying, but not just that—all bets are off. Everything. You'll need to pack up this equipment and get it out of here right now so I can get some entertainment in here. Forget Piedmont Park and don't expect to get within ten miles of any studio once…"

"Whoa," said Glenroy. "Wait a minute. Hold it. This is bullshit. It's a rip-off. You're saying we don't even get a percentage—what kind of shit is that?"

"I'm saying, here's the deal I'm offering you, take it or leave it." He exhaled and shook his head as though to the gods. "All this time, you *still* don't get it. The *risk*," he said, drawing out the word, "is *all* mine. All you're doing is playing a few songs. I've got to rent the studio, pay the engineer, have the records pressed, pay an artist, pay *you*, pay the distributor, pay off all the station managers. A band with one local hit doing their first album? That might sell five thousand copies and might sell ten?"

"Or half a million," Glenroy said.

Grube shrugged. "It's possible. Anything's possible in this world. I mean, Tiny Tim sells a million records, right? It could happen. That's why I'm willing to take the risk."

Glenroy gave a sardonic laugh. "You talk like we're nothing, we're unknown, which is not the case and you fucking know it."

"I know you *think* that. You *think* a lot of things. But I'm not dealing with what anybody *thinks*, I'm dealing with reality, okay? It doesn't matter to me what you do—I can find another band—but whatever it is, decide pretty quick, all right? I've got a club to run."

He turned smartly—then that little walk of his, as he whisked himself away.

"He's bluffing," said Glenroy.

Dartt sighed, shook his head uncertainly. "I don't think he's bluffing about keeping us out of the studio."

"So what? We do it ourselves. Who's got the music—him or us?"

"I want to make an album," said Dartt.

"Yeah, we all do. Who says we have to have him?"

Dartt sighed and frowned. "I don't see anything else at the moment."

"So? We find something else. Look at us, man. We've got something going here. What the hell is he without us? He's got more to lose than we do."

Dartt shook his head. "I don't know." He looked around. "And not play here anymore?"

"Shit," said Glenroy. "There's all kind of places to play."

"It's just—we're on a roll. I hate to lose our momentum."

Glenroy groaned.

"You turn around in this business and you're yesterday," Dartt said.

"We haven't hardly gotten started yet," Glenroy countered.

"Yeah, but look—it's just one record, what the hell? I don't know about you, but I can use a thousand bucks."

"He'll probably take some of that we already did," said Doug. "Add a couple of things..."

"That's not the kind of record I want to make," Glenroy protested. "Our first album? Man, it needs to be *goddamn* good. I'm telling you, that's how the world decides what you are."

"Yeah, but he's going to end up fucking himself, can't you see that?" said Dartt. "Think about it. We need him right now—we're using *him*—but when we make it big, people like him will be coming from everywhere and we can dump him and take our pick."

Glenroy shook his head. "Man, we can't think about *then*—we've got to think about *now*."

"But look," Dartt persisted. "We'll have a *record*. In our hands. That's clout. That puts us in a position to call the shots. And it's just one record. I mean, let's keep things in perspective here. We'll probably knock it out in three or four days. A thousand bucks for three days' work? One record? How many records do you think we can make? Let's get out of this with something to show for it."

"I guess I'm not thinking about anything we might do—I'm thinking about *this* record," said Glenroy.

"So am I. Let's just do it and keep going."

Glenroy sighed and took off his guitar. The music was dead. He stood there indecisively. Doug got to his feet, Dartt unstrapped his bass, and they dispersed. Alma, arms crossed, tarried in the shadows of the back corridor.

"Y'all making a mistake," she said.

———

Some instinct kept Grube out of the way and Boyd approached the project like a moon mission. The musicians eased from the warm May afternoon through the cool portal once more, though this time the charm required coaxing. The cluttered booth and padded rooms and booms and wires and all the amiable disarray of record-making met them like a woman out of make-up.

They dawdled setting up, then drifted into playing slowly, as Boyd scampered tirelessly back and forth. They passed a spiritless hour trying to become a band, fighting the wind that carried them, before the energy came back. It always did. As they gathered around the board listening, it started in the nerves and spread. The universe had contracted to here. Their laughter rang with relief and anticipation.

"I want to start with 'Do Like Me,'" said Boyd.

Dartt rocked his head back as though from a blow. "Why?"

"For several reasons. It cooks, it's straightforward, and you always nail it. Get it right and it'll set the tone for the whole session."

Dartt laughed. "Are you trying to say it's simplistic?"

"I'm trying to say it's a good riff," Boyd replied.

Dartt laughed. "Here we go again. I repeat: why waste time if we're not going to use it?"

"Who says we're not going to use it?" returned Boyd.

"Aw, come on."

"We don't know what we're going to use yet."

Dartt stared at him. "Why not?"

"Because we don't know which tunes are going to work out best."

Dartt blew out his breath. "Whatever. Let's just do something."

After all, it was a fun song to play. Somewhere in the second take they got drawn into it—no way to resist the challenge: the attempt to perform not just a perfect, but the definitive rendition of a four-minute song. It took them until six o'clock.

They listened to the playback. Laughter.

Boyd called and ordered pizza then went next door for more beer.

"Any *theories* about what's going on this record?" Dartt asked.

Boyd smiled. "Some—yes."

"For instance?"

"You mean my idea or..."

"What does *Grube* say? Wherever the hell he is," said Dartt.

"Well, he wasn't really clear," Boyd answered.

"Who's the producer?"

"Him."

"So he'll decide?"

"Well, yeah, but I see it more as a group decision," Boyd explained. "We do as many tracks as we can, see which ones work the best, see what fits together, make an album out of it."

Dartt laughed. "Are you in with him or something?"

"I'm not in anything with anybody. He's paying me just like he's paying you."

"Well, tell me this—why are we acting like amateurs?" He shook his head, laughing. "Is anybody listening?" he asked the ceiling.

"I wouldn't call it amateur—just casting a big net."

"Time," Dartt said abruptly, glaring at Boyd. "It wastes time. You decide what you're going to do and go after it."

"But this is so much fun," Boyd replied in good humor, "and you guys are so good, and it's *his* money. I hate to waste the opportunity."

"The opportunity..."

"To get as much as we can."

Dartt rolled his eyes. "Whatever."

"Anyway, we've already got five or six finished tracks—'Jeez Louise,' obviously. 'Mother Roach'—probably 'Lake Trash' at least." He skipped a beat. "And yours. We add that many, and take the best. Save something for your next one."

Glenroy grunted. "I wasn't really happy with what we did on 'Lake Trash'—what *I* did anyway."

"Okay, we can do it again," Boyd said. "Hell, we can do whatever we want."

"I want to do all of mine again," said Dartt.

Boyd looked at him.

"Well—what are you staring at? We do 'Lake Trash' again, we do mine again. I've got all kinds of new ideas."

Silence.

Dartt laughed. "God, some things never change." He shook his head. "I wonder," he said. "I mean, I just can't help but wonder sometimes. About the whole thing." He stood up and left the room. They heard a muffled door slam.

"Where's he going?" Boyd asked.

"Who knows," answered Glenroy.

"I guess he'll be back?"

"Hell yes, he'll be back."

They were quiet for a moment. "I don't guess you've ever given any thought to another bass player?"

Glenroy shook his head.

"Well, look, I want to tell you. I've been thinking a lot about this record. I can hear it—I can see it. I can see the cover—it's like I'm holding it in my hand. I'm not trying to tell you what to do, but I hope you'll..."

"Hey," Glenroy shrugged. "I'm wide open. I want to make the best record we can."

Boyd nodded appreciatively. "Of course we want 'Lake Trash'—which we can re-do," he said. "But I want that instrumental too. The new one."

A little surprised, Glenroy thought a moment. "You talking about for this record?"

"Absolutely."

"It's kind of long."

"Seven or eight minutes. Last cut on side B. Just what we want."

Glenroy laughed. "You planning to put a gun to his head, or what?"

"He'll play it," Boyd said, and smiled. "We'll just have to bribe him."

Glenroy snorted.

"It needs to be on there, I'm telling you," said Boyd.

———

An hour later Dartt came back and they worked until three-thirty. When they stopped, they had finished rhythm tracks for "Grapefruit" and "Come When I Do." They stepped from the studio into an early morning cool with the scent of privet blooms and honeysuckle and went their separate ways.

———

The next day picked up where the late night had ended.

The process had developed momentum now, consuming them. By midnight they had "Amy, Smile," a new "Lake Trash," and "When You Get to Know Me."

Still no Grube.

Glenroy drove across town blowing a fat roach, tired, anticipating the cool sheets, his heart mind and soul waiting for his body in tomorrow.

———

Boyd perched anxiously on his rolling chair. He could sense they were near the top of the curve.

"'Rainy?'" Dartt said, tasting the word disagreeably. "'Rainy?' Is this for real? That two-hour thing?"

"It's seven minutes," said Boyd.

"So now we're doing jam sessions? I didn't realize we were that desperate."

"It's not a jam session."

"Whatever you want to call it. I guess I don't get it. What's the point?" Dartt asked.

"The point? To make a record nobody else could make," Boyd returned.

240

"With filler?"

Boyd smiled. "It's not filler," he said.

"Oh."

"Like I said, we don't know what we're going to use. We agreed to do as many as we could."

"*You* agreed," Dartt protested.

"Well, this is the one I want to do today."

"I'm not sure I *can*."

"Why not?"

Dartt just laughed.

"Then we'll go on to some of the other tunes."

Dartt set his jaw. "I want to do 'You Can Go Now' first."

"I'd rather save it."

"No, let's do it first." Boyd just looked at him. "You expect me to shoot my wad trying to play some long jam I don't even know? We'll do mine first."

"It's okay," Glenroy inserted. "Let's do it first. It's a good song."

Dartt looked at him, gave a laugh, and comically put his hands to his ears. "What? Oh my God—Doctor, something's happened to my ears. I almost thought I heard him say it was a good song."

"Let's get rolling," said Glenroy.

It took hours. When they finished, they took a break, and then as night crept outside they sat in the main playing room while Glenroy took Dartt through the song he half knew.

The first time they tried to play it they made it to the first bridge and stopped. Then again, and again. Dartt kept faltering, dropping out.

"I screwed up, okay? How am I supposed to remember all this?" he complained.

Boyd sat in the booth, preoccupied, until he realized they were losing ground. All they had was a most unpromising chaotic blob. It was after one o'clock.

His voice came over their headphones, he killed the tape, and came out.

241

"Let's sleep on it," he said. "I know it's here—but I don't think it's here tonight."

Dartt snorted. No one argued. The room seemed to be closing in on them.

An entire day—one Dartt song. All Glenroy wanted was not to think.

———

The next afternoon they started out with a take so fresh the energy in the studio immediately trebled. Glenroy suddenly heard his leads complete, and Dartt, having dreamed some clever bass licks, didn't say anything, just played. There was some confusion with the ending; they worked on it a while, and Doug figured out his solo. Then they played it through several times, wringing it dry. It was timing out at just under seven minutes.

They took a break, came back, and knew this was the final take before they even started. Boyd begged the gods to let nothing happen.

They heard him—granting them seven minutes of pure absorption.

The final note died a long echoing death into the transformed silence, and Boyd, not breathing as he watched the falling VU meters, held up his hand, then gave them a thumbs up, thinking, *by God, if I die tomorrow at least I had this.*

They hardly spoke, almost embarrassed. Glenroy, feeling the oddest sensation of euphoria and depression he had ever felt, wanted a woman more than he ever had in his life.

———

For people to whom it mattered, it was late. He had killed his bottle and stopped for a refill even before he made it out of town, blowing that stupefying red Colombian so rich it oozed amber globules, which he dabbed onto his jeans. A three-man band playing live. Top to bottom, one take. The night city around him looked like something real, remembered.

He woke her up only because he needed her to be awake, then, spent, began snoring almost immediately, driving her out to find another bed.

————

The next day when he lurched awake, indeterminately in the afternoon, his head throbbed, and he felt her absence at once. Scenes of yesterday came back to him like a slide show and as he got to her he winced.

God, he thought, turned over and tried to find sleep again, unsuccessfully. When at last he rose and moved around he understood that she was not on the premises. He dressed, took some coffee to the porch, and after a while she came back, having been he couldn't imagine where.

"Hi," he said.

"Hi."

She didn't meet his eye, but went inside and he almost felt rather than heard the bedroom door close.

He waited a while, hoping she would come out but she didn't, so at last he went and stood in the middle of the room and said, "Hey, I'm heading back to the studio. I'll see you, maybe tomorrow—okay?"

But he heard no response.

————

Running late, he found them sitting around the control room, listening to the rough mixes. The claustrophobia he had felt as he walked in evaporated at the sound.

"Okay, we're almost there," said Boyd. "Let's do 'Moolah' today."

"I want to do 'That's Just Who I Am,'" Dartt objected.

"Let's save it for last," urged Boyd.

"Any particular reason?"

"Not really."

"You mean today?"

"Yeah, today. We get those done, I guess we're through. Start on the vocals."

Dartt laughed to himself.

"Moolah" went fast. They simply realized after the second full take that they couldn't play it any better.

Then came Dartt's song and he started animatedly explaining the many changes—a musical tour of his moods. They were just putting it together when, at last, Grube made his appearance. A woman with tinted glasses followed behind him. It was almost five o'clock.

"I want you to take a couple of hours for photographs," he said. "Down at the lake."

"The lake?" said Dartt, stunned. "We're in the middle of a song here."

"I'm sorry—I didn't know we were going to get Melinda today. And she's leaving town tomorrow. You can come back to it."

"We're working on *my* song—why am I not surprised?"

"You can come back to it," Grube repeated.

"Completely losing everything we've done and basically having to start all over, but why should that bother you? You obviously don't give much of a shit about any of this."

"I've been busy. I left you in good hands. I've been keeping up with you."

"Okay—maybe this is a crazy question—why the lake?"

"It's the concept," Boyd interjected. "Where you started, where you came from..."

"Spare me the concept, okay? It's a long way—right when we're in the middle of my song."

"It's not that far," said Grube. "And you're almost done, I understand. That's good. You've done a good job. We'll have a record by the end of June."

"Boy oh boy," said Dartt.

244

———

Somewhere in the second day of the vocals the sometime secretary slipped into the booth. Doug, slumped in a chair listlessly watching, looked up. Dartt's naked voice filled the room, his headphone-framed face, two windows away, intent.

"I'm sorry to bother you, but you've got a call," she said. She was looking at Doug.

He sat up quickly. "Who—me?"

She nodded.

"Who is it?"

"I don't know."

———

He had spent the day on the couch. When Alma came home after five, he hardly looked up. An FM jazz station was playing so quietly the music was barely distinct from the hum of the fan and the aloof, random sounds outside.

She didn't say anything but passed through the hallway to the kitchen. A few minutes later she returned and sat down with a glass of tea. He rolled his head over and barely parted his lips, as though faintly propelling some mute word of greeting across the heavy silence.

The ice clinked in her glass. The silence seemed permanent until she said, "looks like y'all be in Birmingham this weekend."

He turned his head to her. "He ain't said anything?"

"About what?"

"About—anything. About what we supposed to be doing."

She sighed and laughed together. "One day y'all gone understand about him. I don't know one-tenth of what that man got his hands in."

"He's supposed to be doing something for us."

"A lot of things *supposed* to be." She leaned her head back in her chair and closed her eyes for a moment. "He ain't even hardly thinking about y'all."

"Why not?"

"He's too busy hiding from half this town."

Doug shook his head, reflecting. "I believe that man's evil. Some kind of devil."

Alma snorted sarcastically. "*Evil.* He ain't nothing but a little man driving around in a silver car."

"*Evil,*" Doug repeated.

"Tss!" said Alma. "How much of evil is just people too lazy to do what's good?"

Doug kept silent.

"What *you* been doing all day?" she wanted to know.

He shrugged.

"You can't find nothing to do?"

He shook his head.

"No way to help out?"

"What you want me to do?" he flared.

She laughed. "If you even got to *ask* that…"

"How can I change anything?" he added angrily.

"I ain't talking about changing anything—I'm talking about taking care of things. I ain't never seen a man just roll over and not face his problems."

"You don't know nothing about my problems!" Doug passionately returned. "Something *on* me, something *been* on me."

"That just about make me want to scream when you say that," said Alma.

"It's true."

"It ain't true! People talking about something *on* them ain't but just a way to get out of doing what they got to do."

"You don't understand, Alma. You don't understand, and you ain't never *gone* understand."

246

"Ain't never gone understand what? Like you got the kind of troubles somebody else can't even understand? Like *I* don't know what it feels like to have troubles of my own?"

"I didn't say that."

"It ain't a matter of what you said, it's a matter of what you did—which as far as I can see ain't much."

He shook his head ruefully. "You don't understand."

"I understand your aunt died—who took care of the funeral? Some people in the church took in your mama—did her son lift a finger? And now it look like Kenny and Andrew going up to Cincinnati."

Doug looked at her, shocked.

"And who's been seeing about that?" she added.

"Cincinnati?"

"Yes, Cincinnati."

Doug let it sink in, then rolled his head over with a laugh. "So that's it—I ain't got nobody."

"What you mean you ain't got nobody? What am I?"

"I ain't talking about you—I'm talking about family."

"Your mama ain't dead."

"I know."

"And you act like I ain't nothing but something the dog drug in off the street."

"No, Alma. That's not what I mean at all. You ain't listening."

"It ain't like you ever *told* me," she said.

"That ain't what I'm talking about."

"You still ain't."

"Come on, Alma."

"Come on, what? I can't understand the way you act. Can't nobody tell *nothing* about you. You ought to at least take care of your own mother."

He sat up angrily. "And do what with her?"

"Get a house. Give her a room in it."

"A house? Where?"

"It don't matter where. You and me ought to *been* married by now and made a place for her. If you'd just open your eyes you'd see what you got: somebody love you, help you out with your problems, don't ask for nothing back except you just *show* you know what that means—but no, you just let it drift along and drift along, and I can't blame you when I'm fool enough to do it anyway even if it does make me feel about as low as a snake."

He groaned. "It ain't like that."

"No, it ain't. You're right."

"You just don't know what it *feels* like to me!" he spat.

"What *what* feels like?"

"To be nothing."

"Why you talk like that?"

"Because it's true. Don't even know where I came from. Can't even point to nothing or nobody and say that's what I am. People talking about their family going back all these generations—*shit.*"

"You ought to be ashamed talk that way about your mother," Alma scolded.

"And trying to be somebody, do something with this band. Good God." He laughed. "Can't even pay the rent, you talking about a *house.*"

"What I can't understand is why you put yourself down so low—*you* the one doing it. There ain't no telling how many million people would give everything they had to have your talent."

"*Talent,*" he sneered.

"Yes, and that's something can't nobody ever take away from you. Except yourself."

"Yes they can. They can close you off. Talent don't mean nothing. The only thing mean something is luck. Less you a nigger, then nothing don't mean nothing."

"Don't talk like that!"

"It's true and you know it."

"It ain't true—and I don't like that kind of talk."

"They don't even look at you—don't even see you."

"You ought to thank God for what you got."

"*God.* Now *you* the one talking about something ain't nothing but the way people give up."

Alma shook her head bitterly. "You worse than blind," she said, and went back out to the kitchen.

————

When Glenroy left the studio he knew he would get drunk. The place had constricted around them like a tomb, or an aborted stage set, the props hollow and fake—all imagination, all life, gone dead.

Dartt had already left, Doug shortly after him.

"I'm going to start right in on the mix," said Boyd.

Glenroy responded dispiritedly.

"I figured you'd want to be here."

"I'm just worn out," Glenroy said.

"You must trust me," Boyd replied with a laugh.

"I do." Glenroy gave him a pat on the shoulder.

"You okay?"

"Oh yeah."

Outside, he could breathe again—but the heat was astonishing. During their long sojourn in the cool underground summer had happened.

He was weaving, speeding up and slowing down, and knew it but didn't care. His thoughts skirted around a rotting animal that lay at the heart of him.

When he got to the cabin he heard the muffle of the television as he walked across the weary, junk-ridden porch, and something about the sound ragged his nerves. He came to the door and stepped inside and it was so hot he had the sense of not being able to breathe again.

Her expression, at seeing him, turned odd.

"Hey," he said.

"Hey."

"Watching a little TV?"

She nodded, barely.

"That's creative."

She just shrank into the place where she sat, the look on her face turning his blood cold.

"That's just sort of what you do, isn't it? I mean, I *guess*. What the fuck do I know? But no shit—what the hell do you *do* down here?"

She didn't say anything, looking away.

"Anyfuckingbody else would go crazy, sitting down here on the back side of nowhere staring at the walls watching The Price is Fucking Right. I mean, how do you stand it? Explain to me why you don't go out of your goddamn mind."

She had the look of a dog being beaten, but the rage wailed through him like a storm and he couldn't stop it.

"You don't have any money, except what I give you—do you? You don't buy anything but Slim Jims and goddamn Oreos. What do you *do* down here—you and the catfish and the kudzu?"

"I don't want your money!" she spat with sudden bitter passion.

And then, at the sound of her voice, he stopped. Even as he reached for the next thing to say, he had no words, no fuel—he was spent; and he saw the pain and contempt, the humiliation and shame on her face that was not her face now but her face then, and it was as though someone had reached a fist within him and squeezed.

He rolled his head back, closed his eyes. "Oh my God, Rainy," he said. "Baby, I'm drunk—I'm real drunk—do you understand? I'm just drunk and spouting off, that's all."

In her eyes there was nothing.

He sat down, deflated. He held his head in his hands, rocking it slowly, as little spasms of trembling passed through him.

"I don't even know what I'm saying—I'm drunk." He tried to look up at her, couldn't. He turned, looked out the front windows at the tired scene fixed there. "Rainy—it's not me talking. I'm just...fuck me—God knows, baby, I would give you everything I had if I had anything. I'm just drunk. I'm tired."

She hadn't moved, huddled in her hollow on the end of the couch, staring at the same point on the floor as the television droned irrelevantly on.

He closed his eyes again and his head swirled. He only half heard her get up, and when he looked she was going into the bedroom, closing the door behind her.

"Oh my God." He ran his hands through his hair, drunken tears scorching his face. "Oh my God."

———

The first time he became aware of the girl, he noticed her without seeing her, and the second time, he *saw* her: slender, elegantly frail, features sleepy and pretty, skin the color of coffee with cream, fawnlike, *young*, fixated on Doug. And now he had glimpsed her again, out there, haunting the edge of the stage in a sunhat. They sat in some kind of office, down a cool, carpeted corridor—back in Macon, waiting. Outside, around the pool in the August heat, sales personnel milled over buffet tables and two bars like insects on a log. A blue and white striped awning shaded the empty stage. Some guy made the rounds with a huge hat fastened to his shoulders and his beer-gut torso painted like a face.

Glenroy, gazing out the window, laughed. "The Hil-ton," he intoned. "This is class, isn't it?"

"Yes sir," said Doug. "Big, anyway."

"I like 'em big. What do you figure—it's a joke?"

"It's two hundred dollars," Doug shrugged.

"*Right.*"

"He'll pay us."

"Oh yeah. Maybe even last weekend too. Not to mention the records. Wait a minute—*what* fucking records?"

"They're coming," Doug said reassuringly.

"You really believe that?"

Doug gave a half-hearted nod. "Yeah—more or less."

Glenroy laughed. "How can you more or less believe it? Either there're going to be some records, or there're not."

"I believe the records are coming."

"You taking bets?"

Doug smiled.

"And where the hell's Dartt?"

A brisk man whose face no one would remember appeared in the door. "What's up, guys?"

"Waiting on the bass player," said Glenroy.

"Can you *find* him, please? You're already twenty minutes late. I've got four hundred people…"

"No," said Glenroy, "I can't *find* him. All I can do is wait on him."

The man tapped his watch, made a pissy face, and left.

Glenroy exhaled in frustration. "What the hell is going on?"

"Aw man," said Doug, "don't let it get to you."

"Sorry, but it's got to me. It's got way down to me. What are we doing here? Man, we played for five thousand screaming people."

"We will again."

"It doesn't make any sense."

"We just need to make some money right now—*I* do."

Glenroy looked around, scowling. "I already did this shit."

"Hey, me too, man. But when the records come out—we'll get something on the air again, do the Park—we'll get it back going."

"Drop Grube," said Glenroy.

"Yeah."

"Or kill him." Glenroy looked at Doug. "Let's kill him."

"Wouldn't hurt my feelings."

They fell silent. After a while Glenroy said, "How's your mother?"

"She's all right." He paused. "Staying with some people for a while."

"That's good," said Glenroy.

A brief silence. "Man, I tell you," Doug said. "Seems like you just look up one day and something you had is gone."

"Tell me about it."

"Why couldn't they have made it some other way?"

Glenroy shook his head.

"Man, my aunt—I never even talked to her. And when she died, man, it hit me. She was the only one I could have talked to. Ain't nobody else."

"Talked to her about what?"

"I don't know. Everything," said Doug.

"It's always like that," Glenroy observed.

"And this band, like you said—it's going to be the same thing. Sooner or later."

"Hey, you were just the one saying we'd get it going again," Glenroy said, turning to him with a laugh.

"Yeah—I mean, I believe that. We will. We'll get it going again."

Glenroy just laughed.

"Naw, man—I do believe it. It's just," he paused, "it ain't like this is the *only* band we could have."

"I know that," said Glenroy. "I guess there's just a part of me that keeps hanging onto it."

"Yeah—" Doug shook his head. "Ain't like no other band in the world, I'll say that."

"That's true—you know it?" Glenroy shook his head. "Goddamn."

"Feels like I've been dreaming the whole thing, man."

"I know what you mean."

"What about *your* mother—you get to see her much?" Doug asked.

"Yeah, but not if you ask her. She stays mad at me about half the time," Glenroy replied.

"Not really."

"No, not really."

"At least she can take care of herself." Doug sighed. "I'm going to have to do something, I just don't know what."

"What about Alma?" asked Glenroy.

"I don't know—Alma—I can't seem to do nothing right with her."

Glenroy, with a little smile, looked at him. "What's her name?"

Doug cut his eyes, met his gaze briefly.

"Come on, man, you know I'm bound to notice," Glenroy said. "It's none of my business—I was just asking."

Doug's expression changed. "Tawana. She's..."

"You don't have to tell me anything. I can't say a word. I was just thinking about Alma."

"Yeah—Alma—I know."

"There's Dartt," Glenroy said, looking out the window. "You ready?"

Doug nodded; they stood up. Doug shook his head. "Man, I don't know what to say."

"You don't have to say anything."

Their eyes met. They embraced.

"Man, it's just one long string of shit, isn't it?"

———

At the break—they had played forty-five minutes to an oblivious audience—Dartt seemed surprised. "Three sets?"

"Supposed to go to seven-thirty," said Glenroy.

"I can't go to seven-thirty," Dartt returned.

"Why not?"

"Because I don't have time."

"You seem kind of short on that."

"Well—I am," Dartt said.

"What's more important than the gig?"

Dartt considered briefly. "Okay—I guess I might as well tell you. I don't really think it has anything to do with whatever's going on with us, but I've been sitting in some with Streetcar."

"Streetcar?"

"Yes. Streetcar."

"What are you talking about? You're already in a band," said Glenroy.

"Like I said, it won't affect what we're doing."

"The hell it won't—it's affecting it right now."

"Look, I'm not going to argue about it—I'm just telling you, that's all. Right now, I'm going to scarf up some of this free food."

At seven o'clock, he announced, "Thank you, ladies and gentlemen—we've enjoyed playing for you this afternoon. Hope you enjoy the rest of the evening. Bye, bye."

And ten minutes later, some new girl in his shadow, he took off.

———

Three stiff screwdrivers in about as many minutes—Glenroy made his way back down the carpeted corridor to the office.

The phone rang fourteen times. He had already decided to let it ring indefinitely. The voice surprised him.

"Where's Alma?" he demanded.

"Why's that your business?" answered Grube.

"I'm just asking where she is."

"She doesn't work here anymore."

Pause. "What do you mean?"

"I can't put it any clearer. She's not employed here any longer," Grube said.

Another pause. "Why not?"

"Look, I hire and fire my own niggers, okay?"

"You little son of a bitch."

Silence. "What do you want?"

"What do I want? I want to know what in the fuck's going on," Glenroy said, anger boiling in his voice.

"In reference to…"

"In reference to fucking everything! In the first place, the guy you sent doesn't know a damn thing about sound."

"He's supposed to."

"No shit. The point is, he doesn't. We sound really bad."

"Maybe you're playing really bad."

Glenroy controlled himself. "No. We're playing really good—like we always do."

"Well, what do you want me to do about it now?" Grube spat.

"Forget it, it's too late. And in the second place, we're not even remotely the kind of band for this gig."

"It's the best I could do right now."

"What the fuck's *happened?* We ought to be playing—I don't know, stadiums or something."

"Look, I told you it's the best I can do!" Grube responded, almost hysterically. "I really don't need this right now. I've got shit coming at me from about a hundred different directions."

"We're right there, goddamnit, and we're fucking up."

"I'm doing the best I can!" Grube screamed.

Glenroy pressed on. "And where are the albums?"

"Why don't you let me worry about that?"

"Because *I'm* worried about it. You said we'd have them in June. It's August."

"I know what month it is."

"We're supposed to play at the park in a month, right?"

"That's correct."

"People listening to the record all summer—wasn't that the plan?"

"How much good do you think this is doing?"

"I'm asking you where the damn records are."

"They're *delayed*, okay? It's something I don't have any control over…"

"Will we even have them in time for the Park?"

"Should," said Grube.

"And what is this shit with Dartt?"

Pause. "What shit with Dartt?"

"Playing with Streetcar."

Pause. "I don't know anything about that."

"He left. We didn't even finish the gig. Said he was playing with Streetcar."

Pause. "I don't have any control over what he does in his spare time."

"Spare time? I'm telling you, he basically walked out. What kind of crap is this? He's *in* a band. He's in *this* band."

"Look, if he wants to sit in with somebody else…"

"Sit in with somebody else—what the fuck? We're on the brink, man! How can he be in another band too?"

The brisk, frowning man appeared.

"I've got too much shit coming at me right now!" cried Grube. "He said he could do both. I'll talk to him."

"Yeah, do that." Glenroy hung up.

"That's it? You're through?" said the man incredulously.

"Looks like it."

"Well, we did not get what we paid for." He glared. "I'll give you some advice, friend. If this is how you do business, you won't do business long." He gave a weird little laugh. "All this I *heard*—I don't know, I guess I was expecting something…"

"Oh, fuck off."

Glenroy stopped at one of the bars outside and talked the bartender, Jarvis, into making him up a big plastic cup, half and half, for the road.

"You be careful," said Jarvis with a laugh.

Heading for his car, he caught a glimpse of Doug and the girl, snuggled beside him, as they turned from the parking lot into the street.

———

Something held him in its grip, squeezing. He had a panicky sense of suffocation. His emotions, enflamed by the alcohol, alternated between pain and anger—sad one moment, venomous the next, as the malignant amorphous forces of his life became faces.

He headed straight up I-75 for Atlanta.

———

As he entered the Marathon Club in the summer dusk a couple of guys from the band were doing a final sound check. They stopped and looked at him, but he didn't look back as he crossed the broad floor and marched straight to Grube's office.

He threw open the door, which rocked the flimsy paneled walls of the room. Grube, talking shrilly on the phone, froze. He stared at Glenroy, then recovered. "Just a minute," he said, and covered the mouthpiece. "Do you mind? If you'll wait outside I'll be with you in a few minutes."

"I'm not going anywhere," said Glenroy.

"I'll call you back." He hung up. "Now listen," he said at once, "don't start with me—I'm telling you I don't need any more shit. I've told you I'm doing the best I can with everything. I'm working on it." He looked at him. "You're drunk."

"Yeah I'm drunk. Did you talk to Dartt?"

"No, I have not talked to Dartt yet."

"When are you going to talk to him?"

"As soon as I can."

"What are you going to tell him?"

"What do you want me to tell him? The Trio's his first priority—he already knows that."

"Get him out of Streetcar."

"He's not *in* Streetcar. And I already told you, I can't control what the guy does every minute of his life. I can't control what *you* do every minute of *your* life."

"I need some money," Glenroy said.

"You'll get it."

"I need it now."

"I don't have it now."

"Look, I'm broke. I've been broke. I've got to have some money."

"You'll get it. It's just—cash flow right now," Grube explained.

"What am I supposed to do?"

"Hold out a little longer."

"And eat what? Put gas in my car how?"

"I need you to get off my back!" Grube cried.

"I need some money goddamnit!" Glenroy cried louder.

"What for? Liquor? Dope? So you can drive to my cabin where you don't pay a dime, and feed your whore..."

It was a blind, murderous impulse. He lunged half around half over the desk, Grube put up his hands in defense, and Glenroy had him by the neck, gouging his thumbs into his soft throat. The chair fell over and slammed into the filing cabinet like an explosion. "You little mother-fucker, I'll kill you!" Grube gurgled, kicking his feet wildly against the filing cabinet with loud slams. It was one of the bartenders who rushed in, grabbed Glenroy from behind, and pulled him off the flailing, white-faced crazy-haired little manager.

"Come on, take it easy!" He was a stocky young man and had Glenroy in a bear hug.

Grube sat up on the paper-strewn floor, instinctively smoothed his hair as he ran his bulging eyes over the chaos of his desk, then at Glenroy, still glaring with murder. Most of the crew, along with the band, ogled from the hallway outside.

"Just let me go," Glenroy said, and elbowed himself free. He went out and passed through the hall, past all the gaping eyes, and there at the end, where the hallway met the open room, redressed, stood Dartt. Glenroy stopped a few feet from him, wavered, and Dartt looked back with an odd expression of hauteur and shock.

"You can't be in this band—you're already in a band," said Glenroy.

Dartt tilted his head back, swelled with a deep breath. "I told you I'm sitting in."

"You walked out on us."

Dartt shrugged. "I played. I left."

Glenroy just stood there. Their eyes burned together. "Are you really this stupid?" he said, "You're in the best band in the world—" Dartt rolled his eyes "—and you walk out on it for some third-rate shit like this?"

Dartt laughed caustically. "I'm tired of being used."

"Used?" Glenroy gaped at him in amazement.

"That's right."

"*Used?* How the hell are you being used?"

"Just figure it out." He turned and started away.

Glenroy watched him for a second. "Used? Jesus Christ!" Dartt stopped. "Goddamnit! What the hell are you talking about? What about the rest of us? How many chances do you think you *get?*"

Dartt turned. "You know what your problem is? You never figured out that nobody named you God."

"*What?*"

"Just what I said." He turned and walked away.

The silence screamed. All the gallery stared.

"Get him the hell out of here," he heard Grube say.

———

A week or so later, on the dank and cluttered front stoop of the derelict bungalow, Boyd Ange with two grocery bags, knowing the futility of the doorbell, of knocking even, shouldered open the reluctant malfitting door, scraping it over the arc worn in the wood-tiled floor, and called out "Glenroy?"

The TV droned, and two or three radios rasped statically in different rooms—though the denizen himself had passed through the digestive system of the house to the back porch. At the sounds in the kitchen he came in as Boyd unpacked the bags on the coral Formica-top table. Two half-gallon jugs of vodka, orange juice, a stack of TV dinners, sandwich stuff. From his trouser pocket he took a crumpled ounce lid, and straightening it out, handed it to Glenroy. "Supposedly Mexican. It's not as good as the Colombian—but what is?"

"Thanks, man," said Glenroy.

"It's all right."

"So—are we a band or not?"

"You're a band. Don't worry."

"We still playing?" Glenroy asked.

"If you're not, I don't know about it," Boyd answered.

"What about the record?"

"It's done, but believe it or not they shipped them to the wrong place. I've been on the phone for two days. But they're supposed to be here by the end of next week."

"They'll be at the Park?"

Boyd nodded. "That's the plan."

"And we are playing?"

"Yeah—you're playing. Haven't you talked to anybody?"

Glenroy shook his head.

"Not even Doug?"

"I haven't seen anybody."

"Look," said Boyd. "I know you're thinking about Grube, but forget about him. Remember his ass is on the line too. All you got to do is go out there next week and play great. People love you. They buy the records. They listen to the radio. They tell their friends. That's all—just play great. Then you can do whatever you want."

"What about Dartt?"

"He'll be there. Don't worry. And listen, I want you to know something. This record—" Boyd just nodded for a second "—it's good."

"I appreciate it, man," Glenroy said, reached out and cracked open one of the full, new bottles.

A new beginning.

The Song

Sunday afternoon, Glenroy had dozed off. He moldered on the porch while inside, the TV droned mindlessly—football already. His cousin was away on a four-state swing. The house—moldy, unkempt, the corners holding little spider dramas, jungled over outside, looking for all the world abandoned and slowly becoming a black hole in the neighborhood—was taking on the constricting familiarity of one's own personal purgatorial waiting room, a sensation Glenroy kept at bay by living just on the surface of the place—not his place—and accepting the vague uneasiness of not acknowledging to himself his own presence there. He never answered the phone and, living intuitively, didn't wonder why he did this time. He just did.

Alma, trying to keep a note of edginess from her voice, came over the line. "I was wondering where Doug was," she said. "I thought he might be with you."

"No," Glenroy replied, "I haven't seen him in—a while. I haven't seen anybody."

"Haven't even heard from him?"

"No."

She sighed. "I've never known him not to come home."

"Oh, he's around somewhere."

"I was hoping he was with you."

"No—but I wouldn't worry."

"Is it another woman?"

Pause. "I don't know, Alma. How about you—you doing okay?"

"I'm getting along."

"You working?"

"I have a job with an insurance man. I'm just worried. I don't understand what goes on inside of him," she said.

"I don't think anybody does," replied Glenroy.

"Well, why not? What is it makes him close himself off—can't nobody get inside?"

"I guess he's just that way."

"Just let everything eat him up. It ain't good."

"I know, Alma."

"And it sound like you ain't doing much better."

"It's just kind of a low time, I guess."

"Y'all ought to at least be looking out for each other," she said.

"Well, we do, Alma."

"Don't sound like it to me. It ain't like he's got a lot of friends."

"You're right—we should more. But I'll see him tomorrow—if we play."

"See, you ain't even sure about that."

"Well—everything's sort of messed up. It'll get better," he said.

"Just seem like such a waste," she concluded.

———

Something about the call, the sanity of talking, began to make him restless, and within a half hour he was bored and pacing. Like the sun burning through clouds, the sense that he was sleeping as everything of value in his life bled away finally pierced his mental fog, and he felt a wave of self-loathing and panic. Impulsively he dialed Tomorrow Studio, but it rang and rang. He hung up and looked in his wallet for the other number Boyd had given him—no luck—and came within an ace of dialing Grube at the club—but couldn't. No way. He got in his car, noted sinkingly the fuel gauge struggling, like something rearing from a tar pit, to rise to the quarter-tank mark, then refused to look at it anymore.

Traffic congested the road, lots of people pulling boats, and he remembered it was Labor Day weekend. The time of year he hated—the last outpost, the end.

It would be hard to say exactly when he knew—knowing actually an elusive thing, with its prescient feelers before and myriad echoes after—but it happened before or maybe as he jolted down the familiar dirt road and came over the final slope to the clearing behind the cabin. He parked and got out into a world that didn't at first seem silent, only empty, but then as like a ghost himself he walked toward the house it did begin to feel deathly quiet—he already knew then. After that, mounting the steps and slowly crossing the porch were only stage directions. The door met him closed but not locked. He pushed it open and one glance said everything in mute, foregone eloquence.

It became, as he realized she had left no more material trace than a dream, a quest to find some fragment or clue, some touch, something forgotten. But even the hollowed-out place on the couch seemed to have righted itself, though he looked at it for several minutes as if he might reincarnate her from her fading impression. No article of clothing overlooked, no scrap of paper dropped, no magazine picture nor anything from her hand left. The bed was made, the kitchen clean, the single utensils merged indiscriminately once more with the ones in the drawer, the bathroom vacated utterly, nothing in it but a half roll of tissue on the roller suggestive of any recent human presence at all. No toothbrush, no Tupperware cup. He walked through every inch of the house, slowly, the shock creeping upon him like gangrene, trying desperately now to uncover something, anything.

But his pains yielded him only one thing. And when he noticed it, wadded in the ceramic turtle, his first reaction was not the pain that would come later, but rather, just that desperate and tender clinging to this residuum of herself, this act of her hand. He didn't count it, just took it out and held it momentarily, then put it back where it remained, untouched, until the end.

Then he sat down on the couch and let the desolation come.

———

At Allred's he scoured the floorboards and came up with a dollar and thirteen cents. He pumped the gas and went inside where the place bustled with customers. He feigned looking for something among the shelves until the people cleared away from Big Steve.

He paid for the gas. "By the way," he said, "you know the girl that stays down there—have you seen her lately?"

Steve furrowed his brow. "It's been a while."

"Like a few days..."

"A good week anyway."

Glenroy nodded. "You didn't notice her walking out of here or getting a ride with somebody..."

"Naw," said Steve, shaking his head. "Sure didn't."

He had left out a dime. He had to wait a few minutes as some woman in a big pink and yellow hat laughed about something with somebody, in no hurry. At last she left. Glenroy placed the call.

It jarred him when he got an answer.

"Okay," said Angela shortly, "we'll accept. Jimmie!" Then cursorily to Glenroy, "Just a minute."

The seconds crawled by. Finally: "Glenroy, what's going on?"

"Not much."

A baby was crying in the background. "Damn it's been a long time, man."

"Yeah, I know."

"You excited about tomorrow?"

"Yeah, yeah," said Glenroy.

"We're going early—try to get down front. We'll have a cooler. And listen man, everybody is talking about your record. It's going to be there, right?"

"Yeah, I guess. As far as I know."

"Look, I want five copies. I'm serious. Is there anybody you can tell? I want to get them autographed."

"I don't know anything about all that, Jimmie."

"You know what I'm going to do? I'm going to put two of them up—without even touching them. They'll be worth some money one day."

"Look, Jimmie…"

"Hey, where are you, man? Why don't you come over? We're having a few people over—I'm barbequing."

"Jimmie…"

"Where are you?"

"At the lake."

At last Jimmie paused briefly. "What's going on?"

"I'm trying to find Rainy."

Pause. "She's not down there?"

"No."

Pause. "I don't know, Glenroy. I really don't. Maybe she's just—out somewhere."

"No, Jimmie, she's *gone*. Her stuff's gone."

Pause. "Glenroy, I'm telling you the truth, man. I honest to God don't know. All her stuff, really?"

"Yeah."

"Hmm." He was silent a moment. "Did you call Larry?"

"No."

"I don't know, Glenroy. I swear to God I don't."

"I *believe* you." Now someone else stared, pacing for the phone. He thought about asking for Larry's number, trying him, but the thought disgusted him. "Thanks, Jimmie."

They hung up.

He got in his car and started driving nowhere.

———

Indelible, random music clung mist-like to the old territory, troubling memory like a dark acquaintance from the past. He had taken a jug from the cabin and drank from it now as he aimlessly drove. The indifferent day felt eternal, more like a day caught scent of than a day. Blue sky with towering clouds, trembling with distant shudders of afternoon thunder more felt than heard.

He turned onto county road 41 in a gesture of thoughtless long-ago habit, not realizing, until he got back up to speed, what he had done. *Why would I look for her here?* he thought vaguely—the very idea of looking for her at all absurd.

It had been two years—two and a half. He had left Louis here sealed up in his mind, yet realized now how often he himself returned, loitering. It all looked different—though of course it wasn't; it was only the trick of memory given a little time to work—yet familiar too, the old contours of the road rising and falling, the tracks alongside, the same houses though one once lively with yard rats stood now abandoned and dead, and another a burned-out shell. And then as he got close, the feel of his younger, weightless self passed through him like a surge of morphine. He came around the last curve, slowed, angled into the drive, and stopped.

He turned off the car and sat. A train whistle to the east sounded distantly—coming or going?—and the texture of late summer flowed around him. After a while he restarted the car and crept down the drive, not knowing what he would find, until the still imposing but ruined and empty house appeared through the pecan orchard, commanding still the sloping field, and the view of the lake beyond. The water, catching the afternoon sun, sparkled.

He didn't linger, just looked around for a few minutes, took a pull from his jug, and drove out the way he had come. He turned back onto the highway, and the music followed him for a mile or so, like a family dog, then went back where it belonged.

Still not thinking consciously, he rejoined Highway 11 and found himself driving out to Journey's End. He had heard that Thad had been in the hospital and the place closed for over a year, but he hadn't been out here for longer than that—almost three years. Other echoes met him as he turned onto the bumpy road, and as the long sagging building and its weedy grounds came into view he already felt disillusioned with his little foray into the past. There is no past—only the hot, sucked-dry world it's gone from.

Still, he parked and got out. Not a soul around. The summer afternoon itself seemed the whole point. Boats buzzed distantly. Grass and weeds speared the cracks of the buckling parking lot. He walked toward the building, where most of the darkened windows gaped like eye sockets. The front door stood half open, a smile on a corpse, and recalling a dozen scenes of that very spot he stepped inside the musty cavern. Rats scattered. Maybe half the original tables and chairs sat chaotically shoved about the debris-littered floor. Liquor and beer bottles lay thick as confetti, and someone—kids—had had a field day with spray paint. He saw an empty rubber packet and nudged it with his foot, wryly juxtaposing two time frames in his mind.

Back outside, he went around to the rear where the outdoor bandstand and terrace, like the parking lot, had settled into the comfortable look of abandonment, though the field and the beach down below and the lake looked like the old days. The thought of Rainy came and went like a periodic stab of physical pain; otherwise his alcohol-numbed mind wandered distractedly. Occasionally the elaborate idea that he was looking for her returned, and at this moment he stood on the terrace looking back toward the building as though he might find her in one of the few remaining weathered chairs, perhaps, or just disappearing around a corner.

And so he didn't immediately notice when the door of the trailer half shaded in a grove of trees twenty or thirty yards behind the building opened and a suspicious, disheveled man stepped arthritically down onto the first step, scowling at his trespasser. But he must have sensed his presence, eventually, or heard something, so turned and looked across the patch of ground and time at the wavering, much-changed figure of old Thad Stroop.

He looked as wasted as his once-thriving place—himself the bad nerve of the tooth dying all around him. He must not have recognized Glenroy, for his look lingered mean and distrustful, even as Glenroy walked over to him and stopped.

Still, Thad kept gazing uncertainly until at last some dim recognition softened his ornery and dissipated features.

"Son of a bitch," he said. "Is that you?"

Conjuring a name would have been asking too much. "That's me," said Glenroy.

"What the hell you doing here?"

"Just looking around."

"Ain't nothing to see."

"Looks like it's kind of gone downhill."

Thad snorted. "I'll get it fixed back up. Soon as I get where I can. I been sick."

"That's what I heard."

"Like to died."

"Looks like you didn't," Glenroy replied, thinking he'll outlive everybody. "What was wrong with you?"

"Nothing till them sonafabitching doctors got a-hold of me. Said I was bleeding inside. Shit, they kept me so doped up I didn't even know where I was at. Couldn't do nothing but puke and give them my goddamn money. I'll tell you one thing: if I ever get anywhere near another goddamn doctor, shoot me."

Glenroy laughed. "Sounds bad."

"Boy, you don't know what bad is. What the hell's that you drinking?"

Glenroy looked down at it, having half forgotten he was carrying it. "Vodka."

"Vodka, my ass," said Thad. "Come inside where it's cool and drink you some Wild Turkey. I ain't had nobody to drink with since pussy came looking for me. Hell, come on—I can tell by looking at you you ain't got nothing else better to do."

———

When Glenroy awoke, abruptly, the next morning, his eyes opening onto perfectly foreign surroundings, it took him a sluggish minute to unravel where he was. He had a stab of panic, but it passed as he pieced together the fragments of the preceding night, hearing again flashes of the man's coarse, obscenity-saturated talk, raspy echoes of his laughter.

He had slept in his clothes and got stiffly to his feet. Chilled, and with a brutally throbbing head, he went into the little kitchen, opened the refrigerator, and took a long draught of cold prune juice. Outside, the bright summer morning, well advanced, looked like an alien planet outside the window of a landing pod. The trailer was frigid. A brontosaurus of an air conditioner in the window just above the sofa where he had slept had lumbered at full capacity through the night. He swallowed, wincing at his scratchy throat. Opening the door, he testily descended the steps into the amazing inferno, and went over to the corner of the trailer to take a leak.

He knew what day it was. He came back inside and looked around for a clock. How much time did he have?

He drank some more juice, felt a stomach rumble of hunger but wasn't sure what to do about it, so he sat down at the little kitchen table with its flashes of crazy memory from the night before and became his headache. Eventually some sounds from the far end of the trailer tugged him back to the moment. He looked up, waited, heard the toilet flush, then here came scowling Thad shuffling painfully down the hall. Glenroy looked at him and said, "Holy shit."

"Holy shit, yourself," Thad returned, and then cooked breakfast.

The food helped—a little. The coffee, not to mention the prune juice, sent him on several trips to the bathroom. When at last he discovered the time—almost one o'clock—he felt panicky again. So many details—he couldn't remember the details.

"Can I use your phone?" he asked Thad.

"There it is."

He dialed Boyd, who immediately answered.

"Where the hell are you?" His voice bristled edgily. "I've been sitting here waiting."

"I'm down at the lake," Glenroy answered.

"You need to be *here*. Get up here as fast as you can, okay?"

"Okay."

"I'll meet you at the club and drive you down. You just need to hurry."

"I will."

"Are you all right?"

"Yeah."

"You sure?"

"Yeah, I'm all right."

"You don't sound like it."

"I'll be fine."

Boyd sighed. "Okay. And hey—they're here."

Glenroy, blank, didn't respond.

"The records," said Boyd.

"Oh."

"I took out a few for you."

"Good. Thanks."

"Seems like you'd be excited."

"I am."

"Hurry—okay?"

Glenroy hung up, and Thad, egg yolk in his whiskers, shakily poured some whiskey into his coffee cup.

"You got anything for a headache?" Glenroy asked.

"Hair of the dog," Thad replied.

"Besides that."

"Suit yourself," Thad drained his cup and smacked his lips. "I got something'll knock it out," he said.

"I'll take it."

Thad rose and a moment later returned with a prescription bottle.

"These things is serious," he said. "And I'll tell you something I found out. They don't go with whiskey too good."

"What are they?"

"Strong."

"Will they get rid of a headache?"

"Yeah, and your head along with it."

"How many do you take?"

"One's a plenty."

"Give me two."

Thad shrugged, half smiled and half frowned, and shook out two. Glenroy looked around the room, saw the jug he had left on the countertop the afternoon before, impulsively grabbed it, and swallowed the pills with a long draught of the warm, pungent, pulpy juice.

"My, my," said Thad.

"You couldn't give me a couple of bucks for gas, could you?"

Thad hobbled into the back and returned with a twenty dollar bill. He handed it to Glenroy. "You be careful," he said.

———

Somewhere along the way, the road turned to sponge. The car felt like a battleship wallowing over the highway. Whenever Glenroy dared to shift his eyes from the road to the speedometer he would see that he was going thirty miles an hour and would make a short-lived effort, like trying to flee in a dream, to speed up. But the artillery had indeed taken out his headache and left in its place a pleasant, oblivious numbness—so pleasant, in fact, not losing it had become his dominant concern, so he nurtured it with swigs from his jug, while the air he plowed through became every mile more like pizza dough, and his thoughts like congealing glue.

The ride proceeded luxuriously, his epic migration to Atlanta, as everything urgent dissipated like smoke into the lazy summer sky. He just didn't care.

He had driven into the city for a couple of miles before remembering where he was going, though he had a homing instinct that drew him toward the club. He made his way through town, cars flashing impatiently around him, and at last reached the club and guided his drunk car into a parking space and a half and began the long swim to the building.

But Boyd had been looking for him and hurried out to meet him.

"Thank God!" he exclaimed. "What took you so long?"

Glenroy just shook his head.

"What's the matter with you? I knew there was something wrong."

"I'm all right," said Glenroy, but the words choked his mouth like wads of rubber.

"Can you play?" Boyd asked.

Glenroy nodded.

Boyd appraised him querulously. "Man, what's going on? The Park down there's full of people. Waiting."

Glenroy took a breath, exhaled.

"What do you need—some food, coffee, what?"

"Nah—I'm okay, really." He had depleted his juice, and his few active brain cells occupied themselves in schemes to get more.

"Man, if you're not up to playing, I think it'd be better…"

"I'll be all right, once I get up there, get some adrenalin going."

Boyd nodded uncertainly. "All right—I hope so. You want to see it?"

Glenroy gazed dumbly at him.

"The *record.*"

And at that, a light slowly came over Glenroy's face. *Oh yeah. The record.*

"You can look at it on the way. I've got your guitar. Come on," said Boyd.

At first, he simply stared at it as though trying to establish what it was. And then, as he did, his heart sank; it struck him as cheap. He blenched like a betrayed and wounded child. Black and white, grainy, obscure, cheap! The three of them vague and grim against the washed-out lake and sky and Highway 9 bridge. *Lake Moon*—The Trybald Trio. He turned it over and the words looked sparse and inadequate. The whole thing had an air of tawdry amateur haste. Cheap! Like a flabbergasted boy-father he looked at it, turning it over in his hands as Boyd sped them through town. His mouth moved as he read the song titles again and again. Then, at last, realization slowly dawned. The artifact began to change, or its holder did, who, through some miraculous conversion, now saw the possibility of subtlety in the artist's design—a tasteful simplicity, and his eyes burned at the astonishing idea of this austere complement offered by a nameless and congenial stranger to his rich love's labor.

Then he held it in his lap, drifted away, and looked up in surprise as Boyd guided them past an officer and a barricade, around and through people, and as close as he could get to the stage.

The world came back—the noisy, milling, weighty world—but through the wrong end of a telescope. People spoke like actors in a badly dubbed film, touched him, took his hand, patted him, thrust albums at him for his autograph, as though they meant to hurt him, as Boyd tried to keep them away.

And then, looking all wrong, standing before him: Doug.

"Man, what's going on with you?" he asked.

"Nothing. I…"

"Man—on this one day…" Pain froze his features tightly.

For the first time in his life Glenroy felt the icy shiver of self-doubt. "Yeah, I…"

"Did you see this?" Doug asked him.

His hands thrust something toward him that Glenroy finally took, held it away from his face, and tried to read, though again his comprehension was sluggard.

The poster: "Labor Day Celebration!" Then a photograph, and under it: "Featuring—Streetcar. Also appearing: The Trybald Trio, Enough's Enough, Ben Dover, Bad Marriage, and Fleet Pickle."

His thoughts could not consummate as words. The connections between apprehension, comprehension, and response simply failed. He just looked up at Doug who shook his head and walked away.

Something screeched at the walls. A deflating premonition of losing his high jarred him, and in desperation he began to grasp at schemes to get something to drink. Did he actually say something out loud?

He must have. "I don't think it'd be a good idea," said Boyd, maybe in response to him, maybe to someone else, or maybe he only thought he heard it.

It was too late anyway. Some rumor of their being up troubled the air. Now Grube appeared—but even his face paled beside the crippling dread of coming down. Grube was nothing—it was easy enough to see that now. It was all nothing, everything was nothing.

Then Dartt. Tight black leather pants, half-open shirt, princely hair—cool, indifferent.

And just that blade of studied indifference finally slit his heart and sent him groping through his numb mind for some countering emotion—something artless, intense, and stronger—but paralysis gripped him. Nothing came to a point—all had spilled out and soaked into the dust.

"What," said Dartt, like someone simply interested to know, "'Jeez Louise,' 'Lake Trash,' 'Mother Roach'—something like that? Then go from there?"

"Yeah."

"Anything else?"

Glenroy tried to think, fiercely meeting the bland gaze. "I want to play 'Rainy'—if you can."

Dartt laughed. "If I can? Man, I can play whatever you want. This is your show—you tell me."

A false high note, at last, sounded in the laugh. Glenroy held his eye, then Dartt melted away. Now Glenroy sat on a big black case, the air shrill with some band's ear-splitting harmonica, until he found himself mounting the steps, guitar around his neck like a weight. He stepped onstage and a cheer went up. He could not make himself look at them, the motley crowd spilling over the gentle hillside, Frisbees slicing the air. He only glanced at Doug, settling in, saw the pain in his face—or was it fear?—and looked away. Dartt would not meet his eyes. He had two desires: to keep his high, and not to be here.

Someone introduced them, and then like some kind of cheap joke Dartt counted off "Jeez Louise" too fast—and from the very first Glenroy flagged behind, his fingers numb and slow. He couldn't catch up, he couldn't find it. He listened hard to Doug but heard only mush. He strained for the bass line but couldn't find the thread. Then he stumbled into his lead but had no awareness of his attempt to play it. The end wallowed toward them and he still hadn't caught up and he realized the vaguely troubling sensation in his stomach was embarrassment. The song ended.

There was nowhere he could look. The audience seemed uninvolved, as though they were facing another way, watching someone else.

But Dartt started counting off again—then it was bass and drums for a moment, until Glenroy plunged, insensible of the song. Yes—"Lake Trash"—but too fast! The bastard.

He played by memory and instinct.

Again it ended to a strange non-response, though corrupt with some restive malcontent, as Dartt walked over to him, his eyes bright—and the emotion Glenroy yearned for came at last, a surge of hate so rich it was like love.

"What do you want to do?" Dartt asked him.

Glenroy only glared at him.

"Keep going—or...What'd we say—'Mother Roach?'"

"Yeah."

"Okay, you got it. 'Mother Roach!'" he called over his shoulder to Doug, then turned back to Glenroy. "You counting it off?"

Glenroy nodded, then ransacked his brain trying to remember the song. The indifferent crowd waited. Finally, thinking he basically had it, he just counted. Doug and Dartt began playing, something dirge-like and skeletal, and he could feel them looking at him. Too slow. Way too slow. He glanced at Doug, saw only pained confusion.

I have to play something, he told himself, and started playing something, trying simultaneously to correct the tempo and make it sound like something. All the riffs of his life floated by and he snatched at them, trying to find anything to get him through this. But there are songs after all, and this one was where? He wanted desperately to explain now, strained to concentrate, then like one naked in a dream, he realized all at once the bass and drums had fallen, and it was just him, trying to pull off the coup of making this sputtering nightmare into some kind of eccentric tour de force solo, gamely for a minute or two, at last feeling the whole outlandish sham decaying into bloody rage. With sudden clarity he looked at Dartt standing there benignly, hands folded casually on his bass, watching, and then the music, like a drowning animal, went under.

Icy fire surged through his body like a lethal injection. This had never happened to him in his life.

Dartt took a few steps to him. The crowd murmured uneasily.

"Had enough?"

"Fuck you."

Dartt laughed.

The ominous rumble of the crowd, like bombers approaching, was pierced by whistles, shouts.

"I didn't realize we'd be playing Chinese today." Dartt looked calmly over the audience. "Well—you gave them something to remember, I'll say that."

However it happened, and various versions persist, it was sudden—like a striking snake: Glenroy taking his guitar by the neck, ducking out of it as though in a rehearsed move, and raising it, giving Dartt just the necessary second or two to hold up his own instrument, which, instead of his skull, took the brunt of the blow and let out a thunderous boom that shuddered the park. Then the brandished guitar again, another murderous swing, deflected but stumbling the would-be victim back—then raising it again over the off-balance foe but just at the last second giving it a wild heave instead sending it hurling through the air to crash somewhere backstage with a resounding screech.

Cheers, whistles—and then he collapsed in the grasp of a half dozen pairs of hands.

———

Snakes wriggled toward him, little monkey-faced things, and he struggled against consciousness like death. But he lost the fight, and now painfully awake watched a foggy face resolve into his field of vision. He wanted to scald the air with some indignant imprecation but couldn't, just yet.

Noise, words came from the face.

"What you talking about, boy? You crazy?" he protested.

"I don't think so. But I might be. I'm just telling you, I'm leaving," said Doug.

"What you mean, leaving?"

"I mean I'm leaving. For good. You understand?"

"Leaving where?"

"I don't know. Now listen, this is important. The rent's paid for two more weeks about. Till the first of October. After that you'll have to find someplace else. You hear what I'm saying?"

"I don't hear nothing. Just some crazy fool," Monroe replied.

"You better listen. You can stay here two more weeks. Then you'll have to leave. They'll come and make you leave. You need to go out and find somewhere else."

"I like it here fine."

"You ain't listening to what I'm saying."

"Hell no, I ain't listen to this damnfool talking! I ain't got my sleep out."

"Two more weeks. You better pay attention to what I'm telling you. And all I ask is one thing I want you to do for me. I want you to go see Alma."

"Alma," Monroe said blankly.

"Yes, Alma. Now remember what I'm saying. Tell her..." He sighed. The old impasse—tell her what? "Tell her—out of all the people in the world—I mean, she may not believe it—but there ain't nobody ahead of her, to me...I mean, it may not be the way *she* thought, but..."

"What the hell you talking about, boy?"

"It's love, what I feel," said Doug.

"Me, hell. *You* tell her."

"Can't you just do what I ask you to?" Doug returned angrily, then tried to arrange his thoughts. "Tell her she's too good for me—no, good God, don't tell her that. Just tell her what I said. You understand? Tell her I asked you to come. Tell her I wasn't in any kind of condition…I tried to write a letter but I couldn't get it to sound right."

"Still don't," grumbled Monroe.

"Just do it, please. This one thing for me." He stood up. "And remember—two weeks."

"I think you just crazy, that's all it is. Come around here talking this fool nonsense bother a old man ain't even got his sleep out—yeah, you just crazy."

He turned over and pulled the blanket decisively back over him. His resumed snores punctuated the closing of the door, and the retreating footsteps.

————

Monroe rounded the corner at the end of the block just in time to see the young woman leave the building and start away up the street. Looked like her.

A big storm churned out in the Gulf, creeping north. The day, an almost-October day, brooded drizzily, and he was damp and thirsty. He knew he had business with her, but in his mind his mission had evolved into something more concerned with his own looming crisis. Not that he was particularly clear about that either. The current predicament of his thirst tended to overshadow all other issues.

He limped along and couldn't keep up with her. When he reached the far corner he didn't see her right away, among the other people, then spotted her at the bus stop. Halfway down the block sat a little package store. He debated with himself, took some coins out of his pocket, and counted them. About a dollar would do it. Resolved, he had made it twenty yards down the sidewalk when the bus came. "Shit!" he hissed to himself, and hurried back just in time to slip in the back door. A full load. She had dissolved somewhere among the crowd up front, but that fact scored lower in his thoughts than the vacant sensation of what he'd almost had in his hand.

He missed seeing her disembark, but luckily caught a glimpse of her face through the window, out on the sidewalk, just in time. She had already started away up the street. Grumbling, he shoved and elbowed his way past his affronted co-passengers and just watched her for a second by the bus stand, another liquor store having caught his eye on the catercorner. He didn't squander many seconds in indecision, but hurried across the street and immediately accosted a neatly-dressed young white man on his way out.

"Afternoon, sir. Want to see a old man dance?"

The young man looked at him with a mildly interested sneer.

Monroe did a few steps and sang: "Turn about, wheel about, do jus' so..."

The young man laughed, glanced around him, and found something in his pocket for the old cupped hand.

"Thank you sir, thank you kindly, yes sir."

Monroe opened his hand and looked. He pursued the young man a few yards, got slightly ahead of him, and began to dance some more.

"Old Satan am a liar and a conjurer too, if you don't watch out, he'll conjure you."

The young man stared.

"Yes sir, all I need 'bout fifty cent. I sho be 'bliged to you. Hep a old man out."

Irritably now, the young man fished in his pocket once more, glanced at the catch, and shoved a rumpled dollar bill into the hand.

"Yes *sir*. You are kind, sir, and good luck sho rain down on your head today."

His pocket now satisfyingly heavy, Monroe made the best time he could back to the opposite sidewalk, but he had lost her. He hurried along, briskly for him, until at the first intersection he found that she had turned and saw her far down in the second block, walking circumspectly. He paused, retrieved his treasure, shakily uncapped it, and took a long guzzle.

"Ah-h," he said, and smacking his lips gave a grunt of deep satisfaction.

The woman stopped someone on the sidewalk, questioning him. Monroe repocketed the bottle and started after her.

They had entered a neighborhood of shady streets lined with small houses, many painted in vivid blues, greens, yellows. Monroe had no idea where he was—just new territory.

He nursed no illusion of gaining on her, but he kept her in view. On the next block she stopped and Monroe could see her looking up at a certain house. She hesitated, then at last began slowly to ascend the steps, and disappeared from sight. When Monroe reached the place, he gazed up at the suspected house: a small mustard yellow frame house on a bare-dirt, shady rise gnarled with roots and slashed by a steep rise of concrete block steps. The little front porch, with dying flowers on the railing, betrayed nothing. Must be inside. Nothing to do but wait.

On the preceding corner Monroe's trained eye had taken note of a vacant overgrown lot that seemed to serve the neighborhood as a dump. He returned there now and considered a mangled, evidently abandoned garbage dumpster showing the trauma of some unremembered fire. A little path snaked through old appliance hulls and busted furniture and mounds of nameless refuse (some of this was pretty good stuff), and he followed it to the charred and unsteady bin. Climbing up on an old air conditioner carcass, he peered in. An old piece of mattress towards the back, under the half roof, looked dry.

"Mm," Monroe grunted.

With some difficulty he pulled himself up, got a leg over, then the other.

"Don't you be in here, Mr. No-Shoulders," he said. "And if you is, you leave old Monroe alone."

He settled himself on the mattress and lay back—just him and his Wild Irish Rose, alone at last.

———

"Mrs. Johnson?"

"Yes?"

"I'm Alma Lowe. I'm a friend of Doug Earley's. We've spoken..."

"Oh, yes, Alma."

"I wanted to ask about Miss Vonceil."

"Well...please come in." She held open the door.

The house smelled vaguely of wood smoke and food. The unseasonable weather had the front room feeling damp and cool.

"I hope I'm not disturbing you," Alma said.

"No, we're just staying inside today," replied Mrs. Johnson.

"How is Miss Vonceil doing?"

"Well...she's doing pretty good."

"I know she means so much to Doug."

Mrs. Johnson made a funny little laugh. "We haven't heard from Doug." She looked inquiringly at Alma.

A pained smile came over Alma's face. "I don't know where he is," she said softly, and paused. "I was hoping maybe you did."

Mrs. Johnson pressed her lips tightly together and shook her head. "No," she replied, "we haven't heard from him."

Alma, not knowing quite what to say, only looked sympathetically at her. "Well..." The room fell silent. Then: "I was wondering if I could speak with her."

Mrs. Johnson looked at her, hesitated. "Well...does she know you?"

"I've met her a few times," Alma said.

"Well...maybe it would be all right. But..."

Alma raised her eyebrows.

"Well, you know, there's some things she understands—and some things she gets a little confused."

"I understand."

"You know we try to keep her from having any new worries on her mind."

Alma nodded. "Yes, I understand."

Mrs. Johnson regarded her for another moment. "Let's go see if she's awake."

———

She sat unoccupied in a rocking chair beside the bed, a surprisingly small woman with carefully brushed gray hair and bright, attentive eyes. The room, dominated by her bed neatly made with a frayed quilt, was hissing with a gas space heater and stifling. Little relieved the blankness of the splotchy, yellowed walls but zigzagging strips of tape like the tracks of some mathematical insect, peeling from the cracks they had meant to mend. The side window, fast-covered with a shade, denied a prospect of what could only have been the hard-by next door house; another on the back afforded a view of the hardscrabble back yard, an overgrown gully, and the angled rooftops of the next block.

Her idle hands upside down and cupped together in her lap, she watched with wary interest her visitor being shown into her room.

"Miss Vonceil, here's somebody to see you."

Alma advanced, held out her hand, which Vonceil limply took.

"Miss Vonceil, I hope you remember me. I'm Alma Lowe. I'm a friend of Doug's. It's so nice to see you again."

A peculiar, dawning look passed over her face, then disappeared. Her gaze fastened on Mrs. Johnson.

"Well," said that lady, "I'll let you two have a little visit. I'll go see if I can't find some refreshments."

"Oh, please don't bother," protested Alma gently.

"It's no bother."

Alma watched her, then turned to Vonceil whose gaze lingered upon the just-closed door, then cut back in one swift movement to her. She studied Alma intently, but said nothing.

"I've been wanting to come check on you for so long," said Alma. "I worried about disturbing you, but I just told myself: I'm going to go visit her."

Vonceil kept staring. Alma looked about, pulled a chair closer and sat down.

"Look like we're finally having some cool weather," said Alma. "It feels nice to me after it's been so hot."

Still Vonceil just looked at her.

"I hope you been feeling well, and everything going along all right."

At last Vonceil turned away and began to search through some newspaper clippings on her nightstand. A few moments passed.

"You seem comfortable here with these nice people," Alma said.

Vonceil left off her search, turned her gaze back, grown puzzled, to her mysterious visitor, and gave a short laugh. Another little piece of time slipped by.

A slight tap, then the door opened and Mrs. Johnson reentered with a tray. As she set it on the dresser and began to arrange the things, Alma observed Miss Vonceil acutely watching her. Finally she cut her eyes to Alma, catching her staring and embarrassing her, but surprising her too with her alarmed expression. She held up a finger to her lips. Then her dark look brightened, as though on cue, as Mrs. Johnson finished and turned back to her guests.

"Just some lemonade and cookies," she said. "I'll let you help yourself."

"Oh thank you," said Alma, and turned to Vonceil. "Look. How nice."

Miss Vonceil had fixed a smile on her face.

Mrs. Johnson left and Alma stood up.

"Miss Vonceil, would you like…"

But the alarmed look had returned, in force, and she crooked a finger gesturing Alma to her.

Uneasily, Alma obliged her, leaning her ear almost to the lady's lips, and she whispered: "It's pi-son."

Alma reared back, startled. "What?"

"Pi-son!"

Alma stared at her, baffled.

"But I got me a anti-dope she don't know about. Bring me some here."

Alma poured a glass, brought it over, and set it on the glass coaster on the nightstand, then waited as Vonceil took a small satin bag from her bosom, pecked open the ribbon tying it shut, and took out a small brass monkey with oversized green jeweled eyes. She waved it over her glass and said, "Bring me yours here." Alma walked over, poured herself a glass, and brought it back for a similar ministration, then observed as Vonceil tediously went through the steps of returning the monkey to its haven. "You eat them cookies, you crazy."

The heat and fumes closed in smotheringly on Alma. She sat down, took a breath, patted her face with a napkin, and could only watch as Vonceil carefully grasped her glass with both hands, tremblingly guided it to her lips, and took a deep drink of three long, throat-undulating swallows. The she took a sip herself.

"The devil sly," said Vonceil.

Alma, taken unawares, nodded. "Yes—he sure is."

They fell silent.

"Well," said Alma, "I've enjoyed being friends with Doug these last two years."

Vonceil's face brightened and she looked at Alma with a tender smile.

"We've kept each other company. He sure has worked hard."

Vonceil kept smiling. "He have five medals on his coat," she said.

Alma nodded. "Yes. He's very talented."

Vonceil beamed proudly.

"You don't know where he likes to go?" asked Alma.

Then, by degrees, Vonceil's expression decomposed into perplexity. "Where?"

"I was asking..."

"When is he coming? When is Doug coming?"

Alma shook her head. "I don't know."

Now the puzzlement became pain, and Vonceil cast her troubled look out the back window, her hands gripping the arms of her chair like two old spiders.

Alma swallowed and fought off a queasy wave of dizziness. She took another drink, waved her hand before her face to stir a little air.

"Her arm reach a long way," said Vonceil. One of the spiders rose and opened and closed like jaws. "Born face down on Feb-rary the thirteenth...yes he was...oh yes he was," she sang.

Alma didn't move.

"Slipped goofer powder in the dirt-dobber tea. Cleaned out the fireplace and swept under the bed." She stopped and reached for her cold, beaded glass again, took another deep drink and clattered it back into its coaster. "Ain't nothing worse than see the devil smile. She describe my grave—I feel the cool shade and see the trees. She just full of hate and have the Judas Eye."

"Miss Vonceil..."

"Say she cut my ears off. Say I have a wandering mind all my days."

"Miss Vonceil, I just wanted to say that if you hear anything—I'm going to leave my number..."

"Look in that trunk yonder where my finger's pointing and bring me that cigar box."

Sighing, Alma rose, let back the lid of the trunk against the wall, and saw atop the tightly-packed contents an old, much-handled King Edward box wound shut with a number of rubber bands, many of which had rotted and snapped, held by the others. She took it to Vonceil, then watched with impatience inclining to panic the slow and torturous process of the old hands working at the rubber bands, on the verge of reaching out to do it herself several times, but almost nauseous now from the heat, just endured it.

"A flying lark and a setting dove," said Vonceil as at last she folded back the wobbly, nearly detached lid. From a little trove of odd materials she took a small bulky bag—a kerchief actually, tied off with a piece of yellow yarn—set it in her lap; and then, carefully, a bleached white tortoise shell with a red handprint on its back.

Alma recoiled from the sight of it.

"Here," said Vonceil, handing it shakily to her. "You take this."

"Why?"

"You the one."

"I don't want it."

"It a bring him back."

"No it won't. I don't believe that. It looks evil to me. I'm tired of evil things." She felt quite sick now, knew she must leave at once.

"*Take it*," Vonceil repeated with a look of such imploring intensity Alma took it. "And when he come back—give him this." She held out the bag.

Alma took it as well, mumbled her goodbye, only for one searing flash meeting her eye, and so left her there alone.

———

Cool air streamed sweetly through the opened front door. Alma took a deep breath.

"Are you all right?" asked Mrs. Johnson, pretending not to see what she had in her hands.

"Yes, I just needed some air." She handed the lady a piece of paper. "If you hear anything at all…that's at work. I'm there during the day."

Mrs. Johnson nodded. "You know she's not right."

"I don't know what's right," said Alma, leaving her standing there at the threshold.

On her retreat from the suffocating house Alma paused at the trash-littered corner lot, ventured a few yards in, and gave the painted shell an awkward toss. It nicked the lip of the leaning dumpster, and with a tumbling clatter fell in.

Then turning her face to the coming loneliness, she walked away.